STEALING THE Star Stone

Stealing the Star Stone

He's a galactic heartthrob with abs and attitude. She's a no-nonsense pilot with a grudge and a grudge-stick to match.

They only have to survive a joyride without killing each other.

Instead, a fertility idol shatters, reality twists, and now they're stuck...in each other's bodies.

Arrested, hunted, and mortified beyond reason, the only way to switch back is to find another idol—the one buried on a planet crawling with man-eating vines and carnivorous natives.

Forced into close quarters and very personal spaces, they'll have to navigate body-swapping chaos, jungle horrors, and an inconveniently growing attraction.

Because nothing says romance like sharing a body and stealing an alien relic.

Enemies. Strangers. Now unwilling allies with matching anatomy. What could possibly go wrong?

Also by Sevannah Storm

The Blood of Legends Series

The Huntress

The Healer

*

The Gifting Series

Soul Forged

Fate Forged

Sun Forged

War Forged

Star Forged

Shadow Forged

Earth Forged

Lust Forged

Fire Forged

Time Forged

*

Standalones

Xiaxan Fox

Ire of Silver

GLOSSARY

Amenkar – ah-men-car – Current chief of the Lethari.

Artivar – aar-tah-vaar – space station orbiting Tarnis.

Bigeeli – big-eel-ee – old Lethari woman.

Haeldull – hale-dool – ancient alien race.

Invenire – in-venn-eer-ee – a gallery in Tarnis' welcoming center.

Jedshe – jed-shee – a flesh-eating monster that lives in the lagoon.

Kegawa – keh-gaa-wah – asteroid belt on the outskirts of the Uyes system.

Khepan – keh-pan – the Lethari fisherman

Kovari – koh-vaar-ee – ancient alien race

Laurus – law-russ – Lord Orien's research vessel.

Lethara – leth-aar-ah – name of the moon orbiting Nyxara.

Lethari – leth-aar-ee – people on Lethara.

Messis – mess-is – welcoming port for the planet, Tarnis.

Orien – orr-ee-in – Lord Vex Orien

Qidhari – kid-haar-ee – Lethari meaning god's savior.

Quet – kett – rainbow-colored eels.

Senmut – senn-moot – ancient witch guardian of shols.

Shol – sholl – Lethari for ancient, sentient stone.

Skrillith – skrill-ith – carnivorous pygmies.

Tazoc – tah-zock – a line of witch guardians chosen by the shols to guard them.

Tilqea – till-key – a tree the Haeldull use to see if their females are pregnant.

Vael'Tir – vale-tier – the chief's city.

Viator – vee-ay-torr – Orien's shuttle/s

Vukuub – vue-koob – shimmering crablike spider adverse to noise.

Yuxmet – yucks-mett – massive hair-covered rhinos.

The Uyes System

Uyes – ooh-yes – Red dwarf – center of the solar system.

Scatheon – scath-ee-on –hot, hostile, volcanic – a hellish planet.

Velis – val-is – warm desert world with fast winds.

Auralis – orr-ah-liss – cloud-surfing paradise, bright skies.

Seia – say-ah – dusk-lit and balanced.

Caerule – sea-rule – cold, dreamy skies – ice-cloud surfing.

Tarnis – tarr-niss – deep oceans, lush – food basket.

Nyxara – nicks-aar-ah – tidally locked, cold, frozen – ice farming.

Lethara – leth-aar-ah – name of the moon orbiting Nyxara.

Eli Thorne's Movies

Yeehaw in Zero G – A rootin'-tootin' space cowboy, Nebula Slim, wrangles smugglers on the wildest frontier.

They Call Me Nebula Slim – Gunslinger-turned-bounty hunter Nebula Slim blazes through the galaxy with justice on his hip.

Bang Bang, Binary Baby – A cyborg assassin discovers love is the deadliest glitch in his programming.

The Lost Moons of Andara – Treasure hunters risk everything to uncover a vanished system hiding impossible riches.

Alien in Lipstick – He came to conquer Earth… but first, he has to survive a blind date…as a she.

The Quick and the Quasarian – Two dueling outlaws face off at the edge of a black hole, where only one can ride away.

Shadow Huntress of Andromeda – Queen of the Stars goes on a crusade against the scum of the galaxy with her trusty side-kick, Jax.

Chapter One

On the Entertainment Cruiser (EC) Valiance.

Of all the tourist cruisers in all the galaxies in the known universe, he walks

onto mine...

Year of 2202, May

The oh-so-sexy Eli Thorne didn't remember her. That was clear. A night of passion ten years ago that, as an ex-fan and ex-virgin, Nova couldn't forget no matter how much she wanted to. She rubbed her hip where a tattoo of his name glowed white in the dark. And her poor late husband had thought it meant serenity. That tattoo was one of her more foolhardy decisions she hadn't gotten around to rectifying.

Meeting Thorne again after all this time had her fuming.

She flicked off the sec-vid, not needing to check on her 'honored' guest. The ass had enough sycophants to cater to his every need. Still, he was some serious eye-candy she couldn't resist ogling...when no one watched her.

Before her, spreading out like an antique disco ball, the ship's console displayed their course for the rings of Velis, confirming they would make good time. She huffed a bang off her forehead. The tip of her ponytail brushed her back. She cast a glance at the tiny digital image of her late husband, Seth. If he was here, with her, he'd tell her to take slow, calming breaths and find joy in the moment. That it would steady her. Joy? With Eli on board?

"Listen, Nova..." Petr peeked through the door.

She pinched the bridge of her nose then swiveled the chair to meet the concierge's gaze. "What this time?"

"Yeah, I echoed that...but politely." He ventured into the cockpit, all suave and collected in his deep-burgundy uniform. "Mr. Thorne wants to surf Velis' clouds." His voice took on a pleading note. "We're on our way home. I know, but can't we just do this one thing?" He rushed on. "Captain said to sweet talk you. Said it was my turn." He slumped in the co-pilot's chair and batted his eyelashes at her.

The last stop had been a twelve-hour delay while Mr. Popular partied in Auralis' city, New Liberty. Two nights ago, she'd had to hunt his ass down and peel him from not one woman but two. Bile pooled at the back of her throat, and a shudder ran down her spine.

Now she had to alter course, park the ship, and leave it...unpiloted. At least the ass had the decency to ask when Velis and Seia were visible. It would have been an immediate hell-no had they been nearing Tarnis.

She glared at Petr. "And who's going to surf with him? Do we even have the equipment?" She mentally ticked off what sat in their stores: boards, suits, oxygen tanks. As an entertainment cruiser, they had to cater for...joyrides. "Shit."

"I'm all thumbs when it comes to anything requiring co-ordination. And Captain says he's too old to even think about picking up a board. Sharon will break a nail, and Chef just waved his meat cleaver at me." Petr paled and threw out his hand to catch hers. "Please, babe, do this for me. As gorgeous as Eli Thorne is, I've never had a more demanding passenger."

She could second that. Their 'first' meeting had been when the crew had welcomed him aboard. Thorne had taken her hand, dusted his lips across her knuckles, and said something derogatory about how a little woman like her surely couldn't handle a ship this big all by her lonesome.

What an ass.

Which had become evident a decade ago when his then-assistant had kicked her out of his hotel room, muttering that Thorne's groupies—aka her—weren't as pretty as they used to be. In her youthful madness, she'd sought Thorne out at the next premiere. He'd taken one look at her and treated her like an adoring fan. So, not only had she been a pity-fuck, she hadn't been memorable.

And of course, the years had been good to him, his acting career reaching supernova, his appearance like a fine brandy, and his bank balance with too many digits for her brain to compute. While she'd gotten her pilot's license, met the man of her dreams, lost him in a 'freak' mining accident, and now squandered her days flying spoilt rich folks across the known galaxies.

"It's a few hours delay, nothing more." Petr cleared his throat. "We need this. One raving review from Thorne will boost our dwindling credits."

Business *had* been slow of late.

She scowled. At least she wouldn't have to talk to him...much. "Fine, but I'm in charge. We can't afford to have him die on us."

Petr bounced on the spot, his smile wide. She hadn't seen him grin like that since they'd stopped at Lunar Station VI to pick up Thorne, who'd been nothing but the award-winning pain in the ass she'd expected him to be. Petr had been run ragged.

"I'll record you from here. We might need it for marketing."

"Just don't touch anything else." She waved a hand then tapped keys on the console to add the detour to their trajectory. "Off you go. Tell the idiot he wins."

"Confirming new course for *EC Valiance*; ETA in fifteen minutes," the computer intoned. "Logging change with Artivar Station Docking Authorities."

She pushed off, sliding the chair back on its designated rail. "Send him to the airlock."

En route, she braided her hair—the only style suited to a helmet. Each step she took with sheer will and determination. Three days, that's how close they were to getting home.

She thumped her boots on the polished floors made to look like Italian marble.

The ass's head whipped up as she approached. He frowned, not paying attention to Sharon clinging to his side. "Thanks for this," he said.

Nova met his gaze, tapped a panel, and offered him a suit. "Coming with?" she asked Sharon.

The petite brunette scoffed. "Of course not."

"Then get out of the airlock," Nova snapped. "Or you will be."

"What bee flew up your ass?" Sharon muttered as she sauntered down the corridor.

"Do I strip?" Thorne asked, eyeing the thin spacesuit.

"Yes. Boots are here." Nova opened another panel where various sizes were stacked in neat rows. "I'll fetch the equipment." *And change.* What she didn't want was for him to see the tattoo. Sure, it was in an ancient alien language a xeno-archeologist had discovered in a then-unknown solar system. Still, she couldn't risk Thorne learning about it.

She followed Sharon's disappearing shoulders, intent on some privacy in the cold confines of the storeroom when Petr hurried toward Nova, boards under each arm. *Shit.* And the poor guy had been so happy to be helpful. She waved the suit at him, nudged her head at the airlock, and slipped into the first available room—a maintenance closet. Wiggling into the damn suit took the remnants of her patience. It was designed for short excursions in space, able to take pee, if needed, and keep her warm for a few hours. Across her back, heavy and awkward, sat the circular bracket to which Petr would attach the oxygen tanks.

Leaving her uniform hanging from exposed pipes and her boots on the floor, she padded to the airlock. In time to catch Eli mid-suit. Her heart leaped into her throat, her eyes widened, no doubt to absorb the absolute beauty of this man. Hours of hard work and discipline reflected in every ripple and bulge that formed his chest. His biceps and shoulders were masterpieces. He hadn't been this sexy when he'd had her beneath him.

She forced her gaze away, the cold floor reminding her that she needed boots. The magnetic straps wrapped up her calves, ensuring no air or heat escaped. Same applied to the gloves, from fingers to her elbows. She dropped her pair and his on the floor, needing dexterity to prep him and herself.

"You're not going to help?" he asked, his trademark green eyes narrowing.

"It's a jumpsuit." She didn't flinch, meeting his glare head-on. "How useless can you be?" she muttered, scooping up a glove to peel onto his hand. Sure, his suit had tangled, the fabric almost too thin to feel. But she wasn't touching his skin, even by accident.

He rolled a shoulder and, just like that, he could fasten the suit shut, finally hiding his gorgeous body from her. Petr buzzed around him, adjusting the suit, fixing the tank to his back, then offering him the helmet as she worked on the other glove.

She knelt, taking the boot from Petr and raised her gaze to Thorne's.

He grunted and lifted his foot, allowing her better access to strap on the damn boot. But when he 'lost' his balance, pressing down on her head, she almost threw the offending footwear at him.

"Sorry," he crooned, a shit-eating grin on his soft-looking lips.

A memory flashed of where he'd brushed kisses over her breast.

She scowled. "I don't have to help you. Out there, you could die, and we wouldn't be held responsible." With one violent flick of his boot's last magnetic strap, she stood and grabbed the helmet from Petr, who then shuffled behind her to lock a tank in place. The weight almost bowed her shoulders, but in space, it wouldn't matter. "You signed a waiver, remember?" She beamed at an angry Thorne, showing all her teeth.

Petr's wince meant her pseudo-politeness had come across as a grimace. *Well, fuck that.* She was doing this cloud-surfing bullshit against her better judgment. Niceties weren't part of the deal.

Petr locked the helmets in place then touched his neck. "Check check."

His whiney-twang came through the headpieces loud and clear. "Got ya," she said.

"Same," Thorne said, choosing the longer board Petr had leaned against the bulkhead.

"Fresh fuel canisters on the boards and in the boots?" she asked Petr when he handed her the other board and pressed the controller in her right hand.

"Yup." Then the smiling idiot left the airlock and watched her through the porthole after the doors had sealed.

"When I say we return, we do so immediately," she said to Thorne, clipping her feet to her board. "Velis' clouds contain droplets of sulfuric acid so we can't stay out too long."

He balanced on his board with surprising agility as he too locked his boots in place. The click-click confirmed him good-to-go. "Acknowledged," he said.

She gritted her teeth. That wasn't an agreement. But if the ass wanted to get himself killed, she wouldn't stop him.

While they waited for the airlock to depressurize, marked by the flickering red lights, he angled his head at her. "Don't like me much, I see."

She stiffened. "After your last stunt? Who would?"

The light flashed green, and she shot through the parting doors, micro-jets on the board's tail-end propelling her. Puffs of white engulfed her. She'd parked the *Valiance* close enough as to limit the amount of time it would take to catch the first cloud. Aiming for Velis, she flicked out her legs to change direction.

He whizzed past her, the wall of rolling clouds heading toward them. Two bright plumes of his jets trailed him with every flick of his board. She followed, catching a cloud a little distant from him. His whoops and cheers sparked an answering bloom of excitement. Her breathing became ragged, a perpetual smile spreading her lips. The adrenaline rush was unparallel. She hadn't done this in ages.

Maybe they should add this to their itinerary? They had the equipment so it wouldn't be an additional expense. What else could they do? Climb the peaks on Scatheon? Add the nightlife which had been such a draw for

Thorne. Ice farming on Nyxara? Maybe some unique shopping stops? The ideas had merit, but Captain had the final say.

As she caught another cloud, she had to admit she'd been playing it safe these past years. But never would she thank Thorne for making her realize this. Laughing, she switched off her board's jets and glided back, content to watch him ride cloud after cloud while she caught her breath. Movement to the side caught her attention. She stilled, blinked, then gasped.

That shape was unmistakable. A mining scout.

"*Valiance*," she whispered. "Confirm identification of unknown shuttle between Velis and Auralis."

"What is it?" Thorne asked, heading toward her.

"I'm not sure," she said, lying through her teeth. "Might be trouble. We're sitting ducks out here, and you, Thorne, are worth a fortune...to someone."

"Undocumented Warden Mining Corp scout," Computer droned.

"Shit." She pressed her controller and blasted toward the nearby *Valiance* gleaming like a juicy target. "Thorne," she called, not bothering to check if he followed.

"But—"

"Stay then," she snapped. "Your decision. I can't force you. Computer, note time of passenger's death."

"Sheesh, dramatic much," he said, falling in beside her.

"Mining scouts are notoriously hardy. Which is why they're stolen for nefarious deeds." She waved him past. "Only a heavy antimatter missile can destroy it."

She touched down on the airlock's floor, yanked open a panel, and withdrew a rocket launcher.

"What's that?" he asked.

She gave him a look, vaulted into space, and aimed at the scout.

"Wait!" he called, floating toward her. "There could be—"

"Scouts are drone operated," she said and fired.

The recoil shot her back. She tumbled, head over board, traveling out to space. Usually she wasn't wearing the board and she kept the controller clutched in her hand. This time, she hadn't done either.

"Target hit," Computer said. "Noted in the ship's manifests."

She wanted to scream at it, that now wasn't the time for protocol when she was on the verge of being lost in space. While scrambling for the controller she'd shoved into her pocket, she kept her grip on the launcher. As she closed her fingers around it, she came to an abrupt halt.

"Got you," Thorne said, drawing her into his arms.

Relief burned bright then hit her with the urge to kiss him in gratitude. *Fuck, that's never going to happen.*

With his arm wrapped around her waist, he propelled them to the airlock. She bristled, wiggling to be set free. He only tightened his hold. It didn't help that she was 'upside down' with her ass in his face. The launcher dragged on the airlock's floor when they glided in. The doors sealed, lights flashing red. All the while she fought him, trying to right herself.

"Dammit, Thorne. When gravity's returned, I'm going to hit the floor with my head."

He relented then, letting her struggle on her own. Seconds ticked by. Tension slowed her actions. Screaming, she released the launcher, grabbed the nearest bulkhead, and spun, just as the lights bloomed white. She hit the floor... Hard.

A splutter of curses slipped out, agony spiking along the outside of her knee. "Why is everything with you a pain in my ass?"

She staggered to her feet, gingerly putting weight on her leg.

Petr ran into the airlock, buzzing around them while he removed the oxygen tanks, helmets, and boards. Once he'd left them and nothing obstructed Thorne's face, he cornered her, forcing her to limp backward until her back hit the bulkhead.

"I'm waiting," he said, his voice low, his green eyes more beautiful than the rolling hills on Tarnis.

"For what?" she snapped, squaring her shoulders.

"I saved your life."

"And I saved yours. You're welcome." She shoved past him.

He gaped, but she shut the maintenance closet door on his Adonis-like face. Changing took moments, used to the fastenings of the boots and suit. When she emerged, once more in her comfortable pilot's uniform in burgundy, it was to Petr helping Thorne undress.

Flashes of his well-honed body weren't for her eyes or spank bank. Those days were behind her. She marched off, intent on a steaming cup of Lady Grey.

"Fifty-seven scouts destroyed. Warden Mining Corp has filed a complaint."

Nova settled in her seat, swiveled it to order a tea from the kitchen, then faced the 'music.' "Computer, record this: Undocumented ships of any sort are considered an immediate threat as per the Combined Planetary Alliance treaty. End recording."

She checked the fuel tanks and smiled. "Let's head home," she said, pushing on the big lever at the center of the console.

"Recording communicated," Computer said. "Tea is en route."

She settled back, gazing at the stars and planets in her screens. If it wasn't for that scout, she'd have considered today the worst she'd had since Seth was murdered. With a kiss to her forefinger and middle finger, she pressed them to his digital image. "For you, my love."

Chapter Two

On an L-Class Entertainment Cruiser.

Heading to a movie premiere on Artivar Station. Against my will, mind you.

Year of 2202, May

As exhilarating as the surfing had been, Ms. Bee-up-her-butt had ruined it for Eli. What was Nova's problem anyway? He'd been the picture of charming since he'd boarded this ship. If only she knew how he didn't want to travel to the outskirts of the galaxy to where yet another premiere was being held... He sank onto the couch, letting the pseudo leather embrace him.

Still, he couldn't shake the image of her sexy ass from his memory. She had the best he'd ever seen. And those thighs... He swallowed hard and reached for a bottle of water on the coffee table. Long copper-tinted hair, amber-colored eyes, and plump lips downturned in a perpetual pout? He shook his head, trying to clear it. She hated his guts for whatever reason he couldn't fathom.

The way 'Thorne' snapped off her tongue said it all.

He pushed off the couch, taking the bottle of water to the bathroom with him. The mirror above the vanity showed an all-too-familiar face, one plastered across the media. Fame hadn't been the goal. He smirked and glanced away. Billions of credits were nice, though. What had drawn him to acting was the skills he'd be taught. As a child, he'd marveled at how actors had to learn to ride horses and solarcycles, fence, swordfight, archery, how to use all manner of guns, box, 'speak' languages, fake accents, and romance women. All while being paid. He doubted a better job existed. His last movie had required he learn how to fly speeders.

He hadn't needed to earn his pilot's license, but he'd insisted as part of the contract. Ten thousand hours to master anything, or so the urban legend went. He was far from that, but at least, he'd made a dent.

This cruise to Artivar was supposed to be a break from his many hobbies.

Doing nothing didn't sit well with him when there was so much he didn't know. He hadn't always thought like this. In the early days of his career, the fame had swept him away on a tidal wave of drugs and sex. Those memories he left in the wasteland of his mind.

Although, this trip had introduced him to...Nova. Even her name promised something spectacular.

The shower was topnotch, the pressure almost too much. The spray pummeled his body like a mini-massage, easing the tension he hadn't realized he'd carried.

She'd fired a missile like it was commonplace. No hesitation.

That ricocheted in his thoughts.

But her tumbling away had sent a shiver of fear through him. He grinned, flicking water off his cheeks. Her butt in his face...priceless. She'd filled his arms perfectly for that split second when she'd righted herself.

Just a pity she was such a viper.

Well, challenge accepted.

He washed his semi-hard cock, admitting Sharon's ministrations were acceptable. But taming the shrew, now *that* was irresistible.

"Eli, you there?" Graham called.

"Yeah," Eli said, wrapping the towel around his hips and padding into the lounge. "What's the buzz?"

On the massive screen mounted to the wall, a perfectly coiffed Graham was in crisp focus. "Good. You ready for the premiere? Found a date? Emphasis on singular." He arched a gray brow. "Let's not repeat the last debacle."

Eli grunted, although, said debacle had been fun.

"Galactic Studios wants you for another space western, if you're up for it." Graham chuckled. "If your ass has recovered."

That hadn't been his first...rodeo. Except hours, days, spent in the saddle had hardened him beyond the physical. "How soon?" he asked.

"In about two months. I told them you needed a breather."

Eli smiled. "And that's why I pay you an exorbitant salary."

"You...seem different," Graham said, his tone speculative.

Eli shrugged. "Just got in from cloud-surfing." And blowing up stray ships. How could she get away with that? Surely some owner would be up in arms? And to state it was drone-operated without checking first? That woman was reckless, fearless...

He fucking loved that.

"Did you record it?" Graham frowned. "Publicity matters," he said like a long-suffering father.

"Nope. Was having too good of a time." Eli's heart whispered it was the company, but being snapped at, glared at, and treated like a child... The latter had sucked, but the rest he hadn't minded. For once a woman wasn't swooning over him, telling him how handsome and rich he was. Some tried the 'you're such a good actor' angle. With Nova, he got the sense her hatred was genuine and not a trick to get between his sheets.

His cock hardened at the thought of her beneath him.

Shifting in the chair, he angled his groin away from the screen. He didn't need another lecture on abstinence and how amazing it was for the soul. If Graham wanted to be a monk, that was his choice. For Eli, orgasms were a mini-escape from reality. He could pretend he wasn't stuck on a cruiser heading to yet another premiere. If he could skip those, he would.

It's part of the job, Graham would say.

Been to one, been to them all. Eli learned nothing new except how to waste hours of his life. Sure, his fellow actors made fools of themselves. That was mildly entertaining, but again, nothing new.

He quieted. Now if he could get Nova to be his plus-one...

"You can work miracles, right, Graham?"

The older man narrowed his eyes. "What do you want now?"

"There's a certain pilot on this ship who hates my guts. I want her to be my date." Eli chuckled. Oh, she was so going to love this. Pity he couldn't be there when she was ordered to do it.

"No way, Eli. That's just going to lead to more shenanigans. I'm still recovering from your last mess."

"Except for a reel of me getting champagne thrown in my face or my shin kicked, I don't think it will be *that* bad."

Her flushed cheeks, those amber eyes spitting venom at him, her breasts heaving with each ragged breath... Hell, he couldn't wait. "Do this for me, and we won't have to delay Galactic Studios."

Graham's eyebrows shot up. "Wow. I've never seen you this…interested. Why her?"

"She's amusing," he said.

Her muttered, "How useless can you be?" had been the final nail in the proverbial coffin. Here she thought him spoilt, coddled, his ego the size of this ship, no doubt.

But how could he change her opinion of him? Drowning her in gifts might earn him a slap. His breath lodged in his chest. He was tempted to order a shit ton of goodies just for her reaction alone.

"All expenses paid, of course. I can't have her looking less than perfect." His mind went there, conjuring images of her in a skintight gown, a slit exposing her toes to her thigh, her hair unbound… Fuck, he salivated just at the thought of seeing her curviness celebrated.

"Make it happen," he said, his voice hoarse. "Promise anything."

"Whoa, now wait a minute." Graham jerked back. "Getting women for you isn't in my job spec."

Eli met his gaze. "You forget who you're talking to."

"Yeah, yeah, heart throb of the century."

"I have less chance of her doing anything sexual with me than I do winning an award for my last performance." He grimaced. Space westerns didn't require stellar acting, no pun intended.

"Mm, maybe I should meet this angel." Graham smiled.

"Fair warning; she's more likely to bite your head off than give you the time of day." Eli slid the closet door aside and chose a pair of yoga pants. Tonight, he wasn't interested in anything carnal. Some time alone might just be what he needed. Hidden behind a wall, he dropped the towel and pulled on his sleepwear.

"Got plans?" Graham asked.

Eli peered around the partition. "An early night."

"What? No woman to sing you a lullaby?" Graham sipped from a glass of green sludge: kale, spinach, lemongrass, apple and pear—all imported from Tarnis. "Maybe it's your known philandering that's off-putting."

"Oh, you smooth talker," Eli teased, settling on the couch again.

"Hang on a minute, let me talk to Captain Harolds." Graham's image switched to an 'on-hold' message.

Eli drank from his bottle, content to wait. It wouldn't be long. He couldn't see anyone forcing Nova to do anything against her will. Head-strong, opinionated, all fire, and hell, if she didn't bring a little brimstone with her.

In the past days, what staff worked on board were but a handful. The chef was on par with some of the six star restaurants he'd frequented. But every other task fell on the captain, Petr, Sharon, and Nova. She'd been the one to drag his ass off Auralis, although, he'd been too stunned to react. With the help of the hotel's security, he'd been hustled from between twins and into a shuttle, all in darkness. No publicity had leaked. No images of semi-naked him mid-fuck. No half-lidded blurred shots of him trying to hide his face. Nothing.

Graham should hire her hands down.

But that had been thirty minutes of his life he couldn't recall well. Had he been less drunk, he might have enjoyed watching her move him around like he was a chess pawn.

Yes, she'd be the queen, all regal, standoffish, and proud.

He almost rubbed his palms together, the urge to cackle gripping him. Knocking her off her pedestal would be his interim hobby.

"The captain said he'd talk to her." Graham's face flickered to life on the screen, closer than before. "He sounded skeptical, Eli. Do you have a back-up plan? If you arrive at the premiere without a date, all hell's going to break loose. They'll be blaring it about that you've lost your mojo, are dying, are pining... Oh, dear Lord." He rubbed his face, his manicured fingers trembling.

"Of course I have a spare," Eli said. Although he'd prefer not to take Sharon, he couldn't see her declining a night in the lights. After all, she'd succumbed to his wiles with not much effort on his part.

"Good boy," Graham said, slumping. "Almost had me in a panic. The press would imply you hadn't gotten over Bella yet."

Ah, Bella. The second she'd slammed out of his life, he'd moved on. And yet, she tried every social event they both attended to win him back, turning nasty when he ignored her. As an actor, he saw too many sides to people. Which was fine when he was playing a role, but real life required honesty. Why hide who he was?

"Well, that's it for me. I'll let you know what the captain says."

"Word for word?" Eli arched a brow.

"I'll record it. Happy?" Graham clicked off, leaving Eli alone, in silence, with a muted hum of either the air filtration system or the engines.

He pulled his tablet nearer and typed 'Nova Blake' into the search engine. If he was to get under her skin, he needed ammunition.

Nova Blake. Age: 29. Marital status: widowed.

His finger hovered an inch from the screen, shock stiffening his shoulders. Losing a loved one changed a person. That explained much about her no-nonsense attitude. He flicked through images of her and four women, happier than he'd seen her since boarding the ship. One woman was much older, but the similar features said grandmother. The other three women had to be her sisters.

Top of her class in flight training, said one comment. That he would believe. He doubted she did anything without giving her all. Which meant, she'd loved her husband with her entire being.

What would it feel like to be someone's world? He had no idea.

If it wasn't for his aunt and uncle, he and his siblings wouldn't have known what family meant. His chest ached, and he rubbed it, a sudden homesickness sweeping over him.

Thinking of you. He sent the text, not expecting a response. They knew he loved them. That was one thing his fortune had taken care of...a place for them to call home. How long since he'd visited? Guilt made his heart twinge.

Before the next acting gig, he'd pop by and spoil them a little.

Light tapping on his door stole his focus. *Sharon.* Not that he answered, instead, sinking deeper into the couch and cradling the tablet closer. He flicked through image after image of Nova and her sisters until a man's face stopped him. This had to be her late husband. She clung to him, her gaze adoring.

He tossed the tablet aside. Researching her had done nothing to aid his mission. And he was damn sure not going to let her loss soften his resolve.

What he should do is find ways to annoy her. Regardless of whether she agreed to escorting him to the premiere, he needed more: between now and Artivar were many planets he could force her to 'visit.'

What followed was an hour listing activities that would crack her shell—something he wanted with too much eagerness. Tarnis had orchards and tea emporiums. Nyxara offered ice farming and hot springs. If the *Valiance* had a speeder, stone skipping along Velis' rings would be somewhat new. On Caerule, he could go kangaroo hopping.

He chuckled as he messaged Captain Harolds, copying Graham in the request. Now, if only he could be there when she reacted to this.

He tapped his chin, running his fingertip along the dimple in his chin. "Petr...."

A laugh slipped free, and he leaned back. Oh, yes, he'd convince Petr to share the security feeds or his name wasn't Eli Thorne.

Chapter Three

On the EC Valiance.

Babysitting egotistical, selfish, and sexy Eli Thorne. Did the universe hate her?

Year of 2202, May

Familiar lips grazed the shell of Nova's ear. She whimpered, squirming under the sheets as need pummeled her senses. Her fingers twitched, desperate to test the thick muscles of his chest. He gathered her close, stealing a sweet kiss before traveling lower—one destination coming to mind.

Her thoughts scattered. But each kiss, caress, and flick of his tongue pulsed pleasure through her, evoking scents, textures, tastes, and memories.

Ecstasy loomed, bolstered by pure anticipation. Her breath caught. A tremble swept over her, skittering goosebumps across her skin. Her nipples puckered.

And the alarm blared.

The what?

Her eyes opened to the lights brightening, the window blinds sliding aside to the breathtaking view of outer space.

Sweat coated her, plastering strands of hair to her face.

Desire thrummed, unfulfilled.

For Thorne.

She smacked the pillow and scrambled out of bed. No way was she having sexual fantasies about that ass. And they'd better just be that and not long-buried memories. Both she couldn't deal with. Stomping to the bathroom didn't ease her frustration.

She gritted her teeth, almost biting off the head of her toothbrush. The shower was set to scorching, matching the anger burning inside her. She could count on one hand when last she'd had a wet dream. And this was number two. Both had been about Thorne.

She muttered curses, almost yanking out her hair while shampooing.

Her skin glowed when she stepped out, made worse by the thorough toweling she gave herself. Off went a magnet from her uniform, forcing her to calm herself, to inhale for four counts, hold, then exhale for four. Ruining her clothing would cost her credits, and for what? She couldn't blame Thorne. He'd grin like the egotistical ass he was.

No, this...whatever the hell this was...would go to the grave with her.

Thankfully, no one was in the passages on the way to the cockpit. She might have chewed their head off.

She sank into her seat and blinked at the console. "Computer," she finally whispered. "Anything to report?"

"All is well," the pseudo-female intoned.

"Great," Nova muttered. Nothing had changed in her world. That's what she needed to focus on and not what dream-Thorne had made her feel.

"Um, morning, Nova."

At Captain's greeting, she slumped and pressed her temple to the right of the 'deploy rocket' button. "Morning."

"How did you sleep?"

She spun the chair and glared at him. He couldn't possibly know, right? "As well as to be expected."

"Good." He beamed, then inched closer, his hands clasped behind his back. "I need you to escort Eli to his premiere."

She shook her head, disbelief making her question her sanity. But reality hit harder than 45g's. "You want me to do what?" she boomed.

Her cheeks tingled with the heat flushing them. Her breathing had gone haywire, and for the life of her, she couldn't keep her hands from curling into fists. Sensual visions didn't help calm her heartbeat.

"You're acting like I asked for a limb," Captain said, his warm brown eyes so like a puppy's.

She usually couldn't say no to him, but in this case, there was no way in hell she'd agree...

He continued, not picking up on her cues, "Said they would pay for your time, cover all expenses, and book us for the return trip."

She reeled, the world spun, and she sank into the pilot's seat. "So, not only do I have to schmooze with the ass, I have to fly him home?" A giggle escaped her, bordering on hysterics.

"It's just one night," Petr whispered, coming around to massage her shoulders.

Now that took guts. Anger warred with disbelief with amazement, and here Petr took a chance she wouldn't strangle him.

"And you get to keep the clothes." He offered a tentative smile.

She giggled again, then hiccupped, giving up on the man to face the real authority in the cockpit. "I'll stab him with a champagne flute if you make me go."

Captain winced, then tugged on the hem of his pristine white jacket. "We need this." He raised his sad gaze to hers. "I'm not above begging, sweetheart."

She blinked, switching her focus between him and Petr huddling in a corner like she was about to explode. When Captain didn't back down, she slumped and stared at her clasped hands in her lap, zipping between excuses that lost their shine when she examined them too closely.

"I know," she said, keeping her tone gentle. "It's just that... This makes me feel dirty, like you're not above pimping out your staff. If I wanted to spread my legs—"

"No one said anything about sex," Captain gritted out. "Just spend the evening at the premiere then head home. Or not. Your choice."

"*My* choice?" she squeaked, then pinched the bridge of her nose. "You're bulldozing me for publicity and credits. What's that if not prosti-tution?"

Captain tutted, but he had the decency to blush. Such a gentle soul, and she did adore him, but still. That he thought he could ask this made a piece of her heart shrivel up and disintegrate into a puff of ash.

"You don't like him?" He frowned. "The man's handsome, rich—"

"Lacks morals, has an ego bigger than Jupiter," she ticked off on her fingers, "not to mention his entitlement complex, his arrogance, audacity, sheer—"

"All right, I get it." Captain waved his hands, one missing a wedding finger. "It's a few hours of your time, Nova. Please."

"Tonight's the farewell dinner. Let me get through that." *Without imagining where his lips have been.* "If he can...*behave* himself, I'll think about it."

Captain grinned. "Knew I could count on you."

"I said I'll think about it," she snapped.

He shrugged. "I consider that a win. Come, Petr." He nudged his chin at the door. "Let's leave Nova to her thoughts."

"Good idea." Petr hurried out then peeked at her. "Whatya wearing?"

She glared at him.

He paled then bolted with a "I'll have kitchen send you a tea."

Alone, she couldn't slow her heartbeat nor draw in calming breaths. Be his date? Why the hell would she agree to that? The man was an arrogant ass. And he'd no doubt dress her in something insanely slutty, not to mention parade her around like he owned her.

The evening would be demeaning, and everyone she knew would see her. His premieres were the talk of the town, so to speak. Talk she always ignored as best she could. Now her name would be on every man's lips while women glowered at her.

Would he let her strap a blaster to her thigh? A dagger? Would that make it through security?

"No," she squeezed past the lump in her throat. "Why can't he go alone? Can that man not be single for a second?" She scoffed and shifted in her seat.

"Tea?" Sharon said, walking into the cockpit. She balanced a teapot on a tray, the cup rattling on the saucer. "What's the matter, Nova?"

"Something Captain wants me to do," she said, rising to help the poor girl slide the tray onto the flattest surface in the room—the shifting galactic map built into a side console.

"Well, he *is* worried about his ship," Sharon said, leaning against the doorframe. "At the cost of fuel, he's grateful the ship uses solar."

Not to mention their salaries and other expenses Nova could only hazard a guess at. And here she was, bitching about spending a few hours at a party. She bowed her head, shame lacerating her conscience. "Thank you, Sharon. I needed that reality check." She flashed a smile to soften her words.

"Um, okay. Nova?" Sharon wrung her hands. "What are you wearing tonight?"

"My dress uniform?" she said, gesturing to her clothes.

"Oh? Yes. May I borrow your blue gown?"

Nova studied the slender young woman. "It might be too short for you but sure."

She beamed; a flicker of familiarity to Captain's features—expected of his niece. As young as she was, Thorne should have left her alone. Seemed his morals had dropped lower than Nova had thought. She swallowed past the bile pooling at the back of her throat. A quick sip of Lady Grey eased a hot path down to warm her belly.

"I'll drop it off," she said when Sharon lingered.

"Thanks, Nova," Sharon called as she hurried down the passage.

Nova ached to help Captain at Thorne's expense, but she sure as shit didn't want to spend any more time with the conceited actor than she had to. The trapped feeling made her stomach knot despite her beloved tea.

Sighing, she sipped from her cup while searching possible tourist sports and spots. When she brought the idea to Captain's attention, she wanted to have all the information ready. He'd want to know costs, strategy, the target market.

Cloud surfing off Velis? They had the equipment. Although, a few hardier suits would help against the harmful chemicals.

Clubbing on Auralis? She winced. That didn't align with the other options, considering the amount of trouble guests could get up to when alcohol was involved. The thought of babysitting them made her ass twitch. Getting Thorne out of the hotel and on board without the media finding out had solidified a few connections she could rely on if they had to visit Auralis. They'd have to hire muscle, because if this took off, she couldn't see Petr taking anyone down; bless his soul.

Apple picking on Tarnis? She couldn't find any orchards with seasonal pickings for non-farm staff. Which meant the *Valiance* would be the first to offer this *if* she could negotiate with the orchards.

Ice farming on Nyxara? The cold made her think of a bath, one she hadn't had in so long. Storing water on board for the luxury of a bath was too cost prohibitive. But a dip in hot springs on Nyxara after an hour or two of chopping icicles might have great appeal.

Investigating the feasibility of these would require a hands-on approach. And an expense Captain would need to agree to.

They needed to end the package with something lavish. A special dinner at the end of the known universe? Mm. She'd have to give that more thought.

There were also shopping trips across space stations—all had upper levels targeting tourists, but she also wanted to show them the memorable pubs in the bowels—the best mining hopper, the sticky donuts made by Mrs. Lee on Artivar, where to get fake tattoos that were safe and lasted a while, and the antique book store in New Liberty on Auralis.

She blinked back tears. She and Seth had visited these places during their honeymoon, finding it an adventure to stumble on such hidden treasures. Sharing them with tourists would be an homage to her lost love and former life.

Flicking the tears aside amid sniffles, she scrolled through the first draft of her proposal. When they reached Artivar, she'd pitch the idea to Captain. And hopefully with Thorne's endorsement, this would be, as Gramma would say, a slam dunk.

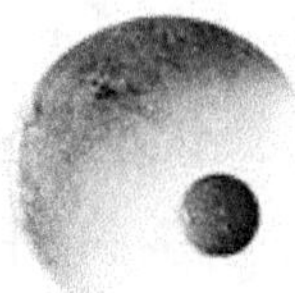

With her focus on the passing space, Nova lost herself in the view. No matter how many times she made the journey, the ever-changing beauty stole her breath. Even when the view was from the executive lounge and she had the 'pleasure' of wining and dining the guests.

"I would officially like to ask you to be my 'date' for the premiere." Thorne's baritone made her ears hum.

She smothered a shiver but could do nothing about her staccato heartbeat.

She met his gaze in the glass's reflection, preferring that to meeting him head-on. Still, her cheeks heated, remembering where she'd dreamed his lips had been. "Why?"

"I want someone I can talk to. As pretty as Sharon is and I'm sure many other women are on Artivar, you I can trust."

His honesty snuck under her skin and hit her in the solar plexus.

"You don't like me." He settled beside her, his shoulder almost touching hers. "Which means there's no silly attempts to take advantage of me." He studied his half-finished water. "It's refreshing not to have to be on my guard around you. Maybe this once, I can enjoy the night without second-guessing everything you say and do." He took a sip, rolled his lips, then offered her a smile. "No strings attached. Just good entertainment, food, and company."

He sauntered off, pausing beside Captain for a chat.

Damn, the man was good. He'd gotten better at it, to be sure. Last time, he hadn't had to do anything and virginal her had let him have his way with her. She scoffed. The poor thing, offered endless sex and adoration? It had to be too much for his sensibilities.

But he was right. She wanted *nothing* from him. Shit, she'd toss him into the pit of hell to save an enemy. She froze at her nasty thoughts. That was too mean of her. No one deserved eternal torment. If she could knock him down a peg or two, she'd snap at the chance.

Which meant...she was going. As his effing date.

She marched to him while he stood next to Captain. "Fine. I'll do it."

Thorne's smile was breathtaking. Had he given her his smirk, she would have rescinded her agreement. But this...was genuine.

"No backing out?"

She bristled. "I'm a woman of my word," she gritted out.

"Thank you, Nova," Captain said, sidling between her glare and Thorne.

She huffed and set the wine aside before she shattered the glass. "I—"

"My agent Graham will be in touch to ensure all's ready for our arrival." Thorne bowed his head, his light brown hair falling across his temple. She'd once flicked it aside mid-thrust.

Anger stole her tongue even while she clenched her thighs together. There was no finding the man sexy. She knew damn well who Graham was. He was the ass who'd called her appearance lacking. Oh, how the tables had turned. She was tempted to ensure she looked hideous.

"Um, Nova?" Petr crowded her, snuck a glance at Thorne, then ushered her to the dessert buffet. "Since we're passing Tarnis—"

"No," she snapped. "We're not going on yet another joyride."

"Tea emporiums."

She froze. That didn't sound bad, and she'd wanted to sample the many teas Tarnis had on offer. "At his expense?"

"Yes." Petr wouldn't meet her gaze.

She narrowed her eyes. "What else?"

"Ice farming—"

"What?" She fake-winced as if the idea was the worst she'd heard. Having just considered it as part of a tourism package, investigating whether it was feasible made sense. Especially when Captain wouldn't have to pay for it. "The next thing you're going to ask for?"

"Caerule."

She arched a brow.

"Kangaroo hopping." Petr's smile was tentative. "I didn't know that was a thing."

Neither did she. By the way Thorne hovered nearby, Captain found the cheesecake fascinating when he couldn't eat it, and how much Petr had stiffened, they expected her to overreact.

What she wanted to do was grin like a cheshire cat with a bowl of real cream. What else could she get him to pay for? That question had her brain spinning with ideas.

Clearing her throat, she fixed a glare on the three co-conspirators. "The delays better be minimal. Artivar's docking fees rise with every change." She scooped up a fruit bowl and sank into a chair next to a moon-eyed Sharon. "What's your problem?" she asked the girl.

"I must have done something wrong... He's ignoring me." She sniffed.

With her spoon in her mouth, the splashes of tart and sweet fruit coating her tongue, Nova couldn't respond. She swallowed, coughing when she choked on a small piece of apple. "He's an actor. He fucks anything that moves, and you think he'll change his ways for you?" She bit her lip. "Sorry, Sharon, that was a little harsh."

A tear slipped over the girl's delicate cheek. "You want him for yourself, don't you?"

Nova laughed. "I'd rather sleep with aliens."

Sharon leaped to her feet and spat, "That's because he wouldn't look at an old woman like you anyway."

Nova blinked at the girl's disappearing back. "Uncalled for but expected," she muttered, digging into her fruit salad. Only for wealthy guests did they offer actual fruit, and no hissy fit from a naïve girl would stop her from enjoying this.

Sharon would come around. Life had a way of teaching the hard lessons. Like self-respect, integrity, honor, and what love truly meant. Arguing with the silly girl made Nova shift in her chair. As the 'old woman,' she should've known to be gentler.

Well, the warning was conveyed however poorly.

She licked the spoon, her gaze on the pants hugging Thorne's fine ass. Perhaps she needed to listen to her own advice. A snort escaped. The chances of her succumbing to anything sexual with Thorne were the same as a wormhole swallowing this ship in 1...2...3...

She chuckled when nothing happened.

"Slim," she mumbled and fetched another bowl of fruit.

CHAPTER FOUR

Despite the forescreens filled with images of domed farms, solar panels, and water tanks, Eli couldn't drag his gaze from Nova's hands caressing the lever. She flew the shuttle with such ease, her guidance delicate—grace in all her movements. As new as he was to piloting, he doubted he would do better.

Once again, she wore her uniform. He'd have liked to see her in an outfit that was more...casual. Though how he'd breach that subject, he didn't know. Maybe a pilot's salary wasn't enough for such...luxuries. Or she was lazy and didn't want to waste the daily effort of choosing something to wear. He got that when his every choice would be scrutinized or worse, taken as endorsement. Graham had a seamstress on call to remove any branding from the garments he bought.

"Tarnis Messis Station, this is *Honor* Sierra Alpha One Tango Eleven. Requesting docking location and sequence." She careened the shuttle toward the circular floating station gleaming white against the bold greens of Tarnis below.

Shuttles, cargo ships, and tourist cruisers littered the space around the station. Not in chaos, but with an impossible synchronicity.

"*Honor*, this is Messis Station. Proceed to dock at Bravo Vector Two," a man droned. "Security has been notified for pre-disembark check and sterilization."

"Copy that, Messis Station," she said, so calm and professional.

Within minutes, the docking clamps budged the shuttle then thunked as they latched and sealed to the sides.

She powered down the engines then leaped out of the seat, almost colliding with Eli, who'd yet to step back.

"Ready?" she said, squeezing between the chair and him without touching either.

"Sure," he said, trying to capture her perfume without appearing to do so. Somehow, her subtle spicy scent lured him to misbehave as if he couldn't go for long without the company of a woman. He squared his shoulders and trailed her. "Any idea where we're going to start?"

"Oh?" She smirked. "I thought this was your joyride." She shrugged on a formal coat in a matching red, then with a flourish, flicked out her ponytail. "I would start with the tea emporiums since we pass those first. Then we can choose a fruit and see if they'll allow us to pick a few." She shrugged before punching a red button that opened the shuttle's door to the tether.

He paused, drawing in a deep breath of the cleanest, sweetest air he'd ever tasted.

She did the same, a dreamy smile making her appear more...approachable. He'd been thinking 'beautiful,' but he needed to get his mind out of the gutter. Sporting a hard-on in public was a nightmare to deal with, press-wise.

"That's it?" She gestured to his expensive denims and buttoned-up shirt made from Ganymede cotton.

He glanced down, liking how his real-leather boots held their polish. "What?"

"You stand out. Or were you planning on adding an obstacle course to the day? I'll let you dodge your sycophants, without spending an ounce of sweat."

"Gee, thanks," he said, but he dug out his sunglasses and slipped them on.

She blinked at him then giggled. "Besides looking strangely more virile, that's not a good disguise." She sighed, opened a closet, and pulled out a matching coat. "Wear that. If I had a helmet, I'd insist on it too. Just your lucky day I didn't pack one."

He pinched the collar of the coat and eyed it with distaste.

"It's clean, and the captain's so it should fit." She marched off, leaving him to debate whether wearing the coat would kill him.

Harumphing, he slid it on then strode after her.

She walked backward, good humor warming her features. "Swagger less. Gotta hide all your signature moves."

That was harder to do than wearing this tent of a coat. But he couldn't help the swell of excitement at her twice complimenting him: virile she'd said, and that she'd noticed his...swagger. This was turning out to be a most entertaining expedition. When he'd rattled off a list of activities, Petr's arching brow at the mention of tea piqued Eli's interest. He didn't much care for tea, preferring pure water. But when the man had revealed Nova's preference for Lady Grey, Eli had succumbed. The chance of spending more time with her was too much to resist, even if he had to sip tea.

"Welcome to Messis Station," a uniformed station-sec said, halting them with an extended palm. His face was half-hidden by a tinted visor. As was his partner's.

"Thanks," Nova said, bouncing on her heels. "Any issues with our identification passkeys?"

"No," the man said, reading something off a tablet. "Scans also confirm no weapons or organic matter on your persons. Please step into the spray and exit only when the light switches to green." He tapped a circular disk at his booted feet.

She took up position and waited as a fine mist enveloped her. Eli did the same on another disk. Mint burned his nostrils, but the stench of chemical cleansers clung to him after the green lights flashed.

"For visiting dignitaries, please wear this S.O.S. device." The guard handed Eli a wrist strap. "Press and hold if you're in danger. We will respond immediately."

"Thanks," Eli said, clipping the strap on. "Do you anticipate trouble?"

The station-sec glanced at his partner. "Of course. It's our job." He swallowed hard. "Your timing could be better. We have a rare event in the Invenire Gallery that has the masses descending."

"Oh?" Eli widened his eyes, his interest piqued. "What's rare about it?"

"Some discovered artefact purported to be ancient alien tech. We have the weirdos, fanatics, and intellectuals on the station. One look at you, we might need to shorten your stay." He cleared his throat. "For your safety."

"I apologize for worsening your day," Eli said. It paid to befriend security, even on a distant station orbiting a farming planet.

"Um, Mr. Thorne?" The other guard inched forward.

Eli knew that expression. He grinned. "Autograph or photograph?"

"Both?" The man glanced away then settled his hopeful gaze on Eli. "My wife loves your movies, made me watch *Yeehaw in Zero G* twelve times already."

Eli fought to keep his smile in place. Nebula Slim had been his worst role to-date.

"You were *amazing* in that," Nova 'gushed,' fluttering her eyelashes and clasping her hands to her chest.

Despite finding her charming, he mumbled, "Quit it."

After posing with the man, Eli signed the tablet on a hastily down-loaded image of the movie's poster. Thankfully, his autograph wasn't legally binding.

Nova hooked her arm through his and guided him toward the outer ring of shops. To the right was a wall of glass, showcasing Tarnis behind it. Along the left were many shops and stalls. The colors were an assault on his eyes with garish signage, lights, and suggestive figures. Worse was the cacophony of sounds from gambling bots and teaspoons hitting tea cups that had the clink of authentic china.

Few loitering tourists snuck glances at him. Some stared without concern. He drew his coat closer and hunched, hoping to 'shorten' his stature. Adding a limp was a temptation, but it would draw more attention than deter it.

"Charlie, how about a cuppa?" Nova cupped his cheeks, dragging his gaze to her upturned face. "You promised me tea," she whined, then stamped her foot while tossing him a pout. She nudged her eyebrows in the direction of the onlookers now whispering to each other.

"I did, *honey pot*." He chuckled, throwing an arm around her shoulders.

Her smile faltered, but she ushered him toward a gaudily lit store. "Let's start here."

The heavy fragrances of incense sticks burned his nose. But her excitement, her wide and sparkling eyes, the way she took in their surroundings... He'd never seen her like this.

"Sure," he said, smothering a grimace.

She bounced inside, her ponytail swaying behind her.

When he followed, pushing through a beaded curtain, the incense faded and the rich aroma of licorice greeted him. He slid into a booth, meeting her gaze across the narrow table.

"Wha' ya want?" an old woman asked, her eyes narrowed with suspicion.

"A little of everything," Nova said, "especially the Jasmine-infusion. Oh, and the granadilla."

The old woman's scowl merged into a toothless smile. "Milk?"

"Of course not," Nova said with a grin. "Are you testing me?"

"I may be." The woman chuckled, but when she focused on Eli, she glowered. "You donna look like the tea-drinkin' type."

"I'm not, but I'm willing to be taught." He summoned his famous smirk. "Rumors have it, a tea goddess is here..." He glanced around the cluttered shop then leaned in as if to whisper a secret. "Only she can convert me to a true tea drinker."

He was laying it on thick, but he wanted the best experience without having a space version of his aunt glaring at him in disappointment.

"Ne'r shall it be said that I, Arell, turned away a student." She waddled off, humming too loudly.

"She didn't need to be charmed," Nova said.

He laughed. "Yes, she did if I didn't want her spit-cleaning my cup."

"Fair enough." She waved her fingers at the illuminated menu above the crockery-littered counter. "Want to try something else?"

"To be honest," he said in a hushed voice, "I don't understand the love of boiled leaves in water."

"Too bitter?" she asked, her hands in her lap. There was no derision in her tone, just curiosity. For once, she was being...polite.

"Too hot." He chuckled. "Grew up—"

"In a scorching climate. I know," she said and beamed at the old lady, who lowered a heavy looking tray onto their table.

He stared over the steaming pots, fascinated by Nova. She'd surprised him again. He supposed his life was an open book.

Arell stepped back, her gaze fixed on them. When he reached for a pot, Nova smacked his hand. His knuckles stung, but he settled in his seat, content to wait.

Arell cackled, grabbed his hand, and massaged it. "That's righ'. Gotta wait f'it to stew." She patted him then waddled off.

"That's it?" he whispered. "No mini-lecture on the origins of tea, what flavors to expect like cinnamon or blackberry—"

Nova snorted. "This isn't a wine tasting." She froze then hummed. "Now that's a good idea. Tarnis has to have vineyards, right?" She shook her head, her eyes wide. "I never researched that possibility."

"Why would you?" he asked.

"Oh, just good to have a general knowledge of our galaxy."

He scowled. "You need to lie better."

She huffed and poured the tea. "This one's granadilla." She pushed the cup and saucer toward him then cradled her cup for a deep inhale.

He did the same, admitting he liked the earthy fruity fragrance. A tentative sip coated his mouth with flavors he hadn't anticipated. The bitterness was there, but the heat of the tea, the subtle granadilla…

"And?" she asked.

"It's good." And he meant it. Enthusiasm to try the next one gripped him, but when she savored another sip, he realized he couldn't down his tea to pour from the other pot.

Instead, he swiveled in his seat and scanned the menu. Fruit teas held some appeal, their flavors mitigating the bitterness. Well, he assumed. After all, this was his first try at drinking tea. He skimmed over rose, hibiscus, lavender, butterfly pea… Lady Grey? He sliced a glance at Nova.

He caught Arell's attention with a wave. "Milady, I'd like to order a pot of Lady Grey and mango passionfruit."

She beamed and disappeared into the back room. When he faced forward, Nova was smirking at him over the rim of her cup.

"What?" he asked before he took a gulp of tea.

"Charmer. You just proved pretty people have an easier life."

"And you're not…pretty?" He arched a brow, blaming his warm cheeks on granadilla-scented steam.

"Apparently not," she mumbled, downed her tea, then reached for the next pot. Gone was her earlier teasing. He'd hit a nerve.

She waved the pot, waiting for him to finish his tea. He hurried to do so while wracking his brain for a safe topic. Even better would be something that would bring back her smile.

This tea, though floral and sweet, was like the taste of a woman's perfumed skin. He grimaced.

"Y'donna like?" Arell asked, her eyes wide with concern.

"I prefer the granadilla."

She shoved aside the jasmine and fetched another cup. With a surprising grace, she poured the mango passionfruit, her fingers not once trembling until she set the pot down.

He cradled the cup and took a sip, his gaze on her. A hum slipped free.

She beamed and scampered off.

When she was out of earshot, he leaned across the table to whisper, "Where did she come from?"

What he wanted to ask was why hadn't Nova warned him?

Why would she?

That thought stiffened his spine and made him realize he had far to go to woo this woman. And why he bothered, he couldn't say. Perhaps because if she did like him, it wasn't because of his fame, fortune, and sex appeal. Her affection would be genuine.

His breath seized in his lungs. If she liked him, it would be for the man he was.

"I wonder," he started, "what this artefact looks like." Safe enough subject and sure to spark a response from her. "Metal with engravings and glowing blue?"

She grinned. "Probably."

"Wanna take a peek?"

"And risk getting spotted?" She eyed him, her cup in one hand as she flicked the other. "The security should be tight. You might have to charm your way in."

"We can ask. If it's a no, then we'll pick apples or strawberries."

She placed her cup onto the saucer, the fragrance of Lady Grey reaching him. "If you get swarmed by your fans, I'm leaving you. No one pays me enough to save your ass."

He studied her, not sure if she was serious, especially after her efforts to get him off Auralis. "Ten minutes. And I'm the client. You're supposed to be doing what I want to do. Nowhere did I sign up for fruit-picking of any sort."

She scowled, huffed hard enough to flare her nostrils, then grumbled, "Fine. We'll go see this silly idol."

Seeing as he'd won that battle, he could be gracious. "I don't want to pour another cup; may I?" He gestured to hers.

With an extended index finger, she nudged her saucer over, the tea barely rippling.

"What do you think of the décor?" he asked, cradling her cup and rotating it slowly, hoping she wouldn't realize what he was up to. It was creepy as all hell, but he ached to place his lips where hers had been a moment ago.

She held his gaze, thwarting him. "I like it. Way better than outside, to be honest."

He gave up and took a sip. The fragrance was floral and citrusy, promising a double whammy of flavor, and yet it was far too bitter for him.

"Not to your liking?" she asked, taking back the cup.

"If I could add honey, maybe…"

She scoffed. "Spoken like a rich man."

He butt-hopped across the seat to rise. Time to end this. As far as he was concerned, nothing beat water.

"Didya likey?" Arell asked, her expression hopeful.

He swiped his wrist over the paypoint. "This was the best tea I ever tasted." Which wasn't a lie, per say.

Nova snorted into her cup as she finished her tea.

He didn't spare her a glance, not wanting to draw Arell's attention to her. "Do you know where the Invenire Gallery is?"

"O'course." She snatched his hand and pulled him out of the shop. With a shaking finger, she pointed to elevator doors. "Take that t'planet. Gal'ry in welcomin' center."

He caught her fingers and pressed a kiss to her knuckles, then left the blushing woman to hurry Nova. His attempts to charm her had been harder than he'd expected. As much as he liked her spitting at him with anger in her eyes, every smile from her was a victory. He wanted her swinging from fury to laughter and back. *Keep them on their toes*, his aunt said.

"Are you done?" he asked, clicking his fingers at Nova.

Her eyes widened, then narrowed, and just like that, the spitfire was back.

He grinned. "Or do you need me to haul your ass out of here?"

She brushed past him, anger in her stride.

He winked at Arell and trailed Nova, content to watch her storm ahead.

"Hope you're not afraid of heights?" she crooned, gesturing to the elevator doors when they opened.

"Not at—all." The elevator pod was nothing but a glass cylinder in a tube. The view was spectacular until they shot down at a speed that should have plastered his ass to the pod's roof.

"Sky elevator," she sang, her beaming smile unpleasant to observe.

Tea roiled in his gut, threatening to spill. He splayed his hand on his stomach and prayed for a miracle.

"Parido Meadows," she said, tapping the holographic map while space whizzed past at a nauseating blur. "We could find out if they'll let us pick fruit or herbs—anything organic." She bounced on her toes, not the slightest bit deterred by their current situation.

He bent over, his face cold, and tea-flavored bile coated the back of his tongue.

"Here." She held out a vomit bag like that was being helpful.

He straightened to glare at her. In that moment, hatred bubbled up and burned his tongue. "You can be nicer. After all, I just paid for your tea addiction."

She laughed. "Bowl a girl over with extravagance, Thorne."

Peace seized his chest. There had to be something wrong with him if he'd missed her snapping his last name at him.

"Jewelry or flowers would be thrown at my face. No, there'll be no gifts for a cranky pilot until she can behave herself."

She huffed and threw the vomit bag at him. "Why don't you hold your breath?" She flashed him a saccharine smile. "Please. I insist." Folding her arms across her chest, she offered him her back as the scenery whizzed past.

He did the same, more so to hide his smile.

Chapter Five

Tarnis' Messis Station
My plan's working.
Year of 2202, May

Nova was torn. Thorne had acted the perfect gentleman and almost childlike in his eagerness to try tea. That he didn't like her favorite didn't bother her, but his charm had. She could almost like him. Squeezing her crossed arms tighter, she willed herself to find nothing appealing about him. The man *had* broken her young heart.

His pale face alarmed her, but after the last comment that she needed to 'behave,' he could faint and lie there in a pool of his vomit.

At least he'd paid for the day's activities. That was her plan and the only reason she hadn't left his ass in Orbit & Oolong. So far, meeting the infamous Arell had been a highlight. And agreeing to seeing this artefact was more to get Mr. Rich-Ass to pay for her research than the desire to spend alone time with Eli Thorne.

The pod slowed when it approached the welcoming center, touching down on a cushion of air. She chanced a glance at her charge, half-expecting him to be green at the gills. Only to whip her focus away.

The ass looked too good: his cheeks glowing with warmth, his sparkling green eyes appearing to reflect the lush farmlands around them.

Noise slammed into her the instant the pod doors opened. People milled about, mothers screaming at their wayward children, and someone even had a pet dog at their heels. A station-sec yelled at a few youngsters banging on the glass walls of the center.

Flashing lights of the paparazzi made her hesitate. "Ready to run?" she asked Thorne.

He grimaced, sliding on his sunglasses, then tugging his coat around him.

His perfect hair tumbled over his forehead in an all-too-familiar style. Thankfully, many men had followed the trend he'd set. She led a path around the edges of the crowds, not wanting to cut a swath down the middle. When they neared, a sec-guard raised his head, studied Thorne, then gestured them to enter.

"Welcome," he mumbled. "We were warned you might attend. Lord Vex Orien will be pleased."

"Who?" Nova asked Thorne when they entered the gallery. The cacophony dampened the deeper they ventured into the quiet confines of art and muted conversations.

"How should I know?" He ushered her past a couple, a hand at her back.

She'd swear his touch scorched her through her coat and uniform. Madness, that's where her thoughts had gone.

"Eli Thorne, what a pleasure." A silver-haired and bearded man strode toward them, wearing an authentic, black-pearlescent leather jacket. He held a glass of champagne in one hand. What impressed Nova was the diamond-studded blaster at his hip when no weapons were allowed planetside.

Thorne flicked off his sunglasses and beamed at the man, his hand already extended for a shake. "The pleasure is mine."

"I'm Lord Orien. Welcome to my exhibition. I'm always on the hunt for new benefactors. Xenology is expensive work, y'know, and finding such treasures isn't for the faint-hearted. Curious about my artefact?" the man mused.

"I am indeed." Thorne hitched a thumb behind him. "The station-sec told me about it, and I must admit, it piqued my interest."

"We're taking it on a tour of the galaxy, hoping to trigger a reaction from it and the general public. Like I said, finding donors is always a blessing. Studies have only revealed its genetic make-up, not its purpose." He led Thorne to the atrium of the gallery where an illuminated plinth took centerstage.

Upon it sat a rainbow-colored stone twice the size of Nova's head. Strange hexagonal and beveled markings were carved into the smooth rock. There were no slips or cracks along the grooves—whoever made those had a steady hand. Whatever it was, it had so much unknown potential.

She eyed it, searching for a flicker of life like a spark or an embryo. "You've just put it on a stand? In the open? What if it's a bomb of some sort? It's alien, right?" She faced Lord Orien, unable to keep the censure from her voice.

He scowled, giving her a once-over that implied he found her lacking. "It is safe, having thoroughly been tested. The natives claim it's a fertility idol." He stroked the surface, the rings on his long fingers gleaming in the bright light. His gaze took on a manic gleam. "Isn't it beautiful?"

"But you think it's something more?" Thorne asked.

"Touch it," Orien urged. "It resonates at a frequency of thirteen hertz. Why, we don't know yet."

Nova tried to snatch Thorne's hand away. "This is madness."

Orien shoved between them, keeping them apart. "If you don't behave, I'll have security escort you out."

Thorne hesitated then pressed a fingertip to the stone. "It's warm," he whispered. "Nova, try this."

"No, thanks." She came around to the other side of him, hoping to rush him out the door. "Your ten minutes are up."

"It's like silk," Thorne mumbled, pressing his fingers to the artefact, "and these marks... I can't feel them."

"Indeed," Orien chuckled, but leveled a glare at her. "They're on the surface yet not detectable by any other sense but sight. Despite the tests we've put this thing through, only the vibrations have been recorded. We've blasted it with everything, from fire to electricity to water. Not even sunlight has an effect on it."

Nova studied the egg-shaped rock, it's myriad of colors blurring into each other, and yet, if she peered deep into its heart, something lay just beyond her understanding. Shapes or words she couldn't decipher. They seemed familiar though. She didn't know when she'd decided to stretch out her hand, but the stone's heat soaked into her fingers almost mirroring the placement of Thorne's.

"Who said you could touch?" Orien demanded. "Only those I invite can meet my stone."

A spark pulsed into her. She gasped, trying to wrench away. She couldn't budge.

"Um, a little help?" Panic gripped her voice. She glanced at Thorne, only to find him in the same predicament.

"What... What have you done?" Orien squeaked, yanking on them both to no avail.

The pretty colors leached out, like the emptying of a water tank. The rock became transparent, and that strange tingling intensified.

"Security," Orien hollered. "You!" He pointed at Nova. "This is *your* doing. Nothing happened when Eli and I touched it."

Nova gawked at him. "Are you insane?" she asked, her mind reeling. "And getting me arrested is so clever when my hand's stuck to your stupid rock."

Orien's face mottled. He unsheathed his blaster, murder in his eyes. "The stone's not stupid. Do you have any idea how many years of my life I've spent trying to find something this worthwhile? It's my...legacy."

Nova blinked at him, not knowing what to say to that load of bullshit. "Well, Lord Orien, *your* legacy has me locked to it."

At that moment, the artefact's last bit of color faded. It shattered, sending shards of crystalized stone everywhere. She flew back from the blast, flung away by an unseen power. Along the polished floor she slid, hitting people's feet before slamming into a wall. Pain radiated outward, her head throbbing, her chest tight. It wouldn't surprise her if she'd cracked a rib.

Thorne was on the floor on the opposite side with Orien dancing between them. His arms were raised in what looked like a rain dance.

That was silly. She giggled, hysteria bubbling to the surface. Tarnis used aqueducts from the planet's vast lakes.

"See how she laughs. This mad woman destroyed my star stone," Orien babbled. "I want her arrested, questioned, find out what she did, how."

Two burly men approached, their black clothes and aura menacing. When station-sec hoisted her to her feet, she offered them a grateful smile. Going with them seemed the safest.

"Eli, do you know her?" Orien asked, fury twisting his features.

Thorne stared at her, then without blinking, said, "A nobody."

Horror sealed Nova's throat. Pain not from the fall consumed her mind, and she let the guards lead her away. Her ears rang, a deafening roar that mimicked the tingling in her fingers. It was minutes later before the realization of her situation sank in. By then, she was in a service pod on her way to jail, no doubt.

"What happened?" she asked no one. "Like I knew his stone would break?" She shifted on the spot and faced the closest guard. 'J. Newman' in gold stated his name. "I get a call, right?"

"Yes, miss."

"Good." She'd reach out to the captain. He had to help her unravel what the hell she'd done to deserve this treatment. But what she truly wanted to do was throw Thorne's belongings off the *Valiance* and leave him stranded. And to do that, she needed to get to the captain first. Thorne with his silly charm and bewitching eyes would claim this was her fault.

Newman pulled on her arm, ushering her into station-sec's central base.

"Now what?" the desk guard asked. "We're full. Damn gallery has ruined my morning."

"Bill them," Newman said. "This one gets her own cell."

"And I'm supposed to find that where? Up my ass?" The man punched his console, moaned, then pointed at any loitering guards. "Go, shift prisoners. I want C7 cleared." He glanced around the crowded control room then settled a beady gaze on her. "Whatya do, little lady? Kill someone? Steal anything?"

"Broke the artefact." Newman nudged her forward.

"Shit," the desk guard muttered. "A murder would've been preferable. Lord Orien's not going to let you off with a hand slap."

"Saw the whole thing go down, Sarg," Newman said, his tone casual. "She touched it, and the colors vanished. It's now worthless shards of glass."

"Pieces? No gluing it back together?" Sarg harumphed then settled a sad gaze on her. "Mm, the way Orien's so gung-ho researching this thing, I'd hazard a guess you're his next guinea pig."

She swallowed past the lump in her throat. No words came to mind.

"I thought so too when his goons loomed, ready to kidnap her." Newman puffed out his chest. "She broke the stone, and justice will be served."

Sarg confirmed her identity, as provided by the docking system. She tapped the edges of the metallic counter, then took a moment to sanitize her hands while shifting from foot to foot.

"Can I call my captain, please?" she asked. "This is a misunderstanding. Why would *my* touch break the stone? Thorne was touching it, too."

Sarg nudged his head at the comm device mounted to the wall. "Get your things in order, miss. You could be staying here for a time."

She weaved through the masses, pressed her thumb to the screen, then when it flickered her identity number, she mumbled Captain's full name.

He answered within two rings. "Nova, sweetheart, you okay?"

"Got arrested," she said, her tone devoid of emotion. More like stunned disbelief. An hour ago, she'd been drinking tea.

"What? You didn't kill Eli, did you?"

Oh, she wanted to. Fury curled her fingers into fists, and she pressed them to the cool wall on either side of the device. "It's...worse."

Captain huffed. "There's no sin more abominable than—"

"Some lord is claiming I destroyed his artefact." She snorted.

Silence met her statement. By that, she had to assume Captain had heard of the incident.

"Has bail been set?" he finally asked, his voice strained.

She arched a brow at Newman hovering beside her. He shook his head. "No," she said.

"Shit," Captain said, and that man never cursed. "I'll talk to Thorne—"

"I'd rather rot here than accept any help from that asshole," she spat.

"Now, now, Nova. He's the richest man we know."

"I don't care. He denied knowing me, told Orien I was just another groupie." Her face flushed, and she pressed her temple to the screen's cool surface. "Take the ship, head to Artivar. On your return voyage, you can fetch me. This...bullshit should be sorted out by then."

"I'm not—"

"Marco," she said, going serious with the use of his name. "They could do a full investigation. It was years ago, but they might just make you pay for it again."

Silence stretched on, so long that she checked the call was still connected.

"Yes, you're right. My...past might complicate things for you."

"Take the *Honor*, too. We can't afford to replace it." She heaved a deep breath. "Docking bay Bravo Vector Two."

"Gotcha. Need any of your things?"

"No," she said. "They're safer with you. I'll get these charges dropped. The gallery has to have security footage. That should clear my name." Oh,

Lord, she hoped so. When credits were involved, a not-so-decent judge could be bought.

"What about Thorne?"

"He can go to hell for all I care," she snapped.

"He's my passenger. We don't get paid—"

"I know. You can deal with him without me. And you can forget about me escorting him anywhere ever again." So much for best laid plans.

She hung up and faced Newman.

"Do you need medical attention?" he asked, gesturing to her torn coat and blue-stained fingers.

She blinked at the color inking her skin. It didn't hurt or tingle anymore, so she supposed that was a good thing. She'd say it followed the lines of her veins, but no, some twirled, others curled, almost in a floral pattern. It could be toxic, slowly killing her, but with exhaustion pummeling her, she'd care about it later.

"I'm well," she managed, fisting and opening her hands. If she wasn't in shock, she'd almost believe the blue was spreading toward her palm and wrist.

"You ready, miss?" he asked, his brown eyes kind...like Captain's. And Seth's.

"Yes." She trailed him along cells packed to the max, faces peering at her through the white shimmering force fields. Close enough and they could shave the hair off her arms. More than that and she'd lose a limb. A decent deterrent.

Newman touched a panel, pressed his thumb to it, and the shimmer vanished, making her realize it had hummed.

Without his instruction, she stepped into the cell, the scent of fresh mint in the air. Well, at least they sterilized. And after what she'd been through, the bench carved into the wall would suit for a quick nap.

But an hour later, she lay there, staring at the cool, unfeeling lights. No solution came to mind, and every time she replayed the scene, anger bubbled up like a well of lava.

If she ever got out, Thorne would pay.

Chapter Six

Tarnis' Messis Station
Terra Lux VIP Bar
Betrayal hurts.
Day One.

Eli couldn't forget the pain in Nova's eyes. The sight of it had been like a blaster shot to the heart. Maybe getting arrested with her might have strengthened their relationship, but he needed to be free to somehow convince Orien the artefact's destruction was a good thing. After all, the xeno-archeologist had been correct in saying nothing had happened until she'd touched it.

So far, Eli had become his benefactor with a decent donation. That was a start. But the hour was late. The Terra Lux's clientele had thinned and yet, Vex and he nursed another bottle of brandy. He drank on predetermined days—to uphold his playboy image. Tonight, he'd bribed the server to water his down, but it couldn't be too diluted. Brandy was all about the rich gold color, and his resembled piss. He'd outright switched to water an hour ago.

Orien slumped in the couch, sorrow in his posture. "Broken, lost my life's work," he chanted. "All gone."

"Is it?" Eli asked, then frowned at the slur in his voice. "After all, you wanted a reaction, right?"

Orien glowered. "I can't study shattered glass. I'm damn furious station-sec took that cursed woman. Did you see her hand?"

Despite the discussions being about this...event, not once had Orien mentioned the blue ink spreading to Eli's palm. He curled his fingers into a fist and shoved it into his pants pocket where he'd kept it for most of the night.

"With the star stone gone, I *could* analyze the effects on her," Orien mumbled. "Will get my lawyers to secure her freedom on one condition." A wicked smile lit the man's dark eyes. "And if she somehow escapes, nowhere will be safe for her." He met Eli's gaze. "Your saw it go down, right?"

Eli smothered a wince. "Can't you find another with additional funding?" He drank from the water bottle, hoping to clear the persistent furriness from his tongue.

Orien shook his head. "Everything in the universe can be bought, except this. We found it by sheer chance."

Stole it, no doubt, and as Eli got to know Orien, his instincts told him the man would kill anyone or anything that might stop him from stealing relics. Who knew how many natives had paid the price.

"I shouldn't have agreed to put the stone on display. The Galactic Scientific Journal begged me to share my remarkable find with the known universe. And look what happened?" He threw back his brandy. "I should sue them, too."

"Where did you stumble upon it, if I may ask?" Eli leaned back on the couch, grateful for the padding. Exhaustion had drained his energy, but he didn't see this night ending soon.

"Some planet on the outskirts of this solar system. I won't bore you with the details." Orien tapped his nose. "It rhymes with pinata." Then he cackled like a mad witch.

"Another round?" the blonde server asked, trailing her fingers across Eli's shoulders.

He blinked at her, trying to remember her name. Belinda? Belle? *Beth*.

"Please," Orien said, resting his elbows on his knees with the empty snifter dangling from one hand.

"Of course, milord," Beth said, offering a smile. She was all professionalism, but lust burned when her gaze lingered anywhere on Eli's person.

He far preferred the hatred in Nova's amber eyes. Not the hurt. She'd jerked back as if he'd slapped her. What he should've done was bail her out and flee in the *Honor*. But like Orien had said, nowhere was safe. Not even if she managed to hide on a backwater station.

Eli glanced at the two men standing five feet behind Orien. They didn't twitch, their expressions didn't change, and not once did they shift on their feet. Blasters were strapped to their thighs, though how Orien had managed to get those weapons past security, Eli couldn't fathom. Maybe because they were *his* bodyguards?

Eli cleared his throat, fighting the fuzziness of brandy blurring his thoughts. "Tell me, milord—"

"Vex. I insist."

Eli bowed his head in thanks. "*Vex*, do you have any women on your archeology team?"

The man stilled, his refilled snifter halfway to his mouth. "Oh, I've given that some thought, too, thinking her gender was the trigger. But no, other women have touched the stone."

"Then perhaps it stores our energy?" Eli set his bottle onto the coffee table. "Something had to cause it to shatter like that. Yours, mine, and Nova's energy combined?"

"I like how you think, Eli," Orien said, a smirk teasing his top lip. "And no, I considered that as well. Alas, without the stone *and* the woman, I can't confirm or deny any of these theories."

"Even if you have the woman, you'd need another stone."

"True." Orien grimaced. "All the viewings will have to be canceled."

"Your reputation's not in tatters when you have evidence of your discovery."

"I do, indeed," the man said. "I should sue the gallery, this station, all of Tarnis." Anger flushed his cheeks. "My star stone..." His bottom lip trembled. A suspicious sheen formed in his eyes.

"Such a waste of effort and credits." Eli spun his water bottle, finding the light reflecting off its surface mesmerizing. "Channel all that into a new stone. I want to know more, y'know. Why the color? Why lose it? Why only when Nova touched it? Could it happen again?"

"Finding another would be a miracle." Orien groaned. "Only to see it shatter again?"

Eli shrugged, growing bored with this topic when freeing Nova wasn't becoming any easier. "Rainbow rocks are easy to come by, but ones that do stuff... This is progress in my unscientific opinion. It reacted!" He jumped to his feet, swayed, then sank onto the couch. "From full-blown color to clear glass, then to a thousand pieces. Boom. You don't get more spectacular than that. If you need additional funding, I can make a few calls. Let's get another stone, monitor it, then throw people at it. Someone has to trigger it again, but this time, have all your sensors ready. See what it does."

Orien stared at him. "You're right. I'll find another and another. There has to be more somewhere. Even if it means clearing all the jungles from that wretched moon." He clambered to his feet, a little unstable. "I'll keep tabs on this Nova. She could suffer from longtime effects or die. Either would be good to know."

Eli rose to stretch the kinks from his back. "It's about time I head back. Release her into my care. I'll guarantee she'll remain in my company. The less we have to deal with station-sec, the better."

"You're too much in the public eye, and I want to keep this under the radar. Besides, I haven't decided what to do with her." Orien slammed down his snifter. "At this precise moment, I know where she is. If I let her go, she'll make a run for it." He gestured to the closest server. "Come, Eli. I have secured for you accommodation."

Eli scowled. He'd thrown his charm and credits at the man, but to no avail. And there was no way he'd head back to the *Valiance* without Nova's freedom secured. Orien was batshit crazy. Eli wouldn't leave any woman in this man's clutches.

When he'd flown across the floor, his focus had been on Nova surrounded by glass, his concern solely for her. That instinct had to be analyzed and prodded. Other than his family and Graham, no one else had intruded on his emotions as much as Nova did. *Damn fool woman.*

The pod ride to the hotel floor was made in silence. One bodyguard had gone ahead, the other crowded Eli and Orien in the gilded cage. When it stopped, Eli exited without thought, then accepted the card Orien offered him.

"We will talk more at breakfast." And the doors sealed on Orien's features.

At last, Eli was alone, standing in the carpeted passageway. Tea time with Nova seemed like ages ago. Should he visit her in station-sec? Would they let him see her?

The expression she'd worn when she'd been escorted away said he'd be lucky if she agreed to talk to him. He swayed and threw up a hand to catch himself from toppling over. No, maybe after a night's sleep, she'll be calm enough to understand his intentions when he explained them to her.

A glance at the keycard drove him to the left, counting down the numbers on each door until he stood before his. The room was luxurious, even by his standards: cream walls, brass uplighters, velvet and satin fabrics. He slipped off the S.O.S. strap, shrugged off the captain's coat, unstrapped his boots, and sprawled onto the bed, uncaring that a feminine-shaped lump took up most of one side.

After the day he'd had, he was done.

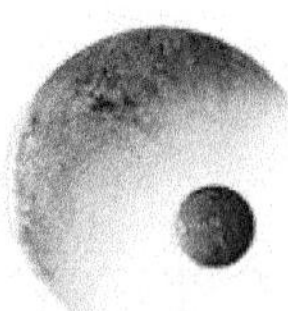

A scream like a peacock snapped Eli's eyes open. He blinked at the bright white ceiling, his mind struggling to register what he was looking at. The bed was ultra hard, and his back pulsed in agony. He moaned, raised his hand to rub his face, and stiffened.

Delicate blue-stained fingers moved as he commanded.

He squeezed his eyes shut then opened them. Had he been drugged? Was he dreaming? He snorted, and ice drenched him. That sound! He snorted again. Nova was here? He sat up and gaped at the white-walled cell. Beyond a shimmer trailed sec officers and their prisoners. None spared him a glance.

What the fuck?

Why was he in a cell? He stretched out his legs, reality slow to dawn. Tiny booted feet? Shapely feminine legs? The red uniform was the clincher. He fluffed the pony tail then slumped, his mouth opening and shutting with but a squeak slipping out.

"I'm dreaming," he muttered, then jerked back at Nova's husky voice speaking.

Panic flared to life, a roar climbed his throat, and he leaped up, needing a doctor.

"Officer," he yelled, striding toward the shimmer and stopping short of it when the hem of his coat sparked and burned. "Officer, please." Each word pierced him, confirming he'd gone insane. "A doctor!"

"Oh, good, you're awake," Orien said, striding toward him.

Eli almost sighed in relief. If there was anyone who could 'fix' this, it was Orien. "Yes, Vex, I need—"

"Who gave you the right to use my name? Do not speak it, you witch." Fire blazed in the older man's eyes.

Eli stepped back, his eyes widening. He'd be an idiot to reveal his current predicament to this madman. The fool might not believe him, or worse, his tests could be lethal.

"What do you want?" Eli demanded, folding his arms across his chest and resisting the urge to stare at Nova's amazing cleavage.

"I'm here for an...apology." By Orien's wince, speaking the word hurt.

"I accept." Eli arched a brow. "Will that be all?"

"No," Orien spluttered, "you say sorry to me."

"For what?" Eli smirked, loving channeling her sass. "Three of us touched your stupid rock. Did you ask Eli for an apology?" He narrowed his eyes. "Or did you just assume I had a hidden agenda?" He strode backward and sank onto the bench. "Neither of us had even heard of your exhibition until we arrived on Messis."

"Regardless, the evidence proves this was your doing."

Eli hummed, unraveling his arms to stroke his chin—his mind marveling at her silky skin. "Something tells me you have mommy issues. That women frighten you."

Orien blustered.

Angering this idiot wasn't wise, but it was oh so enjoyable and exactly what Nova would do. Eli could honestly get behind this woman's attitude.

"And here I was going to offer you a truce." Orien glanced at his goons guarding his back. "Come with me to Lethara to find another stone. Eli has most generously funded my expedition."

Eli stilled. Was that the name of the planet? Rhymes with 'pinata' he'd said. But this about-face had him on edge. Sure, he'd reminded Orien that the stone *and* Nova would lead to more breakthroughs, but still. The man had hardly looked convinced while sulking over his brandy. "Why should I?"

"I'll drop the charges," Orien continued as if Eli hadn't spoken. "A luxurious escort to the jungles covering the Lerathi temples."

"Why?" Eli waited, his gaze fixed on Orien. Last night, he'd been determined to have Nova killed or experimented on. What had changed?

"Eli Thorne suggested you be there when I find a replacement."

Right, pass the blame. Eli shifted on the bench. Her backside was soft, making anything almost comfortable to sit upon.

"So it can shatter again? No, thanks," he said. Slipping into her personality was so much easier than had she been an imaginary character he had to portray.

"Have breakfast with me." Orien flashed a charming smile, making him appear grandfatherly.

Eli eyed him. "For me to accept the invitation, you'd have to get me out of here."

"True," he chuckled. "As a show of good faith." He turned to a mountain. "Make it happen."

Eli's thoughts darted around his brain like cats escaping a bag. What was Orien up to? A chat with Nova was what Eli needed. She had to be awake by now and losing her mind.

He studied her hand, admiring the daintiness of her fingernails and the scar where a wedding ring used to be. Without anyone noticing, he pinched his arm hard. Fire exploded outward and dulled to a heated throb. No, he wasn't dreaming.

This shit's real.

Somehow, he'd swapped bodies with Nova.

And Lord Xeno-Archeologist had no clue what the stone could do.

Eli grinned. "Sure, I could eat."

Staying near Orien was a good start. All there was to know about the Lerathi and their rainbow rocks was in his possession, whether in his mad brain or on some database somewhere.

And Eli had every intention of getting that info. At all costs.

Chapter Seven

Tarnis' Messis Station
Never go to sleep angry.
Day One.

The caress of a hand across Nova's ass snapped her eyes open. What the fuck? She blinked, staring at the lush carpet. The scent of fresh linen dominated her senses when mint was what she last remembered. Furriness covered her tongue, and a headache pinged behind her right eye. She'd almost swear she was hungover. Which was bullshit when she'd been in a cell—

The hand traveled up her back. She flipped over and gaped at the naked blonde in her bed.

"Who are you?" she asked, then gawked at the room. Hotel came to mind. "Where am I?" When the woman reached out to Nova's chest, she scrambled away.

And hit the floor hard.

She splayed her fingers on the bed to rise but stared at a hand not her own. Long fingers, a wide palm, into a masculine forearm? She screamed, lunged backward, and sprawled onto her back. *No! No, no no no no, this* cannot *be happening.* Maybe there were drugs in the minty sanitizer?

Her ears finally came to the party, replaying what she'd said in a deep baritone she knew all too well. "Speak. Now," she croaked, confirming her worst fears.

Crawling across the floor and onto her feet, she bolted for the full-length gilded mirror mounted on a wall. Standing tall was Eli Thorne, all his muscled handsomeness, those deep green eyes. Hell, even his gaping shirt snagged her attention, right down to his bare toes.

"Thorne?" she whispered. His lips formed his name. She flicked his hair off his temple, straightened his wrinkled clothes, and scrubbed a hand over his face. All copied by the reflection.

"Lord Orien said you'd be interested in a little…fun." The blonde woman stepped naked off the bed.

Why would Orien provide Thorne with entertainment? And judging by his fully dressed body, he hadn't done anything with her. Nova didn't swing that way, not anymore, but this beauty would have tempted a monk. She was stunning, perfect, and everything Nova expected Thorne to fuck. Facing the mirror, she arched a brow at the man in the mirror then snorted.

"This is fucking insane," she said, snatching up his boots.

She'd head to station security and bail herself out with Thorne's credits. Then with her body 'in hand,' she'd figure out how to fix this. And there had to be a way. Spending a lifetime like this was out of the question.

When the blonde ran her fingers over his shoulders, Nova shrugged her off and flashed her a glare. "Not interested. See yourself out."

Without a backward glance at the beauty, Nova marched out of the room, hesitated, then headed to the pod. Thorne's long legs covered the distance smoothly, and damn if she didn't wiggle his ass in his signature swagger. Here she'd thought it was part of his act. Seems like he was physically stuck doing that.

Waiting for the pod gave her a few quiet moments to process her new reality. First, she pinched her hairy forearm. A yelp escaped. She'd done it too hard, not used to this much strength. Okay, so not dreaming. She rubbed the offended spot, her thoughts whizzing. When she'd touched the rock, that spark must have been the catalyst. And because Thorne had been on the other side... She stared at his blue-stained fingers and palm. Would this have happened if he'd been someone else?

She groaned, stamped her foot, then glared at the ceiling. *Why him? Argh.*

He was better than Orien, though. Well, to be fair, it might have been entertaining had those two arrogant asses swapped bodies. She drew in a shuddering breath. Now? No, it wasn't amusing at all.

She frowned when the pod's occupant gaped at her. At *him*. Shit. His face was exposed. His sunglasses were...in the hotel room. And the coat. Double shit. Captain was going to be *upset*. Sort of. Under these surreal circumstances, he'd understand.

She hurried across the foyer and onto the wide, well-lit walkway. So far so good.

A squeal snapped her head up.

What now?

"Eli Thorne!"

Like the spreading of an infectious disease, his name turned into a chant amid a group of young women. One broke away, inching nearer to 'Thorne.' Nova wasn't going to wait around to see if they wanted a cup of tea. She bolted, sprinting toward safety with the station-sec signs guiding her. A miasma of perfumes tickled her nose as they closed the distance, driving her on when capture was imminent. Inside station-sec, she skidded to a halt, almost slamming into an officer. Throwing peeks over her shoulder at the many faces of eager women at the entrance, she inched around the desk, placing it between her and Thorne's fans.

"Morning," she said to the desk officer. "I'd like to see Nova Blake."

"Too late," he snapped, not even bothering to meet her gaze.

"What—" she gasped. "What do you mean?"

"Lord Orien dropped the charges and took the woman for breakfast."

"He did what?" *Shit. This is bad. Orien's got my body.* "Why?"

The officer blinked at Nova, then without a word, moved onto the next person in the queue. She eyed the crowds being shooed from the door. Leaving wouldn't happen anytime soon.

"Mr. Thorne?" A muscular man cresting seven feet paused beside her. "I do recall Lord Orien inviting you to join him this morning."

For breakfast, too? *Act the part, woman, or else finding your body is a hell-no.* "Yes. Yes, he did. But as you can see, I'm trapped."

The man frowned, studied the gathering masses, then said, "Follow me."

Nova almost latched onto his ass as he led the way out of the station, cutting a wide path through the women.

"Touch Mr. Thorne and you *will be* shot," he boomed.

Just like that, they dispersed with a few lingering glances. Nova would have done the same. The man was impressive. He hadn't even drawn the blaster strapped to his side. But his deep voice, his sheer size, his confidence...

"You're hired," she said. "That is, if you ever get tired of working for Orien."

She almost laughed. Not even in Thorne's shoes for ten minutes and she was making life-altering decisions.

"My thanks," he said, guiding her toward the domed balcony.

There at its center was the five-star Skycrop Café—too expensive for Nova to ever afford. But as Thorne... She grinned and increased her pace, eager for something warm and delicious to fill the hollowness in her belly. In Thorne's... *Argh*. That was going to get tiresome fast.

Eli watched through *her* eyes as she approached. Dark circles under her eyes had to be from having slept on that hard bench. A quick scan proved Thorne hadn't done anything to her body...yet.

"Lord Orien," she greeted the distinguished man, her memory flicking through yesterday's memories of his mottled face and tantrum.

"Call me Vex," he said, flashing a smile. "How was last night?"

She almost fumbled with the chair when she pulled it out. What happened between Thorne and Orien? "Entertaining?" she hazarded.

He beamed. "Excellent. Beth showed such an interest in you; I had to ensure she fulfilled her dreams."

Beth? The blonde? What dreams? Oh, yes, getting a chance to sleep with Thorne. Nova smirked. Yeah, when that was all the beauty had gotten. Compared to Sharon in looks, Beth was in the stratosphere. Then again, having done the actual deed with Thorne, Nova could say, without a doubt, the woman hadn't missed out on much.

"Lady Grey tea," she said the instant a server appeared. "How was your night...Vex?" she asked, finding it awkward not to.

"Excellent, as usual." Orien gestured to Thorne nursing a damn bottle of water. "Ms. Blake has agreed to discuss traveling with me to Leratha."

"Good," Nova said. "That is if the *Valiance* can spare you." She fixed her gaze on Thorne squirming her body in the seat.

"I'm certain Captain is more than capable of getting me—you to Artivar for the premiere." He winced. "You have piloted as well, have you not?"

She blinked at him. Who spoke like that? Someone who swallowed a digital dictionary? And the thought of him being in control of *her* ship—

"Why don't you go with Vex?" she asked, mostly because she had to keep her body close. Hying off into outer space while creepy Thorne did who knew what to her... She swallowed hard. An image flashed of her hands cupping her breasts and venturing lower— No. No way was she leaving him alone with, well, her body.

Orien flicked his attention between them, confusion in his eyes. "I thought you said she was a fan."

"I said she was a nobody." Nova beamed at the server who slid a cast iron teapot onto the table. Her stomach gurgled, but tea had to come first. "She's also the pilot who hates my guts." She added emphasis to the latter.

"Mm, interesting." Orien smiled at her. "Yes, perhaps you should come, too."

She cradled her cup of tea and savored the aroma. "I can't. The premiere, remember." Surely by then they'd swap back. She had to hope because pretending to be Thorne in the spotlights would be a struggle.

"We can stop at Artivar for that. What's a night along the way?" Orien sipped his orange juice then smacked his lips in delight. Although, she couldn't tell if it was from the ideas she was throwing out there or the sheer luxury of fresh oranges.

"I haven't even said I'll go," Thorne snapped, cracking open another bottle of water and taking a long drink. "He's an ass, and a pain in my butt."

She nodded, taking another gulp of delicious tea. "You agreed to be my date. So if I go with Vex, so do you."

"I can meet you there."

She grinned at Thorne, playing her so well. "No, we stay together. In fact," she laughed, loving what she was about to suggest, "how about we share a suite?" That way, he wouldn't get a chance to fondle the goods. She planned to never leave him alone, not until they switched back.

"With you?" Thorne squeaked. "I would rather roll around in a pit of vipers than—"

"Then it's settled," she said, flicking through the menu on the table's tablet. "The Farmer's Choice," she said, "with extra whipped cream." A selection of fruits, cheeses, and home baked breads? Sounded heavenly.

Thorne's eyes narrowed. He pinched his lips. "Shouldn't you be watching what you eat?"

She chuckled, leaned back, and rubbed his rock hard stomach. "No need."

He dipped his head, but when he raised it to meet her gaze, his expression was one of glee. "Don't say I didn't warn you."

"I see what you mean." Orien waved his fork at her. "She treats you like a child."

Nova whipped her gaze away from Thorne. "Y'know, you're right, Vex."

Thorne huffed and flicked her ponytail.

Nova chuckled. "I do believe I'm going to enjoy this trip. I'll just get my things transferred from the *Valiance*."

She could have insisted they stay with the *Valiance*, but she didn't want Thorne to play the role of Nova Blake amid people who knew her. They were like family, and deceiving them didn't sit well with her. And since he'd gotten her into this situation, a little payback was in order.

"While we're here, let's upgrade your wardrobe," she said to Thorne. "After all, you'll be dining with Lord Orien and myself. I'm sure your current..." She gestured to the uniform she loved so much.

"Fine," Thorne snapped. "But I'm paying for it."

She choked on her tea, then endured Orien giving her back a thump. "No," she managed past the tears. "I cover all expenses, as agreed."

"I get to choose," he said, digging into the fruit platter the server placed before him.

She glared at him.

"I do have business to attend to." Orien flicked a finger at the mountain of a bodyguard behind him. "Frederik will escort you around the center, but do not take longer than an hour. We need to depart as soon as possible. And don't forget. You promised to make a few calls for a little extra funding."

She bowed her head at Orien, then winked at the server when she slid the food onto the table. "I have to admit, I'm looking forward to this adventure."

And a chance to be alone with Thorne, because damn, they needed to strategize.

As sweet and accommodating as Orien was being, she didn't trust him one bit.

Chapter Eight

Tarnis' Messis Station

Skycrop Café

What the hell's going on?

Day One.

Nova snorted when Eli tried to hide a smirk by stuffing slices of pawpaw into his mouth. Like she couldn't see him. She ignored his childish behavior, relishing each bite of the selection of cheeses on her platter. She had to wonder though, why neither of them had lost their shit over this new development? He hadn't reacted because throwing a tantrum in public wasn't something she'd ever heard he did. And he could, now a nobody in her body.

But why hadn't she? When avoiding the paparazzi wasn't instinctual for her. Drawing attention to their situation seemed stupid. Maybe that's why she'd yet to wail at the fates and their silly games. And she'd be forced to 'stay' with him. Pretend to be him while watching him act like her or his perception of her.

Shopping for a new wardrobe wouldn't dent his credits, as wealthy as the paparazzi purported him to be, and she did need clothes. She'd been right about that. And it would give her a chance to 'talk' to him about this insane situation. Traveling with Orien was a risk, but it made sense. She'd expected Thorne to object; then again, he didn't stand to lose his job. He had little skin in the game other than getting his body back.

Solving this took priority. She hummed on a sip of Lady Grey, cradling the cup as if it were liquid gold.

Thorne shoved aside his unfinished meal and rose to his feet. "Let's get this over and done with."

She blinked at him. "What? Now?" Maybe getting this mission started sooner was wise. She set her cup down and rose. "My thanks for breakfast, Vex."

The man waved mid-chew.

"I would like it in writing," Thorne said, playing into Nova's distrust of everyone. "Once we find this rock, I want you to leave me alone." He splayed her fingers on the table and leaned in. "I'm not an idiot, Orien. You're going to want to test my blood. Any xeno-archeologist worth his salt would have noticed we sport the same blue stains. Your rock did that to us."

"Mm, I was going to ask you about that." Orien studied his palm. "I find it intriguing that you two caused such a potent reaction." He peered at them both. "No other effects?"

"I damn well hope not," she said, then winked at Thorne. "Come, Nova, let's get you out of that uniform."

"You can get that thought right out of your head, Thorne," he said, circling the table to reach her. Then with a huff, he marched off, adding an extra sway to her hips, the idiot.

"I do like to watch you walk away, darling," she crooned, smothering a giggle—something a movie star like him wouldn't do. Still, she was tempted.

She trailed him, amazed at how he knew where to go.

Frederik remained on the outskirts of her peripherals; there if needed, so to speak. Probably to keep tabs on them and ensure they made it to Orien's ship. That thing better be space-worthy or else. No way was she going to die in some ill-maintained death trap he called a research vessel. She peeked at Frederik, considering asking him. But she didn't bother when he might not know and she'd find out soon enough.

Thorne veered into a clothing store she wouldn't have glanced at. The items on display were super expensive and made with natural cloth. Synthetics were all she could afford. The ass better not be thinking of slinky and silky. The last time she wore anything sensual was for her anniversary, the year before Seth died.

She wasn't about to dress-up for Thorne, no matter what he said.

Being tall had the bonus of giving her an almost bird's-eye view of the shop's layout. Thorne had already thrown garments over his arm and in colors that might look good on her. They were too dark but at least they weren't in oranges or pinks. She couldn't pull off those with her hair coloring.

"Trying these on," he called, heading to the changing booth.

She bolted, panic widening her eyes and ratcheting her heartrate. Whipping the curtain back summoned a squeak from the shop assistant. "Wife," she muttered to the poor, flustered girl. She took a moment to press a forefinger to her lips like it had to be a secret.

Thorne glared at her, his cheeks flushed. "Get in here, then."

She squeezed in, realizing how big the bastard actually was. "Good," she whispered, checking they were closed in without the shop assistant eavesdropping. "What the fuck happened?"

"You're asking me?" He hung up an array of dresses she wouldn't have chosen. "You touched the damn rock."

"At your insistence." She pinched the bridge of her nose, fighting for calm. "All right. Neither of us knew it would do this, so let's set that blame aside. We need to figure out how to fix whatever this is." She flicked a finger between them. "And this blue shit is spreading. Or am I imagining it?" She sank onto a rickety seat, bringing her gaze in line with her cleavage. "This is all manner of fucked up. And don't think you're going to strip—"

"How else do I try these on? Are you even listening to yourself?" And down went the zip of her uniform.

"I swear, Thorne, if you so much as reveal a nipple, I will neuter you." She spread his thighs, grabbed his balls, and wrenched. Pain radiated outward, and she stiffened. "Shit," she groaned, bending over.

"Yeah, hurts like hell," he said, sliding the uniform off her shoulders.

Thank goodness for her white bra—the better of the two she owned.

"Now you listen to me." He dipped to snag her gaze. "Quit acting feminine," he gritted out, smacking her hand she'd pressed to her chest as if to say, 'moi?'

"Fine, if you walk like you don't have two massive balls between your legs," she hissed.

He rolled his eyes. "You can't go around acting like a woman and telling everyone we're married. That's gold dust to the paparazzi. Hell, I better fill Graham in on this. We're going to need him to curb the fallout from this disaster."

She winced, trying to ignore the fading twinges in his groin. "It explains us living together. You're not getting any alone time with *my* body, Thorne." She wagged a finger in his face. *Her* face. *Oh, Lord.* Dropping his face into his hands muted the moan that slipped out. Sitting up, she sucked in a sharp breath. "Back to the matter. I don't trust Orien, but he has to know something about switching us back."

"The man hasn't got a clue. I tried to find out more last night, only to realize he's our best hope of getting another star stone and undoing this."

"Star stone?" She harumphed. "Well, I'll have to milk him for information. Seems like he's taken a shine to you."

"Yeah, that cost me a small fortune. We need his trust...for now. He had every intention of kidnapping you and doing a full dissection."

"I knew it," she rasped. "Made no sense to release me, then take me to breakfast, all without having an agenda. Well, I'll give him a blood sample like you promised. Maybe that will appease him. But that's it. We're in this shit together, Thorne."

Off went her uniform's top half, leaving her pants in place. He peeled on a dress, letting it slither over her hips to her knees. The lines of the dress were ruined by the pants beneath, but she was grateful she was covered, none the less. The deep red with massive white orchids softened her features.

"Looks like a crime scene," she said.

He grinned. "It does. Next."

"Can't you choose items I'll wear after this is over?" She fingered the fabric of a deep blue summer dress patterned with tiny white flowers.

"I suppose a few boring clothes could be added to the bill." He glided her hands down her waist and over her hips, turning a little to admire the half-bare back. "This one I like."

"Well, I don't," she said, tugging on the bra straps sticking out.

"Mm, shopping for a woman's harder than I thought. Go pick a few things, would you?"

She studied him, trying to gauge whether he'd peek at her intimate bits under her uniform pants. Him seeing all of her was unavoidable. He had to pee at some point. She grimaced, not wanting to even think about that upcoming ordeal. The last time she'd handled a cock was beyond her ability to remember.

"Fine." She left, pausing to close the curtain before pacing along the racks, yanking off pants, blouses, and yes, a dress or two. She'd need evening wear and... Gritting her teeth, she hooked bras and panties off their racks.

Heat scorched her cheeks. She'd wanted the ass delivered to Artivar and out of her life. This... All of this was a nightmare. "These will fit," she said, peeking into the booth. Her stomach churned and she frowned, using an empty hand to press to her abdomen. Maybe his body hadn't agreed with the tea? What else could it be? "Allergic to anything?" she asked. It would be good to know.

"No," he said. "Shoes?"

She huffed, dropped the bundle on the counter, and headed to the racks at the back. Boots, heels, sneakers in black filled her arms minutes later.

"I'll take those," the shop assistant said, her gaze lingering, her mouth parted as if she couldn't breathe. "Is she really your wife?"

"Soon to be," Nova said, forced to remember what the girl was seeing—suave and sexy Thorne.

Said ass strolled out under a mountain of clothes. "All of these, sweetheart," he said, winking at her.

"Are you sure?" Nova gestured with a finger to the shop and beyond.

"Yeah, I'm tired." Thorne pouted and fluttered his eyelashes.

"Of course, *honey pot*," she said, using the worst endearment she could think of. "Frederik, tell the lady where the ship is, please. Have these delivered, miss." She swiped the paypad, trying not to gawk at the amount.

"Very well, Mr. Thorne." Frederik gathered the bags. "I have taken the liberty of having your things transferred to the *Laurus*."

"Thanks," she said, unable to ignore the pressure building in her gut. "I have one more stop."

"As you wish," Frederik said.

"Where to?" Thorne whispered as they headed to the sky pods.

"Orbit & Oolong. I doubt Orien has Lady Grey on board."

"Of course." Thorne sighed. "And you better hurry. You're going to need a bathroom soon."

She glared at him, realization dawning. "You could've warned me," she snapped. "How was I supposed to know you're lactose intolerant?"

"I tried to tell you."

She huffed, stepping into the pod. Crowded in the corner didn't stop her from leaning in to mutter, "You could have tried harder. Watch my weight, indeed." Tarnis below became a blur the higher up they traveled, but what awaited her lay heavy on her mind. "Dealing with your nethers would have been better without an upset tummy."

"Upset?" He chuckled. "Sure, why not call it that. Are you allergic to anything?"

"Besides you?" she asked, arching a pointed brow. "No."

As soon as the pod doors opened, she headed to the tea shop, flashing Arell a smile before ordering boxes of her favorite tea and a box or two of Thorne's. Just in case since she was spending his credits. With that in hand, she gestured to Frederik to lead the way. Of course, Orien's ship would receive priority docking, and damn if it didn't gleam in the weak sunlight. The thing was pretty, all polished silver, white lighting, and state-of-the-art ion engines.

Maybe this trip wouldn't be *that* bad. She could pretend it was a vacation in a den of snakes. Doable if she kept her head down and her ears primed. And made Orien think they were the best of friends.

"We should be honest with each other," she said, climbing the lowered ramp into the belly of *Laurus*. "Have each other's backs, y'know."

"Sure," Thorne said.

"No more surprises." She met his gaze then smiled at Orien striding toward them. "What a magnificent ship," she said, throwing her arms out wide.

"Glad you like it." Orien beamed.

"If you don't mind, Vex, I'd like to freshen up. Shall we meet for drinks in a bit?"

"Absolutely. I'll give you the tour." Orien waved his hand.

Four men crowded them, their gazes menacing.

"Vex?" she asked when one of his men pinned Thorne's arms behind his back. "I thought we had a deal."

"I lied."

Chapter Nine

"Well done in convincing Nova to come with. I thought it was going to be a struggle," Orien said to Nova as if he wasn't imprisoning them.

Eli gritted his teeth. The asshole.

Nova paled, but she was smart enough not to let on that she wasn't who Orien thought she was. "This is a bit extreme. Was this your intention from the start?"

They'd been wined and dined. *Well played, Orien.*

"I must say, your presence is a welcome change," Orien said, striding along as his men ushered them to who knew where. "And sure to boost my funding once word gets out of your patronage."

"Of course." Her smile was strained.

Eli bowed his head. By now he should be used to people using him, but this was life and death. He'd handed himself *and* Nova into the hands of a madman. "Our absence will be noted."

"Pfft," Orien said. "You'll attend the premiere. We all will." He grinned. "But if you thought I'd let you take advantage of my good heart, then you're sorely mistaken. You," he pointed at 'Nova,' "destroyed years of research in seconds. And you," he gestured to 'Thorne,' "thought you could charm me to forgive and forget the disrespect your 'nobody' showed me. I must admit, your credits saved your backside. For that alone, you won't be harmed. I want publicity without the law digging their dirty noses in my business." Orien paused. "Let me be clear. You're my guest. She isn't."

They were marched along a wide passage, white-clad staff hugging the sides as they passed. Glassed labs, canteens, and offices preceded the living quarters. Well, at least they wouldn't be in some sort of cell or strapped to gurneys. They halted in front of an unmarked door.

His heartbeat paused. He held his breath. The door slid open, and they were nudged to enter. A double bed dominated the left, a bathroom leading off. To the right was a small living room. His luggage and their packages sat next to the coffee table. By a wall of windows looking out to space was a table with two chairs. Sheer luxury was in every inch from the lighting to the fabrics to the furniture. The colors were in beige and navy blue, a vase of real flowers adding a little joy.

"What?" Orien smiled. "I'm not a monster, and besides, you asked to share a suite. My team will assess you soon, Blake. Be ready."

The door shut, leaving them alone.

Nova bolted for the bathroom.

Not a bad idea since a pinch-and-pull pressure built in his groin—soon he'd need to pee. Eli wasn't eager to learn how to do that. Men just did a little tap-tap, and they were 'clean.' Women didn't do the same, did they? With how long they were in the bathroom, he supposed they just waited for the dripping to stop. *Damn*. Time wasted, in his opinion. They could use toilet paper and wipe. To speed up the process, y'know.

He searched their room, hoping to find some sort of screen he could use to call Graham. He gave a cry of victory when panels slid aside and revealed...nothing. Whatever had been there was gone, ripped from the walls. How long before Graham worried? Would Captain Harolds say anything other than Eli took his things and disembarked? *Shit*. He should've taken the time to update his manager. Now he was trapped with no one coming to rescue them. Their one chance was at the premiere. With Eli 'missing,' Graham would be in a panic.

He found himself outside the bathroom door. "Nova, you okay?"

"Oh my word," she cried out. "I'm never eating cheese again."

"Cream and milk, too." He leaned against the wall. "It will pass soon."

"Wonderful," she snarked. "Might as well shower. Do you mind choosing something to wear?"

"Sure," he said, grinning.

She was about to wash his body. What would she think when she soaped and rinsed every inch of him? He dipped his chin to his chest, curious about her curves. In the changing booth, her breasts covered in white had tempted him to ogle. He hadn't. He'd taken pity on her sheer panic. Like he'd never see her naked?

It took minutes to unpack his luggage and her new things. And when the shower switched on, he gathered a change of clothes. He didn't do underwear. Neither would she. He chuckled. They hadn't gotten him a negligee, so he took out an old T-shirt.

"I didn't look," she said, emerging from the bathroom with a towel around the waist.

"You can, y'know." Nudity in his films weren't commonplace, but they did happen. So half the galaxy had seen him naked. Except Nova. He watched her expression for any reaction.

She huffed. "No, because you're not looking either. *My* body, Thorne. Remember that." She waved a hand at him. "You're just borrowing it for now."

"Fair enough." He had every intention of disobeying. It was silly when it was unavoidable. "I left you jeans and a T-shirt." He waltzed past her and shut the door in her face.

The mirror was rimmed with steam. He faced it and peeled away her uniform, mesmerized by her white-encased breasts and the way her panties hugged her hips and ass. Her ripped abs truly surprised him. He'd half-expected to find a beautiful softness to her belly. Off went her bra, easy enough for a man too used to disrobing women. Shimmying out of her panties stilled his focus. He forgot to breathe.

This... *This* was hiding under her uniform?

"I knew it," he whispered, spinning to admire the curve of her back into firm butt cheeks. Something caught his attention, and he narrowed his focus on it.

She had a tattoo... In an unknown language that was almost alien-like. Pretty, and familiar somehow.

He eyed the toilet, sank onto the seat like he was going to have a shit, and waited. Not sure for what, though. Like magic, his bladder released. The relief was instant. When it trickled to a few drops, he started counting, wanting to know how long in general he needed to 'drip dry.'

The wetness down there didn't fade. He scowled.

"This is bullshit," he muttered, leaping away from the toilet and spinning to flush it.

While the shower activated, he released her ponytail then stepped into the hot spray, moaning when it coated her tired body. Ah, yes, the hard bench in station-sec's cell. A container read 'bodywash,' it's wet outside proving she'd used it. The fragrances of vanilla and jasmine surrounded him as he soaped and rinsed, trying not to register the silkiness of her skin and the fullness of her curves.

"What's taking so damn long?" she called through the door.

"I'm washing your hair." He flipped open the shampoo to do so, pouring a healthy amount onto his palm.

"Hurry," he thought he heard her say. "I don't want to be alone when they arrive."

He worked as fast as he could, used to long hair. It was minutes later when he finally switched off the water, wrung the last of it from her hair, then got out, drawing a towel around him. It was such a good thing he knew women well. He spent a little time drying her hair before patting the rest of her body with the thick towel. Naked, he marched out, only to halt.

She'd changed the T-shirt he'd wanted to slip into for a complete outfit, right down to the boots.

"I was going to get comfortable," he said, waving a bra at her.

"Hell no when they're coming to 'assess' us. For all you know, it's full body. No need to help them do whatever that idiot has planned."

"You're acting like silk's made out of chainmail." He sighed and clipped on the bra.

Shimmying into a fresh pair of panties was done with way too much wiggle. For shit's sake, he wasn't a woman, but he couldn't help moving like one. Why couldn't she do the same? Why had she brought her feminine ways with her into his...masculine body?

He'd scolded her, but no way would she understand the panic behind his words. At the restaurant, she'd raised the tea cup in a far-too-delicate manner. A scan of the tables around them confirmed they were at the center of everyone's attention. Some were even filming. If he could survive this without damaging his reputation, he'd be grateful. As much as he loved being in her body, he hated not being in his for the consequences alone.

He almost rubbed his palms together in glee. At last, he'd see her in an outfit other than her uniform. Had he left the shopping to her, she'd live in pants and shirts; the proof was the selection sprawled on the bed.

Summer dresses, evening gowns... Lingerie. He grinned, having packed away the latter before she noticed.

"Just..." Her eyes had a suspicious sheen to them. "Take care of me."

"Listen, if I die in your body, there's no guarantee I'll return to mine. You'll probably be stuck as Eli Thorne forever." He caught her wrist and gave it a gentle squeeze. "Besides, I know how to fight."

She winced. "Well, that's comforting. No punches to my face. I like my nose unbroken, thank you very much."

"Yes, ma'am," he drawled.

"This isn't funny, Thorne."

"Don't I know it." But if he was going to be honest, he preferred switching with her. Any other woman would have been inconsolable. Dealing with that and this situation would've been utter torture. Nova had already set aside blame, wanting a solution and teamwork. There was something to be said about a mature woman.

The door swished open.

"How dare you?" she snapped at Frederik. "Can't you wait five minutes?" She gestured to Eli standing there in underwear.

Taking that as his cue, he yanked on the pants and zipped them shut.

"Maybe buttons weren't a good idea." She held out the blouse to him.

"We didn't know," he said, slipping into it.

She swatted his hands away and worked the buttons shut. "We were fools," she hissed.

"Agreed." He sank onto the bed and pulled the boots closer. Socks went on first, then while he did up one boot, she did the other.

"And to think I offered you a job." She glared at the hulking body-guard.

"Why?" Eli asked, then narrowed his eyes at her. "What happened?"

"Just a few fanatical fans." She shrugged. "Mountain over there," she hitched her thumb at Frederik, "saved my ass. Little did I know what he and his sick boss had planned. I think I prefer the fans to kidnapping and experimentation."

The silence ticked on in which said mountain didn't defend himself. When he did move, it was to step aside, sweeping out his arm as if to say, 'after you.'

Eli pushed off the bed, stomped past the man, then paused in the passage. He had no clue where to go, probably to those labs he'd glimpsed.

When she tried to follow, Frederik dominated the doorway. "Just Ms. Blake."

"What am I supposed to do?" She flung out her arms. "Twiddle my thumbs?"

The door shut on her panicked expression.

Eli grimaced. Seemed like they shared a hatred of boredom. Frederik nudged his chin to the passage on the left. Eli marched along it, not even bothering to check if the bodyguard followed.

"Y'know, black is so cliché," Eli said. "I suppose Orien doesn't want you to blend in."

"It hides blood."

Eli pinched his lips. What a mood killer. How would Nova react to that tidbit? "So does the color red. What you meant to say is wet anything. Black's good for that." Yup, that sounded like something she'd say. Sassy to the end. Fearless. He liked that about her.

The lab Frederik led Eli into was blinding white; probably to see all the bodily fluids, wet or dry. There wasn't a stainless steel mortuary slab at the center. Counters formed the shape of an 'S,' with microscopes and other devices across the gleaming surfaces.

Not a medical lab, then.

Odd.

Various staff focused on strange machines on the counters before them. Their gazes whipped up when he entered. And judging by their expressions, they were as pleased to see him as he was to be there.

"We're not used to taking samples from living specimens." A white-clad man stepped forward, his nametag claiming him to be 'K. Doukas.' He shoved a tool into his lab pocket and shambled closer.

Eli frowned. Prepared staff would've been appreciated. Though he doubted his opinion as Nova Blake, aka lab rat, mattered. "What does Orien expect then? Carbon dating?"

Doukas had the decency to blush. "Skin and blood, maybe hair."

"How much blood? A pinprick?" That was doable. Eli couldn't see any of those here able to use a syringe.

"For now. If we find any anomalies, we'll take larger samples." And in the man's knobby fingers was a pin.

Eli took a step back and bumped into Frederik. "You've got to be kidding me."

What followed was a little painful with Doukas pricking and bleeding each of Eli's fingers until ten slides had been smeared. The scraping of his skin was along his forearms. Swabs were taken of his saliva, and chunks of hair snipped off, a few plucked for the follicles.

"Frederik will take you to the cargo hold to be X-rayed. You aren't pregnant, are you?" Doukas paled. "We'll need to know before we subject your body to ionizing radiation."

Eli blinked at him. "No, I don't think I'm pregnant." Shit, he should've asked Nova. This was a serious question with lethal consequences.

"If this was the Haeldull culture, you could pee on a tilqea bark and know in seconds." Doukas offered a kind smile. "If we had any tilqea bark on hand, it would be a sure way to test this legend."

"Don't be an idiot," Eli snapped, channeling his best depiction of Nova. "You need a baseline. If I even consent to pissing on your bark, what does that prove? If I *am* pregnant and nothing happens to the bark, that only shows the legend's wrong. And if I'm not pregnant and nothing happens, then the legend is right, but you still won't know whether I am or I'm not."

Doukas blinked at him like he was mad. "All right," he sighed, "we'll stop at the next station and pick up a pregnancy test kit."

"Lord Orien won't like that," Frederik said. "Any delays will be frowned upon."

"We have no choice." Doukas grimaced. "I'm a xenologist, not a doctor. None of us signed up for this."

"I won't be held responsible for killing a baby," a young woman called from the back of the lab. Nods followed.

"Well, we have some samples to work with." Doukas's tone was that of a man projecting control. "Let's start with that."

The lab's door swished open to a beaming Orien. His timing was almost too spot on. "Status?"

"We've taken what we can." Doukas wrung his hands.

"And did you test healing?" Orien peeled on latex gloves, then raised an ancient-looking bone to the light as if that would reveal its secrets.

"What?" Doukas squeaked.

Orien set the bone on the counter and nudged his chin at Frederik. Within a blink, Eli was pinned to a wall, his sleeve shoved up to his forearm, and a blade slashed across his skin.

He gasped, the burn almost overwhelming against the bright crimson droplets splattering to the floor. "You are a madman," he spat.

Doukas rushed forward with a paper towel, pressing it to the wound. "Lord Orien, this is *not* the way to treat a human."

"My dear Kyle, it is if we're to progress as a species. Now remove your hand." Orien snatched the paper towel away exposing a thin wound beaded with blood. "Mm, pity. We'll try again in a few days. Maybe the star stone's powers are delayed."

"Powers?" Eli screamed. "The stupid stone shattered. That's all that happened. No hidden mumbo jumbo or anything behind it. Maybe your mishandling weakened it. Did you think of that, you weirdo?"

At Orien's mottled face, Eli almost patted himself on the back at his Nova performance. He smothered a smirk at how easy 'she' managed to rile the xenologist.

"We're dealing with an alien artefact. I cannot afford to rule out anything, even if it's in the realm of the supernatural," Orien gritted out. "You have blue fingers. It's possible the stone has hidden...talents. Get her infantile mind out of my sight."

Out the door Frederik dragged Eli, then shoved him into the cabin minutes later.

"And?" Nova asked, her hands on her hips.

"They want to know if I'm pregnant," Eli said, tossing a glare at Frederik. "X-rays soon, then?"

The mountain didn't answer but gestured to Nova, who nodded at Eli in passing.

"See you soon, honey pot," she said.

The silence after her departure was deafening. Eli stared at the blood-splattered silk sleeve, sighing at how they'd ruined a good blouse. He washed his hands and the wound, taking the time to pat it dry. At least it had stopped bleeding.

Powers? What had Orien hoped to discover? Smooth, unmarred skin? Were sparks supposed to come out of his ass? Or superhuman strength? Sure, the star stone had been pretty, but to grant a person magical abilities?

Eli snorted. "What a load of bullshit."

Chapter Ten

Laurus Research Vessel
What's a wo/man to do?
Day One.

Nova didn't miss the blood on Eli's blouse. The sight of it didn't bode well for what awaited her, although, she kind of hoped Orien had meant what he said, that he wouldn't harm her. She'd searched their room, hoping to find a communication device of some sort. Nothing. Typical. Not even an entertainment system to be found, which meant hours of doing what alone in the room with the sexiest man in the galaxy?

She swallowed hard. The one deterrent was having to kiss herself. That felt wrong, like she was twelve and learning to make out with the use of her hand. No, she wanted manly lips on hers, even if 'hers' were currently the more masculine...

She stroked a thumb across his bottom lip, too plump and almost girly. She'd caught glimpses of his magnificent body in the mirror but hadn't lingered. Having just held his cock as she learned how not to pee on the toilet seat, ogling his body would've been rude. *Note to self: don't shake.* Pee went everywhere. No wonder women complained about the mess. Aiming that thing was a nightmare.

Swapping bodies had crossed way too many boundaries. How was this even possible? Part of her wanted to help the investigation, to discover the magic behind the stone. But if the blood stain was a measure of Orien's competence, she didn't have high hopes he'd be of any use.

Lethara? Mm, she'd never heard of it, and she'd studied many a galaxy map. Orien had implied it was beyond Artivar. Maybe near the Kegawa Belt? Every damn month, they stumbled on a 'new' comet, a dwarf star, some unknown metal. Theories changed more than her underwear. The universe was expanding, retracting, stemmed from a massive black hole, dying, birthing, and who knew what else; astrophysicists and their formulae.

"Ms. Blake didn't answer. Do you think she's pregnant?"

She lost a step at Frederik's quiet question. Hell effing no way was she carrying a child. An impossibility when she hadn't been with a man since Seth was murdered. "Why do you want to know?"

"I didn't sign up for harming babies."

She almost snorted. It wouldn't surprise her if Orien had a contract that listed henchmen duties: looming, scowling, general intimidation, proficiency with blasters, then some of the nastier tasks like kidnapping, torturing, and killing. But the mountain had a line drawn in his immoral ground: children, even unborn.

"What will you do if she is, Frederik?" She summoned Thorne's signature smirk. "You're not the type to stage a mutiny."

"Just answer the damn question," the man gritted out.

She shrugged. "How would I know if—"

"She's your wife."

Oh, that. Well, she couldn't blame him for thinking 'Thorne' would know if his wife was pregnant when she'd been the one to announce their fake relationship. But if she told Frederik the truth, he wouldn't help.

"This way, please, Mr. Thorne." A young woman in a lab coat blushed and semi-curtseyed.

Nova blinked at her, not sure what she was seeing. Was this the type of treatment he received? No wonder he had a god complex. She'd quip about not being royalty, but Thorne would milk it. Damn idiot had to be a narcissist.

She flashed a smile. "My thanks," she drawled, then for good measure, added a wink. The poor girl blushed to her hairline. "Where do you want me?" Nova strolled into the lab and eyed the counters. No bed was a good sign.

"Samples of blood, hair, and skin. Then a trip to be X-rayed." A man with gray at his temples and a receding hairline offered a tight smile, but his focus shifted to Orien studying a selection of what looked like pottery shards.

"All right." She thrust out an arm, but when no one approached, syringe in hand, she frowned.

"We're just going to prick your fingertips." Doukas, according to his badge, raised a pin. The girl trailed him, slides in hand. Another technician snipped a few strands of hair, plucking more with extreme gentleness.

"No healing, Lord Orien," Doukas said, raising Nova's hand to show the blood droplets on the tips of her fingers. "Should I make the incision along his forearm?"

"No need. Eli's not to be harmed." Orien waved at Frederik. "Escort our guest to the cargo hold."

"That's it?" Nova whispered to the mountain once they were alone and on their way to what had to be an X-ray machine.

"For now, I guess," Frederik said.

"Any idea what Orien's hoping the X-rays will reveal?"

"I'll tell you if you tell me." He raised his chin in defiance. "Is Ms. Blake pregnant?"

She grinned. *Nice try.* "I can be patient. I'm sure I'll find out soon enough."

He harumphed. "X-ray fluorescence and diffraction is usually what they use the machine for."

She sighed. Not that she knew what either would determine. "No. Nova's not pregnant. Yet." Let the idiot stew over that.

What she did like was the route they were taking, passing what looked like a new shuttle—*Viator IV* emblazoned on its flank. She hoped she could fly it. With the speed at which tech was advancing, she'd need a few minutes to acquaint herself with the controls.

"That's solid, right?" She pointed at the bay door. "What's the odds of being sucked into space?"

He chuckled. "None, unless you hit the emergency override." He nudged his chin at a massive red button to the right of the door. "You can't do that *and* pilot the shuttle. How stupid do you think I am?" He arched a brow. "Pretending to be scared when you've done most of your own stunts? Pathetic."

She shrugged. "Worth a try."

She hadn't heard that about Thorne. Said much about a man who could outrun, outride, and outjump anyone, that is if she could trust the footage in his movie trailers. She'd stopped 'watching' him after her gullible phase.

What followed were hours of shifting position, standing still, then moving again until they'd scanned everything. Baseline was all she could think was the reason behind this effort. It had been a day. No way would the stone have affected them in that short a time. *If* it did, at all.

"I could eat," she said when Frederik escorted her back to the cabin.

"I will inform the kitchen. Any preferences?"

"No dairy," she said, rubbing her bloated stomach. "A tea station and bottles of water would be appreciated."

"Very well," he said, waiting for her to enter.

Thorne sprawled on the floor, midway through a sit-up. He leaped to his feet. "How did it go?"

"Not too bad. Asked for food." She sank onto the couch. "I could do with a cup of tea."

"They cut you too?" He showed her his wound.

"Just pinpricks. 'Eli's not to be harmed,'" she mimicked in her worst impression of Orien. "Does yours hurt?"

"Not much, but get this. Orien thinks the star stone might have granted us magical powers."

She laughed. "You're shitting me."

"Nope."

"All right, why not?" She threw her legs onto the coffee table and misjudged, almost sending them over the other side. "You're not pregnant, but I implied that could change at any moment."

"Nice," he cheered.

"Saw a shuttle we could steal..." She shifted on the spot and leaned back, sinking into the comfortable couch. "It's the how I'm trying to figure out.

If they X-ray you tomorrow, check the ship out. Really open to any ideas here."

"Will do. I've been pacing, working up a sweat, trying to find a way out of this boredom."

"If it wasn't all manner of ew, I'd suggest we fuck."

He stared at her. "It will kill time. Just a pity you're not serious."

"You may get a kick out of kissing yourself, Thorne, but I'm not interested in learning what the inside of my mouth tastes like from the outside."

"I gathered that from the 'ew' part." He sank onto the couch beside her. "I must admit, I'm curious about what it feels like as a woman to orgasm."

She stiffened and faced him. "Hell no are you rubbing one out."

"See. There you go telling me what *not* to do with your body. What *can* I do then?"

She pointed a finger at him. "Nothing sexual, whatsoever."

"So no playing with your breasts?" He cupped one and ran his thumb over a nipple. His mouth parted on an 'oh.'

She yanked his hand away. "No."

He sighed. "You know, it doesn't take much to arouse me." He gripped her knee and slid his hand toward the groin.

A tingle started, sending a rush of heat along his cock.

She clambered over the back of the couch and glowered at him. "Stop that."

"Spoilsport," he said.

"My goal is to end this stupid adventure with myself still intact." She huffed. "I've no idea what your intentions are."

"Wouldn't mind being normal." He folded his arms across his chest then admired his cleavage.

"Honestly, you'd swear you've never been with a woman," she snapped. "Quit it."

"We should just do it; get it over with. That way I'll lose the fascination."

She scowled. "You're a man with self-control."

"True, but it would be sinfully delicious."

She slapped his upper arm. "I don't care if you think it will be heaven-sent. It's a no." She closed the buttons to under his chin. "There, temptation averted."

Sliding her hands over his shoulders, she froze, realizing his gaze was fixed on her. Something sizzled along her nerves. Despite his eyes being hers, the intensity in the amber depths was all him.

The door slid open.

"Knock, y'know," she yelled.

Frederik strolled in and directed a few catering staff to lay out a tea/coffee station, then pack a hidden fridge with bottles of water. A glare at her made her removed her feet from the coffee table, onto which went a platter of sandwiches. On the table by the windows was an array of long-lasting snacks for those midnight nibbles.

"Any chance Eli can call his manager? He's got to prepare for the premiere, right?" Thorne arched a brow at her.

"Yeah, interviews and the like. Not to mention what to wear. Was thinking shirtless this year with maybe a tribal loincloth—" She gasped then glowered at Thorne, who'd pinched her without Frederik noticing.

"I will mention this to Lord Orien. He has invited you to dine with him this evening."

She clenched her jaw, desperate to tell them all to go eff themselves.

"That would be...lovely," Thorne said, giving her knee a squeeze when he'd pinched that spot just moments ago.

Unfortunately, his touch sent a frisson of heat lower. *It* stirred in her pants, and a throbbing ache preceded the forming of a bulge. She gaped at it then hastily threw her leg over the other to hide her crotch.

Frederik nodded and ushered the staff out, shutting the door behind him.

She scrambled to her feet and pointed at her semi-hard on. "What the fuck is this?"

Thorne giggled. "Oh, yeah, that happens."

"How do I make it...stop?" She stroked it and it grew, pummeling her control with a crazy urge to kiss him.

"Think unpleasant thoughts and wait," he said around a mouthful of cucumber sandwich.

She stomped her foot at that useless bit of instruction and headed to the tea station. A calming cup of Lady Grey would do wonders to ground her. As she poured the boiling water into a cup and let the dunked tea bag stew, she took a few moments to breathe in and out.

"I was looking forward to cheese." He opened and shut sandwiches, checking their contents.

"I wasn't." She pressed a hand to her stomach, grateful the gastrointestinal explosion hadn't reoccurred. With tea in hand, she sank onto the couch beside him, cradling her cup against her chest between satisfying sips.

He got to his feet, shoving the last bite into his mouth. "Need to pee." He groaned. "Do I *have* to drip dry?"

Her brow furrowed. "Huh? What are you talking about?"

"Waiting for your bits to dry."

She laughed, almost choking on her tea. "Wipe down, from clit to ass. Never the other way."

Smiling, he disappeared into the bathroom.

When he emerged minutes later, she was halfway through a ham sandwich. "Tell me, do I shake or what? Piss goes everywh—"

"I gently squeeze from base to tip then dab the head dry with tissue paper." He drank from a bottle of water before choosing another triangle. "Any leakage stains my pants and gets my image plastered across all digital outlets."

That sucked. To live under so much scrutiny, she didn't know how he coped. "Accidents happen."

"Not in my world. I 'piss' my pants and it's a full on discussion on my state of mind at the time or whether I was roaringly drunk." He grimaced. "Sometimes they'll go even further, analyzing what medical conditions or drugs on the market could lead to incontinence." He bit into the chicken-mayo sandwich and settled back. "I've had doctors reach out to me, offering their services."

"Shit, you can't be serious?" She licked mustard off a thumb. "And you like living this way?"

"It comes with the job. Good and bad to all things in life." He shrugged. "Graham earns his salary, I tell you."

"I bet he does," she grumbled. Asshole extraordinaire. That one comment had ruined her self-confidence for long after her 'session' with Eli.

"We have dinner sorted. What's that, an hour or two of entertainment?"

"Should've asked Frederik for something to do." She chose another ham and mustard. "I was more concerned about food and tea. I wouldn't put it past Orien to starve us." She waved her half-eaten sandwich at the bed. "Might just sleep the next two days away."

"Yeah, that's right. The premiere's that soon." He drank from his water and smacked his lips. "Maybe we can steal the shuttle then? It would mean sneaking away in the premiere's chaos."

"Doable," she said, rising to make another cup of tea. "Gotta find the planet first. The shuttle's fuel has to be able to reach it. Otherwise we'd need way bigger."

"We could just stay with Orien, since he's heading in that direction." He thrust his hand forward like a ship taking off. "No need to go to all this effort."

"True, but he might leave us on board while he searches for a stone." She tossed the tea bag and returned to pick at the sandwiches, balancing the cup and saucer on an opened hand.

Thorne yawned. "Giving him all the control."

"Yes. I want to find a stone and touch it, not be studied before, during, and after."

"Then it's agreed." He rested his head on the back of the couch, barely reaching it. "*If* we can locate this Leratha."

"A big if," she said.

Chapter Eleven

Laurus Research Vessel

Never dine with a snake.

Day One.

"You do understand this will not be a common occurrence for you, Blake," Orien was saying, a brandy snifter in hand. Behind him was a wall of space, a few stars 'shooting' past as the ship traveled. "Dining with me is an honor and not so frivolously bestowed."

Thank the Lord for small mercies. Maintaining politeness in the face of this man's audacity was taking all of Eli's acting skills. "We'd like to keep ourselves busy: books, games, a television." If Nova insisted on staying platonic, Eli would go insane with nothing to do.

He gazed at her across the dining table lavishly adorned with various dishes and treats. In a black buttoned-up shirt paired with jeans, she'd made him look good, even braided his hair to the side. He was starting to not see himself but the woman behind the eyes. Kiss her? Yeah, he craved to do that, a steady burning in his core urging him to take the chance. To taste those lips.

He'd be on top, riding her. Or would she show a little dominance in the bedroom now that she was...bigger?

"What do you think, Blake?" Orien asked, arching a brow at who he thought was Nova. The fact that the man had yet to figure out something supernatural had happened said much about his intelligence.

"I'm sorry, Orien. Forgive me. This day has been...trying." That was as polite as Eli would play Nova.

"I said, as a pilot, you'd know whether we're making good time."

Eli glanced at the scenery and hazarded a guess when his piloting experience wasn't as extensive as Nova's. Nor had he flown this route before. "Yes, we are. How far from Artivar is Lethara?"

"Five hours," Orien said, staring into his brandy. "We have a day or so before we reach Artivar." He met Eli's gaze. "Where the law will be waiting."

He froze, casting a glance at Nova before glaring at Orien. "What? Why?"

"For destruction of property. Or did you think you were going to get away with what you've done?"

Eli pushed off the table. "Then why pretend to be civil? And you can fucking forget about any more tests. I should sue your ass for—"

"Nova, honey pot," Nova crooned despite the fire in her eyes.

"No, this bullshit is kidnapping. A galactic offence. Which this asshole has done to us *both*." He pointed a finger at Orien, whose cheeks had flushed. "He lies to our faces. Here I thought we'd find another stone together. But no, he has to torture us, too." Eli swept a hand along the wound on his forearm.

"Vex, please, put our minds at ease. Why the impending arrest?" she asked between sips of champagne. Her 'calm' didn't travel to her tense posture.

"Yes," Eli snapped, anger rising. "Didn't you want me near the stone when you find it?"

"There are no more stones," Orien snapped, losing his cool for a moment. "That's a fool's dream. It took me years to find this one."

Eli sank into the chair, chills racing down his spine. "What?" he squeaked.

Nova met his gaze, fear twisting her features. *We're stuck like this?* was in her expression.

"Escorting you two to Artivar allows me the chance to run a few *harmless* tests." Orien waved his empty glass for a refill, which a server hurried to do. "Regardless, Blake *did* break my stone. Justice needs to be served."

"Served? When you probably stole it from the natives? Where's their justice?" Eli demanded.

Orien shrugged. "Part of archeology."

"Stealing?" she asked, at last joining the argument.

"Discovering cultures and their artefacts, and educating our species about our galaxy."

"At the expense of said culture? How did they feel about you helping yourself to their stuff?" She folded her arms across her chest. "I bet that star stone was sacred to them."

"The survival of the strongest." Orien hummed on a sip of champagne. "Been true for millions of years."

She met Eli's gaze, helplessness tugging her lips into a pout. "I...can't afford bad publicity, Vex," she managed to say. "Not only will it impact my reputation, but it would make garnering benefactors for you a harder."

"I know, which is why station-sec will be meeting us in orbit. Fewer people to witness her arrest." He beamed, so proud of himself. "Then you and I, Eli, will enjoy your premiere."

At his nonchalance, they both rose, leaving the asshole to his dinner.

"Not interested in dessert?" His chuckle followed them out.

In silence, Frederik led them to their 'cell.' The heaviness of their situation continued after he left them alone. Eli readied for bed, slipping into that T-shirt he'd set aside earlier. He sat on the edge of a couch, sipping water while Nova used the bathroom. When she emerged, she marched past him to the tea station.

Sitting beside him, cradling her precious Lady Grey, she mumbled, "What are we going to do, Thorne?"

"We find our own stone," he said, though how, he couldn't say.

She'd been right to suggest they steal a shuttle. Hell, if they made it to Artivar, he'd charter a ship. They'd probably need supplies, too. When he'd starred in *The Lost Moons of Andara*, deep in the last jungles of the Amazon, the entourage had been extensive, taking care of the tents and catering. Heading to an unknown planet without planning would be suicide. But with no means of communication, he couldn't prepare anything.

Nova snorted, dragging him back to reality. "We'll be lucky to make Artivar. We can't trust a word that asshole says."

"I know." He stood and abandoned his half-drunk water. "Bedtime for me."

"I'll sleep here." She eyed the too-short couch.

"We'll share, woman," he said. "The bed's big enough that we won't even touch."

She eyed it in silence then set down her tea cup and marched to the left side. A sense of the space consumed him as if he knew the exact amount she took up...with his body. Her back to him didn't detract from her comforting presence. He slid between the sheets and stared at the door, tucking a hand under the pillow.

"You made me look good tonight," she said, long after he thought she'd fallen asleep.

"Thanks," he said. "We didn't buy any cosmetics."

"Or sleepwear for you." She gasped, and the bed bounced as she rolled over. "Wait, you know how to apply make-up?"

He grinned and peeked at her over his shoulder. "Learned how in *Alien in Lipstick*."

She winced. "Missed that one."

"Yeah, got the Galactic Arts for that role." A proud moment. Sadness coated his heart, that he couldn't share this with her. But it was in the past, and perhaps a good role worthy of another nomination was in his near future. He faced her. "I like the way you did my hair."

She stroked the braid. "I struggled. They cut off chunks."

"Same," he said.

"How's your wound?" she asked.

"Healing...normally." He smirked, but it faded. "Think we can do this?"

"We have no choice but to succeed." She rubbed her nose across the pillow, hiding her expression. "This wasn't on my bingo card for this year."

He chuckled. "I didn't see this one coming, either." He ran his fingers from her cheek to the jawline.

She swatted his hand away. "Quit it. You know how much touching affects your...appendage."

"It does?" He arched a brow.

She had no clue how to fight this attraction, blaming his body instead of her lack of control. He smothered a smirk. Women didn't need to worry about unexpected reactions to stimuli. Her ignorance could be entertaining. He stilled. Since meeting her, he had to admit, he hadn't been bored, even with nothing to do in the cabin. Sure, he'd spent the time she was away doing a little exercise, but his mind had been active, trying to figure a way out of this while not worrying about what they were doing to her.

He'd like to have said his concern had to do with her inhabiting his body, and for now, he'd pretend that was the case.

She harumphed and offered him her back.

He smiled, wishing he could pull her closer. But he couldn't be the big spoon, and a cuddle from her was less likely to happen than Orien setting them free. "Night," he whispered.

She said nothing.

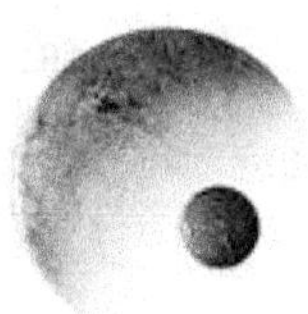

Laurus Research Vessel
A man's body is a minefield!
Day Two.

A scream snapped Eli's eyes open, and he scrambled off the bed, spinning on the spot to challenge the intruder. No one was in the cabin with them, and the lighting had changed to that of the rising sun, mimicking morning. When his foggy brain cleared, he blinked at a shaken Nova.

"What the fuck is this?" she squeaked, gesturing to her crotch where an impressive hard-on projected prominently. "I didn't touch it, I swear." She waved her hands like her palms were innocent.

"Are you sure?" he teased, unable to help himself.

"I need to pee but have this incredible urge to fuck, too. How do you cope with this thing?"

"It's morning wood." He sank onto the edge of the bed, adrenaline no longer flooding his system. "It just means you're desperate to piss. Head to the toilet, and be patient."

She stomped past him, slamming the bathroom door behind her.

Her pink cheeks alone had lifted his mood. He chuckled.

"I can hear you," she snapped. "This isn't funny."

It sure was. "Think about strangling Orien, and you'll be good to go."

A minute later, she was peeing like she'd been holding it in for days.

"Breakfast should be soon," she said, her words a little muffled by a running tap as she washed her hands. "I'm starving."

His stomach gurgled on cue. Dinner had been sparce before Orien showed his true colors, again. He crossed the cabin to the closet and sifted through her outfits. Taking off a woman's underwear was done in the heat of the moment, but putting them on wasn't turning out to be as much fun. Admittedly, it had only been a day, but he'd changed clothes multiple times, including the shopping spree. Nova was just lucky he had nimble fingers and vast experience.

He grinned. Sure, she'd consider herself 'lucky.'

"I don't think I had as much familiarity with my husband's cock as I do with yours," she said, striding past him to yank out gray cargo pants and a baby pink T-shirt.

"You haven't sucked mine."

Her cheeks flushed, and she shifted her gaze away.

He paused. Or had she? His breath hitched, and he dipped his chin, hiding his expression while he sifted through his memories. Regret slammed into him with the endless faces blurring into one another. No, he couldn't recall ever meeting her. He'd have remembered someone as dynamic as her. Maybe the blush was because she'd been thinking of sex with him or her late husband.

He'd take that as encouragement. "How many cocks have you known?" he asked, and received a slap in the face with a T-shirt.

She waltzed off, swinging her ass. Gone was his swagger.

He started to berate her, but the door slid open.

"Frederik, for fuck's sake." She leaped in and stood between the bodyguard and a semi-dressed Eli. "Didn't your mother teach you to knock?"

"I *could* knock, but I'll enter whether you allow it or not." He shrugged. "So why bother?" He stepped aside for the breakfast trolley. "And never mention my mother again, Mr. Thorne."

Ice slithered down Eli's spine when the tension in the air thickened to menacing. He whipped on the closest thing, which, judging by the silkiness of the fabric, had to be a summer dress. If he had to protect Nova, being fully clothed was as prepared as he could be. Under the circumstances when he had no weapon. He eyed a stiletto and grabbed the pair.

"Thank you for breakfast," he said, sinking onto the couch to slip on the shoes. It was years since *Alien in Lipstick*. He hoped he hadn't lost the agility required to walk in six-inch heels without falling.

"And these." Frederik flipped aside the trolley's cloth to reveal a stack of weathered note books and a deck of cards. "All I could gather."

Eli beamed. "You're such a sweetheart," he said.

The aroma of bacon teased him off the couch to lift the largest cloche. Layers of crisp bacon, rows of sausages, and a heap of scrambled eggs made his mouth water.

"How long before the tests start?" Nova asked, shoving a plate at Eli, who'd plucked a sausage with his bare fingers.

"I'll collect you in half an hour," Frederik said, watching their interactions. With a shake of his head, he left, granting them a little privacy.

Eli waved the half-eaten sausage in her face. "Quit doing that."

"What?" she asked, scooping bacon onto her plate, a slice of toast, a pat of butter, and a dollop of marmalade.

"Trying to shield my nudity."

She harumphed and flopped onto the couch. "It might be okay for you that the entire galaxy knows about that mole on your ass, but I'm not like you."

"What do you expect from me?" He swept out a hand, pointing to the door. "I have as much warning as you do."

She huffed, shoving a forkful of bacon into her mouth. Silence followed as she chewed. He should've known it wouldn't last for long.

"Have you had that mole looked at?" Up she jumped, heading to the tea station. "Dark, irregular, growing—all the markers."

He frowned. "I have, and it's fine. My dermatologist offered to remove it, but it's like a trademark, y'know."

She giggled, which was odd on a grown man. "Sure, the mole's what makes your butt recognizable."

"It does," he said, biting into his toast.

"So the double dimple in your left cheek has no part in this?"

He stilled, heat scorching his cheeks, traveling down his throat to his breasts. A slow ache built. Was this what desire felt like for a woman? "Nova, how do you know that?"

She shrugged. "You have the galaxy's most photographed ass."

"Um, no." He sucked butter off his thumb. "All outlets and photographers know to hide the dimples or I sue."

Her face paled, and she swiveled, giving him her back. "I saw it somewhere." But her voice was soft, a rasp.

"A scar from when I was ten."

"I peeked," she hurried to say.

"Yeah?" He arched a brow, knowing damn well she was lying. The way she wouldn't meet his gaze said it all. And her cheeks had yet to regain their color. "Show me where."

"In the bathroom mirror." She waved a fork in that direction.

"No, where exactly on my ass."

"I don't know why you're reacting like this." She sipped from her tea cup, trying to appear nonchalant and failing. "I saw it. The end."

"You, my dear infuriating pilot, need to learn how to lie better."

She opened her mouth to argue then snapped it shut, choosing instead to browse the breakfast trolley.

"Women are cuter when they're quiet." Then he ducked, a sausage whizzing past his head. "Oh, I must have hit a nerve." He chuckled. "Now, when Frederik takes you to the lab, try and seduce someone. We need allies."

"Seduce—" She coughed, choking on a bite of toast. He threw up an arm when crumbs flew everywhere.

"For me, there isn't much to pick from. I doubt Doukas can even get it up." He poured a coffee and settled back, cradling the mug in his cleavage—what a perfect spot. "For you, the blonde might be a good start."

"I'm not fucking anyone in your body," Nova snapped, then shuddered. "Argh, just the thought gives me the hives."

"You'd swear I was asking for a kidney. A wink, a drawl, a kiss... Do it. We need this."

She flicked a messy braid aside. "I'm not pimping myself."

"Fine. I'll do it. Female, male, it won't matter."

She blustered, garbling any words she tried to utter.

"Yeah, yeah, this is *your* body. I'm just *borrowing* it." He pulled an apple pastry closer. "You won't mind a few extra pounds on your hips and ass, would you?"

Her eyes narrowed, anger burning in their depths. "Two can play at that game."

He sighed. "True. I just have this craving for it. I've never been one to indulge."

Her interest perked up. "Oh?" A smirk crawled across her lips. "Let's hope we've swapped back before then."

As warnings went, that one reached into his gut and twisted it. "What? Why?"

"You'll have cravings, mood swings, sensitive body parts, and if you're stuck in me forever, then welcome to the monthlies."

He froze, his mouth falling open.

"It ain't pretty," she drawled, standing to rub her stomach. "I wonder if—"

A chime pinged through the cabin a second before the door opened. "I knocked," Frederik said. "It's your turn for X-rays, Ms. Blake."

Eli lowered his coffee and rose, teetering on his heels. "Call me Nova, Frederik." Eli cast a glance at Nova. "See you in a bit."

As Frederik led him along the passages to the cargo hold, Eli tried to map the path while learning how to walk in heels. Nova had said there was a shuttle they could steal. Finding it easily would be step one of any plan. And yes, they strolled past it with *Viator IV* in gold. What had happened to the three earlier shuttles bearing that same name?

Regardless, its fuel wouldn't be enough for a lengthy trip, especially if they escaped now. Orien had said it was five hours from Artivar, which meant, sneaking out of the premiere was a definite.

He showed no interest, marching past their possible escape route to where a young man waited. His dirty blond hair was parted down the middle, and he had a lovely pair of blue eyes. He was handsome in a bookish way, even though his chin was a little soft. Eli added an extra sway to his hips as he wobbled toward him, praying no one noticed how unstable he was in the stilettos. He flashed the man a smile, testing out his charm in Nova's body. She was a beautiful woman, and men did fuck anything on two sexy legs. He had to hope this was the case for X. Payne.

"Oh," Eli gasped, splaying his fingers across his cleavage. "What does the 'X' stand for?"

"Xander," the man said, a telltale pink splashing across his cheeks. "I'll take it from here," he said to Frederik.

"We'll be fine," Eli said to the burly bodyguard and followed Xander into the lab. "Thorne didn't mention you. How long have you worked for

Lord Orien?" He flicked his hair aside, wishing he'd taken the time to brush it. "Sorry, I'm a mess."

"Not at all," Xander said, catching Eli's hand to guide him to stand before a strange panel.

Frederik stood guard at the door, his arms folded across his chest. A ferocious scowl contorted his features. Eli tossed him a glare.

"Do I need to strip?" he asked, casting a glance between Frederik and Xander as if nervous. "He's seen me naked too many times." He hitched a thumb at Frederik.

The man scoffed and offered his back, making it clear he wasn't leaving.

Fuck. With a resigned sigh, Eli let the opportunity pass him by. Convincing the young man to forsake his future couldn't be done under Frederik's steady judgment. Eli needed privacy, in case his vast experience made not a lick of difference in Nova's body.

Chapter Twelve

Laurus Research Vessel

Gaining an unexpected ally. Without pimping.

Day Two.

Nova didn't think Orien's archeology team knew what they were doing. Her right hand stung from yet another round of pinpricks. Again, they took samples of her hair and skin. What they'd done with the others, she couldn't say. Burned them? She wouldn't put it past them to perform some sort of pagan ritual.

With a cup of tea in hand, she sat on the cabin's floor, a scruffy notebook between her thighs. It took a moment for her eyes to decipher the scrawl, then she was off, paging through it. Rough galaxy maps were barely recognizable, but she got the general idea. Like she'd guessed, the moon Lethara was in the Kegawa Belt, except, it had been discovered two decades ago. No wonder Orien's stone was such a big hit. His funding must have dried up, and finding anything worthwhile meant renewed investments. And the ass was greedy as all hell. Thorne had donated a fortune, so he'd said, and yet, Orien wanted more. Seemed to her that having a lordship didn't come with generational wealth. Or maybe, he'd squandered that already.

The moon was labeled as GJ 172 A e. Sir Allan Teher had named it Lethara when he'd met the first inhabitant. She flipped from page to page, studying the scribbles.

When she snapped it shut, she sat there, her mind reeling.

One, they knew nothing about the artefact, other than the humming. So, what did they hope to learn from these tests? She was starting to suspect it was nothing more than an excuse to punish them for destroying the stone.

Two, why had Frederik given them these books? Was it at Orien's instruction, who'd, no doubt, be laughing in his brandy? Or had Frederik done it on the sly, having a hidden agenda?

She scowled into her cold tea. Not knowing bothered her. She'd have liked some descriptors about the moon, too. Was it a jungle, a desert, a water world? She had to assume it had breathable air. Hell, a photo would've gone a long way in calming her fears.

Eli glided in like a model in those heels. He waved a fist at the shut door, muttering curses she couldn't quite catch. "Cock blocked." Then maybe, "Neanderthal."

"What is it?" she asked, trailing him with her gaze when he sank onto the nearest couch.

"Xander Payne, remember him?" He arched a brow, then leaped to his feet to grab a bottle of water. "Cute young man we could've swayed to our side if the mountain hadn't watched me every second."

Ah, a failed seduction. Good.

Gripping his bottle, he stopped behind her, peering at the spread out books. "Anything interesting?"

She tossed a journal aside and chose another. "Rough idea where this Lethara is. That's a start."

"It is." He sat beside her, removing the heels. "Hand me a book."

She did, and the scrape of pages turning filled the silence between them.

"Mm, this writing... It's like your tattoo." He ran his fingers across the letters scratched onto a page.

"It does," she said, leaning in to study the delicate, almost romantic alphabet—a mixture between Mayan and cuneiform. How did he know? She froze, her head whipped to the right, bringing her lips so close to his. "You looked."

"Of course I did." He dipped his gaze to his cleavage. "Woman, your body's a work of art."

Her face flushed, the compliment making her heart twinge. She nibbled on her bottom lip. Had he remembered that one night she'd been such a naïve groupie? "When?"

"Yesterday."

Fire exploded within her, masking the warmth of relief. She curled her fingers into fists, trying to stem the urge to slap him. "I told you not to, Thorne."

"I got it out of the way," he said, not even glancing up. "Besides, you peeked. Fair is fair."

"When did I—" She clenched her jaw, crushing the words. The double-dimple discussion from earlier... Never would she reveal she'd seen his gorgeous ass so many years ago.

His touch along her cheek, neck, and across her collarbone dragged her back to the moment.

She shivered, liking the caress more than she should.

"I don't mind if you admire my body, Nova," he whispered, the intensity in his eyes darkening the amber to gold.

A flood of heat rushed to her groin, dulling her thoughts, and ramping up the urge to fuck. She jerked back, now sporting a semi hard-on.

She cupped his cock. "Stop it," she hissed.

"You can't resist me forever," he sang, then tossed her a charming smile. "And I'll be waiting for your sweet pleas."

She bristled. "Not a fuck—"

"Oh, no, not singular. Many," he said, flipping through the pages. "So looking forward to it, too. Your irritability is probably because you haven't been laid in a while."

He'd flabbergasted her, again. She wasn't wearing a neon sign stating she was celibate. So how had he figured it out? Sex hadn't been a priority for Seth. They'd loved each other's minds. But sexual releases were medically good for them, so they'd scheduled their bedroom time to once a week: Wednesday morning, post-shower.

Many a time she'd been disappointed, not finding the fulfilment she'd craved. They'd been happy, and it had seemed selfish of her to raise her discontent over this one aspect of their lives. Older her—wiser, maybe—realized how stupid she'd been. Cracks weakened a relationship, forming a fertile ground for anger, resentment, and unforgiveness.

"I'm sorry. I didn't mean to make you sad."

"I'm not..." Tears dripped off her chin. She wiped them aside and sniffled. "Was thinking of Seth, my late husband." She settled beside Eli and took up a discarded notebook. "There has to be a clue somewhere."

"Are you wondering the same?" He waved at the scattered books. "Why do we have these?"

"Either they have tons of information we can use or nothing."

"What we need is a tablet, a way to make notes." He held his place with a finger between the pages. "Orien mentioned the stone hummed at a frequency too low for humans to hear."

She shifted on her ass to find a comfortable spot, her thoughts ricocheting. "And it was multi-colored until we touched it."

"Yeah," he frowned, "but why us?"

"Exactly." She thumped the book on her thigh. "And was the humming consistent? Did it react to anyone else?"

He shook his head. "If it had, they'd be in the labs with us, losing their hair."

"True." She slumped. "It's too much to hope that these," she swept out a hand, "are gifts from an ally."

"Well, we'd know if we find a useful nugget of info."

She divided the unread stack into two. "We've got to be thorough." She flashed him a grin. "Up for the challenge?"

He chuckled. "I had other plans tonight, y'know."

Time ticked by as they sifted through the scribbles made by various archeologists who hated Orien's guts. That was made abundantly clear when on nearly each page, the man was cursed or disfigured with words amid vows for revenge.

"Today, the stone did something odd," Eli read. "Deep in its depths, a spark flared white, then clear, before returning to a dark magenta. And all I did was touch it." He met her gaze then resumed. "I didn't mention this to Orien when X didn't either."

"Ex?" She clambered to her feet and stretched, working the kinks out of her back. Eli trailed her with a heated gaze when she looped around the couch to reach the tea station.

"Could be Xander, an actual ex-lover, or a mystery," he said, smiling when she brought him a bottle of water.

"Huh. They must have stepped away from the stone, breaking the contact, or..." She frowned. "I'm not okay with thinking the thing's alive. Sentient rock? What's next, plants that talk?"

"Same, but when we've eliminated all other possibilities, we're left with the probable."

She lowered herself beside him, careful not to spill a drop of tea. "Still, why us? This just proves we're not an anomaly."

"The star stone was egg-shaped. Do you think it carried a creature?"

"Could be," she said, taking a gulp of the hot liquid, then humming when it warmed her from throat to stomach. "I didn't see anything that resembled a yoke or embryo. Rainbow-colored jello as embryonic fluid? From an alien world, maybe. And its zap might be the transfer of its life force?" She showed her palm where the blue tendrils had spread to her wrist.

"Mm, why isn't this a curiosity?" He set aside his book and sipped his water. "I'd like to see the X-rays. On you, they'd find many a healed bone. I've forgotten the number of times I've injured myself."

"Broke a pinky once, pretending to karate chop with my youngest sister." She chuckled, but her good humor faded. "I was hoping to visit my family on Artivar. Now, I'll be lucky not to be arrested."

"Yeah, I wanted to visit my family, too."

It took something this traumatic to make her realize what mattered in life. "After this...adventure."

He raised his bottle in salute. "Sorry about being a pain. I just wanted to spend time with you."

She froze. "What? Why?"

"Besides Graham and my family, most people don't show me their genuine side. You weren't playing a game and had no hidden agenda. What I see is what I get." His smile was tight.

He'd said similar things the night he'd asked her to be his plus-one for the premiere.

"Well, now you get to spend loads of time with me," she said, trying to fill the awkward silence.

He chuckled. "Sure. More than I intended."

"Way more than I expected to."

He met and held her gaze. "I'd like us to at least end this as friends."

She studied him, respecting his sincerity. "Let's survive first."

"Fair enough," he said, opening his book.

By the time Frederik served lunch, they'd stumbled on a few 'nuggets.' Once the catering staff left, she hurried to prevent him from leaving, standing dead center in the doorway.

"Do you have a moment to chat?"

He leaned back as if she'd threatened him. "How may I assist, Mr. Thorne?"

"We'd like something to write on and a pen or pencil, please, Frederik." She pointed to the stacked books, going around him so he wouldn't feel trapped. "So far, we've gleaned the barest of details: a rough location where

Lethara is, the destroyed star stone was found in a cave, and," she lowered her voice, "that Orien killed the natives when he stole it."

Frederik stared at her, making her doubt that he'd help them. He cleared his throat. "I shall gather what you need."

The door closed on his disappearing shoulders.

She faced Thorne. "Now, I'm worried."

"Eat," he said, gesturing to the lunchtime spread. "We'll need our strength, either way."

She harumphed but conceded he had a point. Not ten minutes later, with half a bowl of chicken soup and three toast points in her belly, the door chimed. Frederik marched in, placed a pen and notepad on the coffee table, and left.

"Thanks," Eli called, then grinned. "That's a good sign."

She mumbled around a mouthful of soup, "Sure is. Pity he can't whisk us out of this. It's been two days, and I'm done with waiting."

"It goes against everything in me to let them do 'tests' on us." He chose a bowl of fruit, picking out slivers of apple, and dropping them onto an empty plate. "We're co-operating to stay alive, but it still grates."

"Okay." She waved her spoon in a circle. "What if we could escape now? Let's run through the scenarios."

"Ah, planning is better than surprise, right?" He moaned when he bit into a strawberry.

She dipped her chin, trying not to react to the blatant *and* cliché sensual imagery, but nope, his cock responded as if on cue. Stupid thing revealing her emotions so willy-nilly. She kept a glass of orange juice over her groin, hoping to hide a semi hard-on.

Desperate for a distraction, she said, "We're in a shuttle; let's not dwell on the how."

"Heading to Lethara. What are we looking for?"

"A cave system of sorts." She nudged her chin at the stack of books where she'd been sitting. "I earmarked a crudely drawn map of where they've looked. We start on one they haven't visited, yet."

"I'm loving this...planning our adventure." He chuckled, licking cream off a spoon—the lucky bastard.

She shifted on the couch, raised her glass, and crossed an ankle over a knee. The full erection was making demands she desperately wanted to ignore. "We need to land somewhere and head into the cave."

"Sounds simple enough," he said, then met her gaze. "But it won't be. We'll need the proper gear, a light source, a weapon..." He pointed with his spoon at a discarded stiletto. "Not much good against cave monsters."

She slumped. He was right. Even if they managed to steal a shuttle, that didn't guarantee they'd make it to Lethara, land safely, find a cave *and* a star stone inside it, or flee the moon unscathed, having swapped their bodies.

But they had to try.

A moan snapped her back to their dismal reality. Thorne had dropped the top of the summer dress and removed the bra. He cupped *her* breasts, giving them a good rub.

Her mouth dried at the sheer bliss in his expression. "Thorne," she spat.

"Feels so damn good. Let me be, Nova..."

"Quit it," she hissed.

"That thing's a torture device," he said, tossing the bra aside before fixing his dress. "This experience has opened my eyes, Nova, seriously."

"Right," she scoffed. "Like you'll stop thinking a woman in a bra's sexy."

Even though it was with her lips, he flashed his signature smirk. "True."

She pulled her fruit salad closer, thankfully without cream or ice cream. Food wasn't the top priority, not when a knot had twisted her gut. But she'd need her strength.

Something had to give, because letting Orien get away with this gritted her teeth. No matter what happened, the ass had to pay.

But so far, he'd outwitted and outplayed them.

That smarted, too. If she had to be brutally honest. Losing her free will hit a primal instinct within her to rebel. And damned if she would lay down and take this...without a fight.

Chapter Thirteen

Laurus Research Vessel

Not all bad things happen in the 'dark.'

Day Three.

A looming shadow yanked Eli awake. He blinked, not sure what he was looking at in the softer lighting. Nova snuggled into him, a solid arm wrapped around his waist. So who—

Frederik!

"Ms. Blake, you and Mr. Thorne *must* come with me."

"What?" he whispered, nudging Nova with an elbow.

"Hurry." Frederik cast a glance over his shoulder as if he expected an interruption. That gesture alone sent a frisson of cold fear through Eli.

He sat up, shoving back the duvet. "What time's it?"

"Two."

Eli stared at the man like he was mad.

"What's happening?" Nova asked, pushing herself up.

"Frederik wants us to go with him," Eli said.

"Get dressed." Frederik marched toward their closet, tossing pants, shirts, and jackets at them.

"This sounds ominous." Eli snatched up jeans, pulling them on without panties. He eyed yesterday's bra, grimaced, and clipped it on, mumbling when his nipples ached. For no damn reason.

Nova was scrambling into cargo pants, peeling on a T-shirt, then sitting on the edge of the bed to put on socks and boots. Getting dressed was so much easier for men.

"What's Orien up to, Frederik? Can you tell us that?" Nova demanded, grabbing their notes from last night, the books with the maps, and a few bottles of water. She held the box of tea, hesitating, then threw that into the bag, as well, darting around the burly bodyguard.

"This isn't from Lord Orien," Frederik announced.

Eli stilled, glanced at a pale Nova, then stood, stomping his feet in the boots. "What do you mean?"

"I've prepped the shuttle."

A slow smile spread across Nova's lips. "You didn't."

"We must hurry. The pilot has flown past Artivar, bringing you closer to Lethara. The delay might not be noticeable if we can make it to the station-sec rendezvous before Lord Orien awakens."

Eli reeled, unable to believe they'd found an ally without realizing. "I love you, Frederik."

The man scowled. "Do not say such things, Ms. Blake." He ushered them out of the cabin and along many passages. As he did so, he said, "The shuttle's stocked for an expedition. Lethara is programmed into its navigation. That's all I can do."

"You've done more than enough," Nova said.

"Good. I'll be fired or jettisoned out of an airlock when Lord Orien finds out." He dropped his head. "Does that job offer still stand?"

"Hell yes," Eli said. "Please, if you get a chance, let Graham Whitney know what happened to us. He's Eli's manager. He'll take care of you."

"Will do." He stepped aside to let them enter the *Viator IV.*

"Why the change of heart?" Nova asked. "Why now?"

"Since we're supposed to hand Ms. Blake over today, Lord Orien ordered shock therapy and an MRI. First thing in the morning." Frederik frowned. "Only you, Ms. Blake."

"Well, then thank you, my friend," Nova said. "I won't forget this."

"Good luck," he said, smacking the button to shut the shuttle's door.

She faced Eli and squealed. "Can you believe this?"

"We couldn't have asked for better assistance. Now, can you fly this thing?" Eli tapped the back of the pilot's seat.

She stilled, glanced at the console, and approached, sinking into the chair while running a delicate touch over the keys. "I hope so. This is state-of-the-art. Some of these functions I don't know."

"To be expected of an expedition shuttle." He looped his hand through a ceiling-mounted strap.

"We don't have a choice. I have to figure this out. I suspect, the moment I start up the engines, Orien might be notified." She tapped a few keys but nothing happened. "Why won't it— Oh, yes." She grabbed the lever with her hands and flicked a button on it. "Extra safety feature. Okay, here goes."

A steady thrum burst into life, sending a tickling vibration up Eli's feet.

"Docking bay opening," a computer intoned in a feminine voice. "All personnel evacuate for your safety."

Eli leaned forward, hoping to catch no glimpses of Frederik putting himself in danger.

"He's gone. Seems he must have charmed *Laurus'* pilot." Nova swiveled the shuttle, bringing the gaping mouth of the bay door into line of sight. "Only two ways to open that door: pilot or emergency button. And since Frederik's nowhere to be seen..."

Out they shot, exploding into the black vacuum of space. Never had Eli felt freer, like a weight had been stripped from his shoulders. Excitement merged into a waterfall of butterflies, from his chest to the pit of his stomach. They could do this. Find a stone. Swap bodies.

With his free hand, he squeezed Nova's shoulder, grateful to have been stuck with her. Sure, he could try and pilot this thing, but he'd learned on a chaser, not something designed as a mobile lab.

"Do you think anyone's noticed our escape?"

She flashed him a smile. "Besides the pilot and Frederik, no. But this thing has no tracking on it as far as I can tell. Even if the galactic armada was on our ass, we wouldn't know."

"Destination Lethara is in two hours, twenty-seven minutes, and fourteen seconds," the computer said.

Eli chuckled. "Feels surreal. Pinch me."

"I know, right?" She hitched a thumb behind her. "Check the stocks. See what he prepared for us."

"Good idea." Eli released the strap and started opening-closing panels. "Dry foods, water, some mining gear too new to touch. Oh, these are nice." He pulled out leather coats, lined and with hoodies.

She laughed. "Any weapons?"

"Getting there," he said, trying on the coats, then holding up a few to measure the width of her shoulders. Tossing one over her lap and shoving his into the bag, he said, "Sorted. Next." Tap-tap went the panels as he searched. "Nothing yet, except for a few devices of unknown purpose."

"Weapons, a fire starter, a space blanket or two. If we're trapped in a cave overnight, I don't want to freeze to death." She spun the shuttle, checking behind them, before resuming course.

"We have hours to sort through this thing." He pointed to the console. "Isn't it on automatic pilot?"

"Yes, but if we're chased, I don't want to be on the other side of the compartment."

He ran his hand along an unmarked panel, not expecting it to pop open when it didn't resemble the others. A light flashed on, illuminating a toilet, basin, and a tight shower. "Oh, they have a mini-bathroom." Which meant water stores were on board.

She bolted out of the seat, striding past him, then snapped the door shut in his face.

He grinned and moved onto the next cupboard closest to the shuttle's main door. The panel was taller—that looked promising. Sure enough, laser rifles, blasters, machetes, and daggers were clipped in place. "Found the weapons," he hollered.

"Great," she said, striding out while zipping up. "I miss bladder control. Yours is like my gramma's."

"Y'know, I've never considered it, but you're right. I'll pee though, just in case."

There was a slight pressure building, but he somehow knew, he was in no hurry. He didn't bother to shut the door when she'd returned to the seat. And as confined as the bathroom was, for his petite stature, it was quite spacious. He washed his hands, gazing at his reflection in the mirror.

The shock of seeing himself through her amber-colored eyes had dwindled. Now, he noticed his messy hair and a little sleep at the corner of one eye.

He was becoming too comfortable in her body. Gone was the initial shock or the excitement to know aspects of her he'd never have gotten the chance to. If they did stay this way, it would sadden him to say goodbye to his body. But being stuck in hers wasn't so bad.

"Water?" he called, going through the panels to find the one holding bottles upon bottles of purified water—and the brand he liked, too. "For now. Pretty sure there's a coffee station somewhere in this shuttle."

"That would be too good to be true. Coffee, tea, something hot." She uncapped the water and sipped.

"On it," he said, giving her a salute. "Gotta feed the addictions."

Silence settled around them. The swell of hope filled the space with simmering excitement. Beside the console was the final panel, and when he opened it, the sight of a hot-water pot summoned a smile. All good so far. He dug out her box of tea and ordered a coffee for himself. The aromas were an added comfort as if their escape had been blessed by the tea/coffee gods.

When he placed the cup in her hand, her joy was unparalleled.

"I can't believe we're doing this." She hummed on a sip.

Her expression, those lips, the flop of hair across her brow and the waterfall of it down her back added to the zing tightening his nipples. The urge to kiss her blazoned across his mind. She'd slap him for sure. And coming from a big hand, it would hurt. Drawing in a calming sigh, he said, as a distraction, "Let's go over our strategy."

She arched a brow. "When it's as basic as you can get?"

He grinned. "True. Steal a shuttle. Check. Heading to Lethara. Check. Find a cave?" He yanked up the knapsack and took out their notes. "A cave system north of the equator. Dense forest; maybe they skipped it because it's unnavigable?"

"Mm, instinct says we try it, but if we can't land…" She changed the holographics overlaying the forescreens. "Here's a basic map."

He reached around her and tapped the general location of the cave. "I think it's here."

She hadn't moved away in time, and the warmth of her breath across his cheek made him meet her gaze. Intense emotions swirled in the dark-green depths of her eyes. The tension thickened. His heart leaped into his throat, and he glanced at her lips.

"You're dangerously close to kissing yourself," she whispered.

"I'm not the one leaning in," he breathed.

She ran her gaze over his face, her chest rising and fallen with every ragged breath. But when she shifted, instinct told him that kissing wouldn't happen anytime soon.

She pulled back, and with a clench of his teeth, so did he. The sense of loss cinched his chest, strangling his throat. He struggled to focus on what they'd been doing. "You could…" he coughed to return his voice to normal, "drop down and machete a clearing. If it's jungle. It would be a bitch and time consuming, but the trees might help to hide the shuttle."

"From a distance, but above the shuttle, no," she said.

Back and forth, he shifted his hand as if he stroked velvet. "If we drape the cuttings over the shuttle?"

"You're assuming we're being hunted." She winced. "Which we should when Orien's such an asshole."

"This would only work if it's a jungle. Sand dunes would be out in the open. He'd have chosen this location for its lack of hinderances."

"Ice would be the worst." She nudged her head at a book. "It described the location, right?"

"Yeah, as inaccessible."

"Let's check it out first before we plan a landing." She zoomed out until the 3D map of the moon spun before them. "South is another location near a lake. The map says it's called 'Vael'Tir'"

He shook his head. "My guts with you on this one. I like the first spot." He studied his hand and wrist, the blue flowery spirals were halfway down his forearm. Two ends had formed familiar symbols. His breath caught. "Um, Nova, does your arm look like this?" He shoved his in front of her face.

She lifted hers and held it against his. Identical. They hadn't noticed that before.

"Huh," she said. "Did we bring the book with the alphabet?"

He lunged for the bag and stacked the books they'd earmarked. Sprawled on the hard metal floor didn't bother him as he flipped through and tossed aside book after book. The second-to-last one had him slumping. He rotated the page, trying to align the symbols to those on his arm.

"It's..." He swallowed hard. "A countdown. That's a number two?" He clambered to his feet and brought the book to Nova.

She studied it, comparing the alphabet to her tattoo. "Yes. One, two..." She met his gaze, her eyes widening. "I think you're right, Thorne."

"How long do we have? I mean, we've been stuck like this for two days. That's not a coincidence. But does the countdown end when it reaches our shoulders..."

"Or our hearts?" She stroked the blue symbol for 'two.' "Could be a toxin, killing us if we don't switch back before an unknown number of days." She raised her chin and offered him a sweet smile. "Well done for spotting this. It's something even if it's scary as hell."

"We never considered there'd be a time limit."

"No." She squared her shoulders. "It just means we can't afford to fail."

The severity of this discovery settled on him like a solid weight. Gone was the excitement of earlier. Now, only dread remained, growing until it almost consumed him.

"We'll tackle this one step at a time." She lifted her chin in a show of determination or courage.

He tried to smile but couldn't. Then he lurched, the force snapping his head forward.

"Shit," she yelled. "Someone's shooting at us."

"What?" he gasped, scrambling to his feet to grip a ceiling strap.

Her fingers flew across the console, making it flicker in a kaleidoscope of colors. "We've gotta push the engines."

"We're still an hour away."

"I know," she said. "I'll head for the Kegawa Belt, maybe lose them amid the asteroids."

He gaped as the forescreens filled with endless bands of rocks that had to be the size of moons. "Nova, can you navigate through that?"

"I have to," she said, squeezing and releasing the lever.

"Auto-pilot deactivated," the computer intoned. "Manual override in place."

She rolled her shoulders back and veered toward the belt. "Fifteen minutes before we'll need to start dodging. We can make it."

His gaze was transfixed while his senses waited for the next hit. When it struck, jerking the shuttle forward, he shuddered. "Any damage?"

"Just photon blasts."

Like he knew what that meant.

"Keep a look out for anywhere we can hide."

He blinked at her. *Is she serious?* "We're in outer space. There's nowhere!"

"I can try hiding on an asteroid."

Fuck. She's serious. "You're mad."

"We need more speed. Maybe if we slingshot around Nyxara."

His mind reeled. *Is she even listening to herself?*

"The shield might not hold." She giggled. "Or we could crumple this shuttle like a tin can."

Great! He gaped, horror widening his eyes. "You're enjoying yourself."

"Beats dying in a lab on *Laurus*."

"In an explosion? Our bodies obliterated in an instant?" The insanity of their situation, that somehow he'd become the voice of reason, had him laughing. "Sure. Let's show them, Nova-honey."

Chapter Fourteen

Viator IV Shuttle

I knew it was too good to be true.

Day Three.

With her focus on the largest asteroid, Nova asked, "Computer, who's chasing us?"

"Assessing scanners," the voice droned.

"Why didn't we think to ask sooner?" Thorne's good humor was still present in the curve of his lips.

His good humor had gone a long way to easing the tension in her shoulders. As did the residual hot tea in her belly. Frederik was a godsend, having prepared them better than she could've hoped.

"The ship's markers are not in any known database," the computer said.

"Pirates? What are the odds?" Thorne hurried to the weapons locker and started arming himself.

She grinned. "Fat lot that's going to do you when we're jettisoned into space. And the odds are pretty high. Space beyond the station-sec's boundaries is a free-for-all. Computer, plan an escape route with Lethara in our sights."

"It can do that?" he asked, kneeling to strap a blaster to her thigh.

She swiveled the chair to grant him access while keeping her hands on the lever. "Let's just hope they don't have tracking missiles. All this weaving will be for nothing."

With him between her thighs, she relished his shoulders nudging her, the dip of his head, the brush of his fingers, all while praying none of it aroused her. Sporting a hard-on now would be so inconvenient. Regardless of her opinion on the matter, life stirred in her groin. As soon as he leaned back, she faced the console, tempted to fold a leg over the other.

It was his cock, after all. Surely she need not hide its misbehavior from him. But what she was truly trying not to reveal was how he could garner such a reaction out of her. She'd stated no kissing. No anything, and yet, they'd been inches away from doing exactly what she'd claimed was disgusting to her.

In two days, she'd gone from seeing him as an intruder in her body, to just seeing him. The outer appearance no longer played a role in her impression of him.

Another jolt hit the shuttle's ass.

"How much more of that can we take?" he asked, sliding a dagger into her boot.

"Shields are at 72 per cent," said the computer. "Escape route planned."

"Take control," she said, flipping a switch.

The shuttle veered right, away from Lethara. She opened her mouth to ask why, but the forescreen altered, showing the projected path. *Oh, now that's brilliant.*

She grinned. "Clever."

"What?" Thorne asked, stuffing the knapsack with bottles of water, and her box of tea—the sweetheart.

"She's taking us past—"

"She?" He paused.

"Yes," Nova snapped. "*She's* taking us past a research station in the Kegawa Belt, barely manned but still in use. That would put the pirates in station-sec's territory."

"And once they've abandoned the chase, we can head to Lethara." He chuckled. "That *is* ingenious."

"Found any space blankets?"

He frowned. "None. Damn things are so tiny when compressed. Could be a sheet of paper and I wouldn't know."

"You've done well so far." She met and held his gaze. "We can do this."

"One step at a time."

She pursed her lips then admitted, "I hate and like that we're working as a team."

He laughed. "That's because I'm not fondling parts of your body."

"True." But it wasn't. Not anymore. Besides the breast-jiggle from last night, he'd been amazing at keeping her clean, dressed—for the most part—and STD free. Though it had been touch and go there with Xander Payne.

"*Viator IV*, do you require assistance?" A woman's face appeared on the screen. "Oh my word, is that Eli Thorne?" she gasped, glanced away, then a man joined her.

Since they were both in station-sec uniform, Nova pasted on a broad smile. "Hi, yes, we're on a joyride and have been shot at by what our computer says are pirates."

The woman squealed. "No one's going to believe we rescued *the* Eli Thorne." She cleared her throat, fluffed her hair, and gave Nova a seductive look. "We'll come up behind you as a deterrent. Can you confirm your destination?"

"Lethara," Nova said.

The woman jerked back. "But it's overrun with Lord Orien's xeno-archeologists." Her face scrunched up like she'd touched an unknown jelly-like substance. "They don't take too kindly to station-sec interference."

"Yes," Nova said, "well, let's hope we don't cross paths with them. I'm hoping to find suitable locations for my next movie. It will determine how I develop the character. Doing my part for my fans, y'know," she drawled.

The woman fanned herself. "Oh, yeah, how sweet of you. Are you filming this?" she hissed to someone on the side.

"It's a surprise, of course," Nova went on, giving the woman a wink. "I need to reach Lethara before the paparazzi do, y'know, to get settled. Then the press can have their field day."

"We'll keep your secret, Mr. Thorne," the man crooned.

"Oh, call me Eli," Nova said.

"It'll be in the news the moment this call ends," Thorne whispered. "And I don't say 'y'know' all the time."

Nova huffed, then cleared her throat. "Any chance you can escort us to Lethara? We're trusting the navigational system to know where it is."

The woman hesitated, tapped something before her, then grinned. "Yes, we can certainly do that for you, *Eli*."

"You two are amazing," Nova gushed. "I'm so happy you stumbled upon me."

"Us," Thorne hissed.

"Confirming pirates are withdrawing," the woman said. "We'll loop around you to lead the way, and make sure there are no more pesky delays."

"You have my eternal thanks. And should we ever meet in person, I'd like to invite the two of you to dinner."

The woman giggled. "Why, thank you, Eli." The screen blanked.

"Computer, abort the escape route and follow that station-sec," Nova said.

"That was a little thick," Thorne said, coming to stand behind Nova.

"We need all the help we can get. Besides, what's a dinner with fans?"

"They'll want sex. They always do." He slumped against a panel. "Asking for an escort was genius, by the way. Is it wrong of me to be happy it's pirates and not Orien?"

She smiled. "Not at all. With that kind of riffraff, we know what to expect. Orien's as slippery as they get."

"We're armed and ready. So far, so good."

She stood for a stretch. "We need to find the cave and fast. Once the paparazzi gets wind of this, Orien will know, too." Since he'd packed away the tea, she'd settle for a coffee. Not her favorite, but it would do.

While cradling the hot cup to her chest, she went through the panels, browsing what was stacked inside. "The usual, and that's a theodolite. I'd say to pack it, but I don't know how to use it. A source of light would be great. Did you find a flint, matches, a lighter?"

"Got a solar-powered torch." He laughed. "If we get to charge it first."

"I suppose if we fired the blaster at dry kindling, it might light it."

"I doubt it." His brow furrowed. "Let me search again. It's not much of an expedition if we can't start a fire. You think we'll need to?"

"I want to plan for it, just in case. I don't know what's on that moon. If the fire only serves as a deterrent for the local wildlife, it would be good to have." She headed into the bathroom to pee—again—and splashed water on her face. Dark stubble had formed along her jaw. She scratched it, finding it semi-itched. "How many times a week do you shave?"

"Once." He popped his head through the door she'd forgotten to shut. "I could get the follicles removed, but if I have a role needing a beard, I'd have to sit for hours in the make-up chair."

"What *is* your next role?"

"Another space cowboy." He winced. "More time spent in the saddle."

"On a horse?" she gasped.

"Yeah, or something alien-looking. Days of having a sore ass. Maybe this time, I'll get to ride a speeder, instead."

"Why not suggest it?" she asked, flipping her hands under the sunbeam—a flash of heat that sterilized.

"I haven't seen the script yet. Besides, family first, remember."

She smiled. "I do. Might as well tell me about them, just in case we get stuck like this."

"Then we're getting married," he said, with all seriousness.

She froze, raising her gaze to his. Logically, it made sense. If anyone found out they'd swapped bodies, it wouldn't be medical examinations they'd have to worry about, but psychology assessments and possibly the psych ward.

"No one would believe we 'fell in love,'" she said. "Everyone knows we hate each other."

He didn't answer, taking his time to study her. "Hate's a strong word."

Her heart leaped into her throat; his expression sparking a fire in her belly. "It is," she managed to say. "One step at a time."

"Yeah," he said, cupping her cheek and running a thumb along the stubble. "It's going to start itching."

"It has," she said, resisting the urge to nuzzle the palm of his hand. "When you said lactose intolerant, does that mean chocolate, too?"

"Unfortunately."

She pursed her lips. "Forsaking all things chocolate is sacrilege."

"I know." He shifted back and massaged his breasts. "Could sure do with some now. Why do these ache? And why are your nipples so damn sensitive?"

"You don't like?" she teased.

"No." He scowled. "Not the good kind of sensitive. It's on the verge of painful."

"All par for the course," she said, slipping between him and the door.

"You women hide this discomfort so well. I never knew." He lifted his forefinger in a 'eureka' moment. "They should teach this to boys."

"Vice versa," she said, ticking off on her fingers. "Horny all the time, never kick a man in the balls, teensy weensy bladder, never shake after a pee, and hair in all the strangest places."

"What hair?" he asked then laughed. "And how do you know this?"

"I told you I peeked." She touched her ear, pulling back with a long hair pinched between her fingers. "What's this?"

"Ah, the stylist usually takes care of those."

"My point, exactly." She opened the weapons locker, now missing a few pieces. "Frederik... What an amazing man."

"Indeed. And we have you to thank for his help."

"Me?" She touched her chest then lowered her hand when he stared at her.

"Yeah, offering him a job might have started him thinking that working for Orien wasn't his only option in life."

She shrugged. "He saved me from your fans with such ease. The poor guy must've been used for his size his entire life."

"Trust you to go all soft like that. A man wouldn't think about his childhood and how he was bullied." Thorne leaned his shoulder against the panel. "With his size, he could've done the bullying."

Everything within her rebelled at that suggestion. "No, his heart's too big. He would've protected those weaker than him."

Thorne's smile was sweet, sincere. "You think he rescued injured birds and kittens."

"Don't you?" She splayed her fingers across his cleavage. "Aren't we the kittens in this scenario?"

Thorne covered her hand with his, trapping her. The padding beneath her touch was intriguing. "We were hours away from Artivar. He could've left us to Orien's devices, let me get arrested, and walked away. We wouldn't have blamed him since he was only doing his job."

"But he saved us," she said, trying to move away.

"True," he said. "And will be rewarded for that, as soon as we're...fixed."

"Or not."

Into the silence, the computer said, "Destination in thirty minutes."

Thorne released her, only to wrap his arms around her waist, and press his cheek to her chest. It was odd hugging someone shorter than her when she'd been the short person. And yet, enfolding him in an embrace felt right.

A tingle on her arm had her pulling back. Before her eyes, the blue tendrils spread to the inside of her elbow, then formed another symbol.

"Day three," he whispered, comparing tattoos.

"Shit," she said. "It *is* a timer."

"I wonder if I can decipher your tattoo." He sifted through the books until he waved the one holding the alphabet.

She paled. "Now?"

He raised his gaze. "Don't you want to know? Maybe the tattoo artist wrote something stupid instead, like 'no regerts.'"

"It was so long ago, Thorne. Whatever it is, it doesn't matter. I'm having it removed when I reach Artivar."

"I'm still curious." Then, to her shock, he unzipped his jeans and exposed his ass. "What's the first letter?"

She tried to hide a grin. If she had to describe each symbol, then she could mislead him. "That one," she touched the symbol for the letter 'N.'

'No regerts' it is.

Chapter Fifteen

"No, you're shitting me," Eli gasped, disbelieving the words. "It doesn't spell that." He laughed, shaking his head. "What are the odds?"

"I should be angry, but I've had it for so long," Nova said. "Good thing I'm having it removed."

"It's pretty, though," he said, zipping up his jeans.

"It glows, too," she said, sinking into the pilot seat.

A blue-green-purple moon drew closer, filling their screens. The station-sec saber-class cruiser took up the foreground. In the background was the frozen mass of Nyxara.

"Safe and sound," station-sec said on the comms. Her face didn't appear and wouldn't if he judged by the ship veering away. "Good luck, and we'll hold you to that dinner."

"Absolutely," Nova said. "And thanks for the rescue."

They were alone, no longer being fired at, and traveling to yet another adventure. Things were going too well. "Any damage?" he asked. "We good to land?"

"I hope so," Nova said and spun the shuttle, catching a glimpse of the departing saber.

A slight whir in the engines made him stiffen his spine. Maybe he was being paranoid. When she resumed their path to Lethara, the strange sound settled into a hum.

"Mm, maybe take it easy when we land?" She didn't glance at him. That didn't bode well.

"*If* we can."

He wasn't a praying man, but the urge to start pressed on him. Gazing at the ceiling seemed silly. He did so anyway, sending up a quick prayer for a good landing, survival, and overall success. He followed with a quick apology for being silent all these years. The last time he'd spent any time with the Lord was after his parents died.

The forescreen flashed, mapping out their trajectory with a dashed line. They breached the red-tinted clouds, barreling along tall, asparagus-like trees. Three feet or more below their tips, thick foliage began, hiding the ground below. The engines whined, and when the shuttle dipped then righted itself, the sudden movement left his stomach in his throat. He swallowed the rising nausea.

She gripped the lever, her knuckles white and strained. "We're nearing the spot," she said. "See any clearings in the canopies?"

He scanned the almost-phallic trees, trying to find a break where they didn't look like porcupine quills. "Nothin—"

"Destination reached," the computer intoned, flashing a green icon on the screen.

She yanked back, the ass of the shuttle scraping along the tips of the trees. They hovered there.

"Caves without mountains have to mean an opening going underground," he said. "Any guns on this thing?"

"Computer, can we blast a clearing?" she asked.

"This is a N-class expedition shuttle, designed to be a scientific personnel carrier. It does not have security features," the computer said.

"There we go," Nova muttered.

The computer continued. "A suitable landing location is 2.43 kilometers due west."

Nova grinned. "Thank you." She propelled the shuttle forward then jerked it to a halt. The suggested spot was on the apex of an orange waterfall where a narrow strip of dark riverbank jutted out.

"Shit," he hissed, tension hardening his spine. "Can we make it?"

"We have to," she said. "Good to be near water, though. Computer, land this shuttle." She removed her hands from the lever. "Goes against my better judgment, but she'll do it better than I can." Nova offered him a smile. "Docking, no problem. Landing, mm, not my best skill."

"Now you tell me?"

"Think you can do it, Thorne?" she snapped. "How long have you had your pilot's license?"

How does she know about that? He pinched his lips. *But she has a good point.*

What should have been a gentle touch down turned out to be an extreme joyride. The shuttle shot up, then dropped, leaving his stomach pinned to the ceiling. His feet left the floor then slammed down, reverberating up his feet into his knees. A horrendous whine pierced the air.

"Engine malfunction," the computer stated. "Overriding auto-pilot. One moment, please."

Up they flew. This time, he couldn't hold on and hit the floor, the chair's edges scraping his ribs. Nova stayed in place, having strapped herself into the seat. She tried to grab him, but to no avail.

The final descent rattled his teeth, and the crunch of shattered rock had to mean only one thing.

They'd landed. Metal creaked, and the distinct odor of chemicals pierced his senses.

"Chance of exploding are?" he asked the computer while keeping his gaze fixed on Nova.

"73.7 per cent."

"And the air's breathable? Water drinkable?" Nova hurried to ask.

"Affirmative," the computer droned.

"Let's not delay then." She jumped up, tugging the coat off the back of the chair and pulling it on. "What else do we need?"

"So, we're not hiding this thing, right?" He eyed the trees visible in the forescreens. Chopping them with a machete would take days.

"We don't have to. Pirates attacked us, not Orien. There's no reason why he'd find us." She opened the weapons locker, slipped a laser rifle over a shoulder, and hefted a machete.

He took a machete but left the rifle, not sure he could carry that *and* the bag. With the blaster and dagger, he was more than armed.

"Ready?" she asked, then punched the red button beside the door.

It swished open, flooding the compartment with fresh air, the likes he hadn't enjoyed since Tarnis and filming *Yeehaw in Zero G.*

She jumped out onto the pale-gray rock of the riverbank. When she veered around the tail-end, he followed. The tinkle of cooling metal reached him and that same stench from earlier. He came to a standstill beside her, gaping at the wreckage. Grooved into the right engine was a deep gash, exposing layers of metal and mechanical parts.

"We were lucky," she said, stating the obvious. "Could've blown at any second."

Lucky? He scoffed. They'd been close to getting splattered. He wasn't sure if that was an improvement to torture.

Spinning on the spot, she scanned the area. "Any idea where east is?"

He hitched a thumb past the ass-end of the shuttle. "That way. You didn't swivel, heading in a straight line from the cave's location, so yeah..."

"Good enough for me, Thorne."

He stared after her, her long legs carrying her along the bank with such speed. Sure, he'd spent a lifetime adjusting his stride to align with the shorter people around him, but it sucked being on the receiving end.

She stopped when she skirted the treeline. "Want me to carry that?" She gestured to the knapsack.

"No, I can do it."

She frowned. "We need to make good time. *If* Orien's on our six, I want to be as far from here as possible."

"He'll know where we're going."

"True, but he can't land near to the cave or us." She grinned. "We took the last parking spot."

He handed over the bag. "This doesn't look inaccessible." Hiking two kilometers through these tall trees seemed doable.

"There has to be something we don't know," she said, palming the machete. "Come. Stay close."

"Then slow down," he snapped, sounding more like Nova when he'd first met her.

She glanced at his legs then nodded. "Sorry."

As they marched through the trees, the weak sunlight obliterated by the thick canopy, a green glow came to life on the bark, north-facing. It gleamed as if wet, and where it dripped, it hissed.

"Don't touch anything," he whispered.

"And watch where you step." She sprinted ahead, smoke rising from her bootheels.

Yelping, he did the same, leaping onto the same boulder she balanced on. "Acid?"

"Could be that same green goo." She eyed the path they needed to take. "We're going to have to make a run for it. Think you can?"

He frowned. "No other choice. I'm not standing here like a sitting duck waiting to be captured again or worse."

She grinned and bolted, taking off down the hill. Every chance she could, she took a rock outcropping or a patch of thick ground cover. He stayed on her, a little behind but kept her in his sights. The stench of burnt leather singed his nostrils by the time they paused, this time on a fallen tree. He eyed it, not sure it was safe.

"Don't think about it," she panted. "Just...catch your breath."

"I'm not *that* unfit," he rasped.

"Neither am I, but we don't know the percentage of oxygen in the air."

Why hadn't he thought of that?

A squeal pierced the sky. Glancing up was flipping useless when he couldn't see through the tree cover.

"Animal or mechanical?" she asked.

"Fuck knows." He peered into the shadows, half expecting something to charge him. "Let's go."

She did, leading the way. Being a little out when they started would send them in the wrong direction or missing the cave. Hopefully, the entrance would be gaping and massive. She rounded a corner and was gone.

Sheer panic gripped him. He hollered her name, tracing her steps but not finding her. A blast of goo splattered his boots. He stared at the smoke sizzling off the leather. A flash of light snapped his head up with the realization that something was firing at him. There, hovering above the treetops was a shuttle looking like *Viator IV*'s nastier brother—a canon was mounted to its side. Its neon-blue light burned brighter, warning him of an impending shot. He ducked behind a tree, but when nothing happened, he peeked to find the shuttle had for some reason moved on.

A boom and a cloud of fiery smoke made him duck. It had come from the direction of their shuttle, but he wasn't a hundred percent sure. Not that they could've flown it again, but its destruction resonated with finality. He broke into a run, casting glances over his shoulder.

Then darkness engulfed him, swallowing his scream as he plummeted—wind whipping his hair back. Vines grabbed at him, wrapping around his arms with slime coating and stinging his skin. One sank its teeth into him. He cried out. In the meager light, all he caught was white suckers like an octopus. Around each one were tiny fangs, drawing blood. In disbelief, he stared at it. When his thoughts slammed into his head, he began to struggle, making the pain worse.

"Quit wriggling," Nova yelled.

He froze at hearing her voice. Despite the warmth of relief, he twisted to find her on an illuminated shore, a rifle on her shoulder. "Don't! You'll kill me."

She fired, hitting the rock beside his face and showering him with shards.

"Nova," he hollered.

"You're distracting me," he thought he heard her say. She aimed again, striking the nearest vine. It squealed—the sound piercing.

And he was falling, his scream lodging in his throat.

He hit the soft soil and crumpled.

"I think Orien found us," he managed, digging a foot out of the mud.

"Pirates, sure."

He met and held her gaze, her face painted blue-white from what looked like fairy lights climbing up spiraling stalactites. A little to the right and he would've skewered himself.

"Nova, honey, something exploded, and the other shuttle was like *Viator IV*." Circular bite marks littered his arm, and a tingling sensation burned his fingertips. Not good signs.

She blinked at him. "Shit. I didn't expect him this soon."

"Yeah, so not only does this thing have us on a time limit, we now have Orien closing in without a way to get off this moon." He swept his gaze across a burgundy-colored lake, its orange waves lapping at the shore. "Pretty."

"Not how we planned it, but we found the cave."

"How's this inaccessible?" he asked again.

"The carnivorous vines, maybe? We've got to find a way out of here. If this is part of the cave system we targeted, we might not be in the right section."

"I'd say it was." He tapped her shoulder and gestured to behind her. Across a rock wall were familiar carved letters. "Can we decipher that?"

Dread settled over him. He stilled. That made no sense... It felt like it was coming from Nova. He shook his head. This experience from the stone shattering to reaching this point had been traumatic, possibly messing with his mind.

"Give me the bag."

She hesitated but did so. "This was too easy."

He hummed in agreement while he dug for the brown-leather notebook that held the alphabet.

"We don't have time for this, not when Orien's men could—"

"We need a direction to go. If there's a slim chance it's telling us to head left, we have to unravel this." He handed her the book while he readied the pen to paper. "Come on, let's start."

He wrote down each letter as she translated it, his ears primed for any danger. Fragments were easy to make out, but the message was long. His hand had cramped by the time they reach the final symbol.

"What you seek is not here. Look to each other for the source," he read off.

"That's no fucking help." She huffed. "I should've expected that from an alien moon with body-swapping geology."

"It's a riddle, right?"

"The first part isn't. It's pretty clear." She rested her hands on her hips. "And the rest is some mumbo-jumbo any idiot could make up."

"If we set aside the frustration, what could it mean?"

She glared at him. "I'd rather we hadn't found this silly message and figured out where to go on our own."

He hid a smile. 'Look to each other for the source' might mean choose a direction. She was right. It was nonsense. He folded the paper in half and shoved it into his pocket. "Okay, where to?"

She studied the message. "Left."

He pinched his lips to swallow a chuckle. "Guessing's not helpful either."

She pointed at the symbols. "The 'h' has an arrow in it. Maybe it's a design feature, the author being exuberant. Then why does the 'o' and 'n' have the same squiggle?"

He laughed. "Left it is." Scooping up the bag, he tossed the leather-bound book in and set off along the shore. The lights dwindled when the sand narrowed until they came to a point where only water awaited them. "Maybe they meant right?"

"Give me the torch."

He dug in the bag and took out the lantern-shaped torch. "It's probably not charged."

She grimaced, smacked it a few times, then handed it back.

"We could use my ass..."

She smirked. "I doubt the tattoo's bright enough." She spun on a heel and stomped back, marching past the message. The shore curved around a pillar of rock.

"Wait," he whispered, pointing at a standalone symbol. "Isn't that an arrow?" He ran his fingers over the 'o.'

She whooped. "Yes, we've got this."

A garbled scream snapped his gaze up. The bottom half of a man hit the ground, blood and innards spilling across the sand. Riddling parts of him were hundreds of bite marks—similar to those along Eli's arm. Many vines must've latched onto this man and torn him in half.

Her eyes were wide when she said, "We better hurry."

Panic gripped him, and he froze. Again, not his emotion, but something external lashed at him.

"Nova, breathe." He cupped her shoulders and forced her to inhale and exhale, trying to test if that unknown anxiety would subside. When it faded, he bit his tongue. Now wasn't the time to tell her he was sensing impossible things. No way could he *share* her emotions. It would be all kinds of stupid to even consider that possible.

She pulled away. "Okay, I'm good." She hurried along the shore, dodging incoming waves that thankfully washed away their passing.

"It could be me," he said, "but doesn't the moon affect water like this? I mean, why would it have waves?"

She stumbled to a stop. "The other side didn't have any." She swept a gaze at the disturbed lake. "Maybe we should run?"

"Hell yeah."

She exploded into a sprint, the butt of the rifle slapping her on the ass. "Up ahead is a sliver of darkness. It could be a doorway."

"It could be a pit," he called.

"No choice," she said, stopping in front of the carved archway. "Now that's interesting. Look at the symbols."

"He who passes through will die?" he offered.

She snorted. "More like, 'Only the worthy may enter.'"

He winked. "Well, you're worthy in my book."

She met his gaze, her breathing slowing, and yet a staccato heartbeat reached his ears. Without breaking eye contact, he pressed two fingers to his wrist, measuring his pulse. It didn't align to the thundering in his...mind...

"Come," she said and slipped into the shadows.

He hesitated. It had looked like black quicksilver, engulfing her in an instant.

"Thorne?"

He followed, allowing the icy liquid to coat his skin as he stepped through it.

Red-tinted sunlight streamed through a crevice in the cavern's ceiling. A jungle had grown at the base—tall trees, vines, with birds circling the oasis. At its center was a gigantic flower, long petals dipping to the floor. From up high, a waterfall cascaded into nowhere.

"So pretty," she rasped but when she faced him, she paled. "Thorne, the archway's...gone." She darted around him to slap solid stone.

He gaped. "We're trapped."

Chapter Sixteen

"Fuck that," Nova squeaked, inching closer. "It's vanished. Doesn't that scare you?"

"No," he said.

And yet a wave of sourness washed over her. She stiffened. Either he was as shit scared as she was, or something weird had made their gathering a party of three. Traveling in space, she'd seen many a thing she couldn't explain. She'd shoved them to the recesses of her mind to never be poked.

But nothing this wild.

She tapped the rock, the coldness of it solidifying its existence to what she'd hoped was an illusion. "All right, let's hope Orien can't follow."

She studied the next step in their adventure. "It's beautiful." Shuffling back, she surveyed the wall of rock, searching for a symbol. "Which way?"

"I'd say we travel along the circumference. Map this area, so to speak."

"Sounds like a plan." She glanced at him then scowled. "Quit it."

He stopped rubbing a breast. "But it's sore. Does it look bigger to you?"

She rolled her eyes. "They swell...when my period draws near."

"Really?" Horror contorted his features.

"Yup. Welcome to womanhood." She chuckled as she headed clockwise.

"Not funny," he called, stomping after her.

A vision of his swagger in denims with the coat flapping behind her had her spinning to arch a brow at him. Sure enough, he was staring at her ass. Instead of responding, she faced forward, trying to unravel how she'd known his thoughts, had seen through his eyes. This planet had to be affecting her mind. Could be the air? That made sense since she hadn't touched anything. With machete in hand, she hacked at the fauna, making a path for them while keeping the side of the cavern in view. Hours ticked by, sweat formed, and the thought that they were going in circles ate at her.

She stopped when Thorne offered her a bottle of water. "This place is huge."

"Yeah," he said, after a long drink from his bottle. "I haven't seen any lettering or alien-made objects to guide us." He grimaced and hitched a thumb at the center of the oasis. "We could try there. If I was an alien culture, that's where I'd put a marker or shrine."

She gazed in that direction. "I'd build it into the rock walls on the circumference."

He stilled. "No, we're not splitting up."

"It would cover more ground, and you can't get lost."

"When you fell into a hole? Who's to say there isn't another? Or a massive creature swallows you in one bite?"

"The problem with actors is their overactive imagination," she said, taking another gulp of water before capping the bottle. "I just want to reach our starting point, to make sure we're not missing arrows or other instructions. Then we can head to the middle."

He peered over his shoulder. "I haven't heard anything other than the wildlife."

"Same." She dipped her head, fear building in her spine. Orien wouldn't give up, not if their footprints led to a solid wall of rock. He'd find a way in.

Thorne flashed his smirk. "We're lost, thanks to you. I've been kidnapped by the sexiest man in the galaxy."

She laughed. "Humble, much?"

"Nominated for that title two years in a row, I believe." He puffed out his chest then sighed. "Everything's sore, Nova. This jungle-forging isn't for the faint of heart."

She nodded. "To the beginning, then we stop for lunch."

He grinned. "Sure, protein bars sound good about now."

She marched on, slashing or holding back snapping vines. Great silver leaves moved aside as if sensing their approach, coating the ground with a fine layer of white pixie dust. She stomped her feet, trying to keep the stuff off her boots. Who knew if it was like acid or a narcotic. She'd rather not find out. But with every thump-thump, a fresh cloud of white rose. So, she gave up on that futility.

When Thorne stumbled, she spared him a glance. Sweat drenched the T-shirt to his chest, and he'd looped the coat through the bag's straps. The temperature, its warmth to be expected of a jungle climate, wasn't hot enough to cause discomfort. They'd been walking for hours, but her body was in pique condition.

She paused at a pool of water that disappeared under jagged rock. It was orange, and so clear, she could see the bottom where iridescent eels swam between silver weeds. They seemed to be the length of her arms, and tiny green fish trailed each one. Beyond that was a shore then more jungle. Somehow, she knew, they were close to the start. Then they could head to the center.

"What bothers me," she said, facing Thorne who'd dropped the bag and sank onto the sand. "Where's an exit? We need to get out of here. Up isn't an option—no rope."

"Didn't see any on the shuttle," he said before drinking more water.

"Which means into another hole or cave or through a secret archway." She wiggled her fingers. "Gimme a bar. Might as well eat."

His smile was weak, but he did as asked, handing her a purple-wrapped bar. "Blackberry."

She took a bite, chewing around the 'berry' pieces. "Want me to investigate the opposite shore while you rest?"

He bit into his and moaned. "Didn't realize how hungry I was." Waving his bar at the pool, he said, "Be my guest, but stay within line of sight."

With the bar gripped between her teeth after every bite, she hacked a path around the pool until she reached the other shore. She waved at him before heading deeper into the foliage. The cavern's wall was to the left, rising high with nary a carving. To the right, the ground climbed a little to the middle of the oasis.

She struck stone and glanced down, finding geometric rocks stacked high. "Found something," she called.

Excitement tempted her to carry on, to not return to Thorne until she had more to share. After all, this could be nothing, even though the precise corners said otherwise. They'd been chiseled into shape. A quick stroke around their sides revealed no lettering.

Reluctantly, she trudged back along the path, crushing flowers in pinks and blacks beneath her boots. The potent fragrances intensified, so sharp her nostrils burned and a headache pinged at her temple. Stepping onto the shore gave her a moment to breathe.

Thorne lay on his back, the half-eaten bar clutched to his chest.

The ass was napping.

She growled and stomped to him, ready to shake him awake. When she approached, he stirred, angling his head to meet her gaze. His hand flopped down, exposing a thousand pinpricks in his arm, each one tainted blue-purple.

She gasped, hurried to reach him, then sank onto her knees. "Why didn't you tell me?" She took his bottle and poured water over his wounds.

"Didn't think to pack a med-kit. Didn't see one," he slurred, offering her a wobbly smile. "Nothing we can do, honey pot."

"But find a way out. I stumbled on a piece of a wall. Could be ruins. I don't know." She shrugged off the rifle and set it near at hand. "Use this if anyone but me comes near you." Maybe those vines had venom? She couldn't be sure. And bandaging them was impossible with them being all over his arm. She had to try though. Shrugging off her coat, then her T-shirt, she sliced the latter into a long spiral, like peeling an apple skin in one go.

Thorne blinked at her, a silly smile in place. "I like you, Nova Blake."

"Oh, Lord," she muttered as she wrapped his arm. "You're delirious."

He pouted. "You don't like me back?"

"I do," she said, tying a tiny bow at the end, just under his armpit. "I've left the rifle. Your water's here, and finish your protein bar. I'm going to see if there's a way out of this place." She shrugged on the coat, better to have a layer of protection, then dug in the bag for the leather-bound book.

"I'll stay here then," he mumbled, shutting his eyes on a dreamy sigh.

This wasn't good. She could carry him, but with nowhere to go, that was pointless. No, there had to be an arrow somewhere. "I'll be right back."

Without thinking, she pressed a kiss to his cheek, then jerked back. *Shit.*

Stunned, she rested on her haunches, fingers pressed to her tingling lips. *Why did I do that?* Argh, it had been instinctual. His eyes stayed shut. He must not have noticed.

Scrambling to her feet, she hurried along the path, only stopping when the pillar was before her. Whack-whack, breathe. On she went, exposing cobbles beneath her boots, a few more pillars—all bare of writing. Her shoulders rose in hope then slumped in despair when each one offered no guidance. A breeze, cooling her sweaty skin, gave her pause. She turned, staring at the unmoving leaves and branches. Where was the wind coming from? A writhing vine reached for her, but she slapped it back with the flat of the machete's blade. That's when the corner of her eye caught a flutter.

Obscured by deep blue flowers, the top third of an archway sat at the base of the cavern's wall where it met the ground. She'd have to wiggle through to reach what lay beyond. For now, it was all darkness, and not the liquid kind from before. She squealed when she brushed aside a few elongated petals and found letters.

Her fingers trembled as she withdrew the book and paged to the alphabet. It didn't take her long to decipher its meaning.

"To find oneself is to face the shadows. Yes!" Back she sprinted, uncaring if she disturbed the pixie dust or if a vine tried to bite her. "Thorne, I f—"

She skidded to halt on the shore. He floated on his back in the pool, eels squirming over him. Throwing aside the machete and the coat, she waded in, registering the water as refreshing and thicker than normal, almost viscous. The eels and their entourages scattered, one slithering from under his T-shirt just when she reached him.

"Eli," she gasped, gripping his shoulders. "Are you okay?"

His eyes were closed, but his chest moved…barely.

"Eli?" A chill shot down her spine. The bites… They were gone, now silver circles of tiny scars. "What the—"

His eyes opened.

Relief exploded in her, bathing her insides with joy. She hugged him, crushing him to her chest. "You scared me," she snapped.

"Sorry," he whispered. "I was hot, and the water looked so inviting." He tightened his arms around her, keeping her near. "I feel better too. For a moment there, my mind wasn't—mine." He leaned back, sloshing the water, and cupped her cheek. "Find something?"

"I did." She beamed, caught his hand, and led him to his side of the pool. "Grab your gear."

He hefted the bag over a shoulder and offered her the rifle. "You called me Eli."

She scoffed but glanced away. "Thought you'd drowned."

"Mm, so I've got to be dying before you'll be nice to me?"

She frowned. "When haven't I been nice?"

He arched an accusatory brow.

"Yes, you have to be dying." She strode off. "Keep up. The hole's this way."

Through the overhead crevice, the sky was changing into pinks and reds, promising night. They were running out of time. Did the countdown take planetary rotations into consideration? A few hours ago, they'd been waking up on day three. The sun setting this soon could mean they'd been cheated out of a day.

"What does the writing say?" He stroked the lettering along the arch.

"To find oneself is to face the shadows."

"Sounds like the right direction." He dipped and peered into the darkness. When he re-emerged, he said, "White fairy lights are here and there, but nothing else. I don't know if we're falling into nothing, water, or rock." His eyes widened. "It's a leap of faith."

An explosion scattered the birds and sent up a cloud of pixie dust from across the oasis.

She froze, peering through the jungle like she could magically see Orien and his men. "They must have found a footprint. I was pretty sure the waves were washing them away."

"We better hurry. We've left a trail..." He gripped the top of the archway and went in feet first.

She blinked. He was gone in a second.

"Shit," she scrambled to the opening, then did the same.

The last thing she registered was the bite of stone under her fingertips.

Chapter Seventeen

The moon, Lethara

Into a dark cave.

Where the hell am I?

Day Three.

To be weightless twice in a day was new to Eli. He fought the urge to scream, to snatch at air like that would slow his descent. Have faith, the writing had said. And oh boy, did he. One moment, his mind had been filled with sensual images of Nova, the way she'd looked bare-chested, the kiss on the cheek, her admitting to liking him. The next, he was plagued by sorrow. Someone had died. A man...with platinum hair, a scruffy beard, and the brightest smile. His gaze held such love. But it was snatched away, drenching Eli with ichor. There was no other way to describe the dense sadness. Images flickered, conveying the passing of time.

And yet, the wailing of despair echoed in his mind.

Only to be awoken with eels tickling his wounds and wrapping around his limbs.

"Eli," she said, her voice snatching him from a troubled sleep. She'd called his name. Hugged him.

Cold water engulfed him, breaking his fall. He surfaced, peering into the shadows while trying to swim away. Nova would follow, and landing on him would hurt. She hit the water next to him, coughing when she came up for air.

"See anything?" she asked, touching his shoulder.

"A blue flame." He squeezed his eyes shut then opened them again, just to be sure he hadn't imagined it. "Over there." A flicker of light had to mean something good.

"I wonder if we can use these little lights, like a torch?" She started swimming toward the flames.

"Yeah, I kind of don't like the idea of navigating a new cave by touch." He brushed his fingers along her sides, summoning a chuckle from her.

"Thorne," she gasped around a giggle. "No fair. You know your tickle spots."

"Where are yours?" he asked, smiling in her direction.

"My feet, alas. Oh, land. I can touch down." She stood, then waded out of the water.

It was a minute or two later before he could follow—another downside to being short. He shivered, standing on shore, drenched and cold. Two burning sconces marked the entrance to a cobbled path. On either side, stone pillars ran the illuminated length. They were covered with letters glowing in the torch light.

"I think we hit the motherload," he said.

"Shit!" She wiggled and pulled a sopping wet book from the back of her pants. "It's ruined." She flipped through the ink-coated pages, stopping at the alphabet. Some of the lettering had blurred together.

"Keep it open. Let it dry."

"I'm such an idiot," she mumbled.

"We can still read most of it," he said, throwing an arm around her waist for a quick squeeze. "And if all else fails, your tattoo can help."

He moved back and almost tumbled over when his heel hit the first cobble. Light illuminated the path for about three feet, then shut off when he leaped away.

"What was that?" she squeaked.

"I..." He rested his booted toe on the cobbles, and again, the path lit up, each letter carved into the stones glowing blue.

"Yes!" She danced on the spot, the rifle smacking her ass. "All right, let's do this."

He stared at her offered hand, then grabbed it. She led the way, marching along the stones. They glowed only for as long as needed, going dark after they passed.

"Have faith," she said, "With each step testing us."

"The path could fall away, and we wouldn't know until it's too late." He almost wished he hadn't said that when the lights wavered.

The stairs down yawned, darkness engulfing its depths. With one step, blue carvings exploded into life, showing them the way. Nova turned to help him as if he didn't have two legs of his own. He did appreciate the constant warmth of her hand, keeping him grounded.

"I'd love to know what this place is like. If we had a drone, tons of lights..." She released him to twirl, then she laced her fingers through his and drew him nearer.

"We'd be the first people in a long time to see it." Gemstones embedded in the walls glowed violet, crimson, gold, white—so beautiful that he slowed. "Looks untouched," he said, the weight of millennia draping over his shoulders. "I hope Orien doesn't find it."

"Same." She sighed, dipping her chin to her chest. "We've led him right to it, though."

"Do you think it has a stone?"

The narrow path opened to a hall, its high ceilings enshrouded, but massive pillars dominated the space, too wide for him to hug. As they ventured deeper, circles of light glowed beneath their feet.

"There?" She pointed to the far end at a deep alcove—an eerie red glow emanating from it.

At the end of the rock-lined alcove, a pedestal on a dais took up center-stage. Floating above it was a star stone, a red ray of light bathing it.

"Seems too easy," she whispered. "Walk up to it and touch it; that's all we have to do."

He studied the cobbles, any holes in the walls that could fire darts at them, a slab in the lowered ceiling that was loose? "Yeah, I'm distrusting this, too."

She rocked on her heels. "Let's run for it. Together. We *both* have to be on the other side for this magic to undo."

"Magic?" He smirked.

"What else would you call it?" She ran a hand over the nearest glowing letter in the stone wall. "Want to tell me how your aura's powering this place?"

He chuckled. "Fair enough."

"On the count of three?"

He nodded.

"One... Two..."

As she counted, he admired the sparkle in her eyes. This was it. They were so close to being free.

And yet, his chest ached. Everything within him wanted to head the other way.

"Three."

They bolted, sprinting across the cobbles. Something flicked his hair back, stinging his cheek, but he didn't stop to see what. She reached the dais first.

The floor disappeared beneath his feet, crumbling in a deafening roar. He screamed and threw himself forward, catching the edge of the dais' lowest step. A glance down showed nothing but darkness below his dangling feet. His arms began to burn, unable to hold him in place for much longer. Then he was safe, whipped onto solid ground with her hands under his armpits.

"What the hell," he snapped, gaping at the chasm. "I...I couldn't pull myself up, like your ass is too heavy for your arms."

"I can carry my weight," she said, peering into the darkness below.

"Pfft. I doubt it. This body of yours is useless," he muttered, touching the sting on his cheek only to stare at the blood on his fingertips. "No upper body strength."

"Excuse me?" she gritted out, slapping her chest. "Not everyone can bench press planets."

"Yeah? Well, your body's clearly allergic to mine because I swear it's been blushing since we left orbit."

She leaned in, jabbing a finger into his borrowed chest. He shortened the distance, nose-to-nose, the light flickering red over them.

The tension thickened. Thoughts faded, and he shifted, bringing their faces into kissing distance. Her ragged breathing rubbed her chest over his breasts, tightening the nipples. He'd be damned if he kissed her first, as much as he longed to. She had to do the conquering, proving she wanted this. No more denials. This was sexual. An ache twisted in his gut.

Their lips collided.

He blinked, not sure who'd moved.

A moment of silence followed as he stared into her green eyes wide with shock.

She recoiled, scrambling back like she'd been electrocuted. "You kissed me!" She waved a finger at him.

"Uh uh, you kissed yourself," he said, fighting the urge to touch his lips where the imprint of hers still lingered.

"This doesn't count," she said, straightening her spine.

"We shall see," he said, casting a glance at the chasm that could've been his grave. "Thanks," he mumbled, jumping away from the void where the floor had been. "We're trapped, again."

She caught his wrist and guided his palm to the warm star stone. "Thorne, we're here."

A spark zapped his fingers, but he didn't pull away. She touched the other side, meeting his gaze over the egg-shaped stone.

"It's been an adventure," she said.

Minutes ticked by.

He released a breath, allowing the tension to drain from his shoulders.

"I'm still in you," she said, frowning and slapping the stone. Slap, release, slap again—nothing happened.

"Yeah, and it's *still* colored. Last time, we broke it."

"We?" She scoffed. "Now you admit it wasn't just me?"

He grinned, not about to admit to anything.

She glared at him then dropped her hand. "This isn't working. See what those symbols mean." Smacking him on the chest with the book, she sat on the edge of the dais and hung her legs off the edge.

He switched his gaze between the wall and the book. "These symbols aren't in the book. Maybe a different dialect or some ancient language, but if I had to hazard a guess, we need two stones," he said, drumming the wall where one of two figures held a star stone to their chest.

"Two!" She pinched the bridge of her nose. "Orien swore getting his hands on one was hard, and yet, boom, here's one. We can't be lucky enough to find another."

Eli trailed a finger along wavy lines. "Flowing water?"

"We have to go back over that?" She pointed her toe at the chasm.

"Yeah, we're sitting ducks if we stay here. These pictograms say something about taking a river and jumping off a cliff."

"Off a what?" she squeaked, clambering to her feet to study the ruined alphabet then the wall. "I don't know how many leaps of faith I can take."

"So back we go." He eyed the chasm. "Dunno how without dying."

She huffed and circled the pedestal. "If I was an alien culture, I'd put in a secret exit."

He smiled. "I like that idea way too much." He tucked the book into the bag. "So touch everything?"

She laughed. "Yes," she said, running her hand along the top of the pedestal.

"Wait, we have to take the stone first. If the floor swallows us, I don't know how to get back here. We need this." He tapped the star stone, then adjusted the bag on his shoulder.

She wiggled and poked random corners, even kicked the pedestal, before leaning against the wall with a groan. "This is madness," she mumbled, throwing her hands up in despair.

As entertaining as watching her was, he had to somehow remove the stone from its floating nothingness. He grabbed the top part and cupped the base, then yanked.

It didn't budge.

Again, he tried, eventually placing both feet on the pedestal and using all his weight.

"Here, let me help." She inched him out of the way. Even with her strength, the star stone didn't shift. Her face flushed red, a low growl escaping. "Damn thing's stuck. Listen here, you stupid stone. I'm not about to fall through carnivorous vines, walk through a magic door, traipse around an oasis, jump into darkness, and cross that chasm just to bring you another stone. You're coming with us."

Lecture delivered, she gave it a firm nod.

She's adorable. The urge to kiss her hit him hard. He sent that thought to the back of his mind and pressed his side to hers. "Looks like everything's in twos."

He placed his hands around hers.

The stone came free, sending them flying backward. Half-expecting to hit a wall, a strangled cry squeezed past his throat as he tumbled down a slope to sprawl in a stream.

Nova was face down in the mud, the stone between them. "And Orien wonders why I call it silly, or stupid." She clambered to her feet, dripping mud down her cheeks. "I'm a lady, and ladies don't swear." And she proceeded to call it all manner of things, kicking water and mud onto it.

He chuckled at that nonsense since she'd been swearing for as long as he'd known her. "Sexiest lady I know."

Up went her finger. "Don't you start with that bullshit." She scooped up the stone. "Now open your damn bag."

He did, grinning at her while she wrestled with the bag and the stone.

Done, she flicked wet hair off her temple. "Right, so where are we?"

"Some sort of tunnel," he said, gesturing to the late afternoon sunlight streaming into the narrow opening.

Water trickled past them underfoot, not strong enough to sweep them away. The thunder of a nearby waterfall reverberated through the tunnel, promising something substantial. Not like the one that drizzled a fine mist over the oasis.

"This isn't good, Thorne," she said, inching to the edge. "One, it looks like freedom, but by my count, we're missing a stone. Two, this's probably said cliff those symbols were talking about."

Down below was a sizable pool surrounded by a wall of rock. One massive waterfall tumbled into the water—its dark orange implying it was deep. Except, they were high up, about fifty to sixty-five feet—terrifying as leaps of faith went.

"No way am I jumping," she said, gripping the tunnel's side.

"It wants us to go in that direction." He pointed outside.

"I'm not keen on going splat." She marched back to peer up the slide they'd fallen along.

He balanced his feet on the middle of the entrance, clutching the bag to his body. If he threw himself off, she had to follow, right?

He leaped, keeping his form tight, his legs extended.

"Thorne, you asshole!" trailed him to the pool below.

He burst out of the water, wiped his face, and waved to her glaring at him from the tunnel's opening. It was higher than he'd thought, but he'd survived.

"I'm going to kill you. Just you wait," she yelled, then sat on the edge, dangling her legs off.

He stilled. Was she afraid of heights? In his distraction, she'd managed to haul her ass over and was now hanging by her fingertips.

"You can do it," he called, wading out of the water and onto the shore.

Her curses came and went as she glanced at him, down at the pool, into the tunnel, then at him again. At last, she inched her way over the edge, finding toeholds and grips. It was painful watching her inch down, making him hitch his breath and send up prayers. Especially when she slipped and scrabbled for another hold.

Ten feet to go, she let go. Her trajectory was clear, and it was bad.

Had she jumped, she would have cleared those jutting rocks. She bounced from one to the other like an antique pinball machine. Her garbled curses rose in pitch, until she landed, legs akimbo on the final rock not an inch from the water.

Clinging to the rock, her face changed from pale to green to purple. Laughter exploded out of him. Tears fell unhindered. Unable to help her down, he could only focus on getting himself under control. Having been kicked in the balls before, the pain was excruciating. He winced in sympathy.

"I'll…kill you," she managed to rasp, her eyes squeezed shut.

"Slow inhales and exhales," he said, mid-chuckle.

"Fuck you, Thorne," she yelled. "Fuck all of this." With a gut-wrenching groan, she slipped off, her hands clutching her groin.

She sank underwater mid-grumble.

He shrugged off the bag and dove in, finding her with ease in the orange water. Her face was scrunched up, her cheeks pale as he dragged her to safety.

"Anything else hurt?" he asked.

"Can't tell," she gritted out through pinched lips. "Give me a moment."

"Well, you made it," he said and received a glare for his trouble.

Standing, he assessed their location. The light was almost gone—the vestiges of daylight in the crimson and pink on the horizon. They'd have to sleep here tonight, under the canopy of rock. It would protect them if it rained, and maybe hide them from prying eyes above.

Except, they had no blankets or fire.

He gazed at her, pain leeching from her features.

"We're going to have to share body heat." He glanced away, hiding his delight.

One stone in a day? They *had* been lucky.

And now, he'd get to spend the night with her, naked, snuggling.

Damn, things couldn't have ended on a better note if he'd planned them.

Chapter Eighteen

The moon, Lethara
A punchbowl waterfall
All out of faith.
Day Three.

With each second that passed, Nova could breathe a little easier. She'd never kick a man between the legs again. Well, maybe if she wanted him incapacitated so she could run away. Her groin was in excruciating agony. She tried to stand, to assess their surroundings, but could barely rock onto her knees.

"That was a dick move," she hissed.

"You were supposed to leap, not fall." He set the bag against a wall under a canopy of rock—a good place to spend the night.

She tried not to dwell on his warning. The idea of sharing warmth with him made her skin tingle, and her balls twinge, or was that the residual pain leaving her body? Damn, she hoped so, but the sane part of her knew it wasn't.

He peeled off his coat and sprawled on a nearby boulder to dry.

She shivered, four times drenched, once covered in mud. At least she was clean. Not much of a consolation as cold as she was. She'd started to dry after finding the star stone, her damp jeans chaffing her inner thighs.

Now, as she stood there, watching him reveal every inch of a body she knew too well, aches began to register. Her thigh, a hip, and a shoulder burned, no doubt bruised from hitting those rocks.

"Want a bottle of water and a protein bar?" he asked, digging in the bag. He was naked, his almond-toned skin glowing as the light faded. Chunks of hair stood on end, almost sheared off at the scalp. Why hadn't she noticed that before?

A muted yellow light rose from the pool, at the bottom slithered the eels and tiny green fish.

She stripped, splaying out her coat beside his. Boots, socks, jeans followed, then she marched into the orange water and floated.

He came to the edge and watched her, the underside of his breasts painted an eerie blue.

"Eels heal," she said, catching her breath when one nudged her chin in passing.

"Well, that explains this." He waved his bite-marked arm. "In the excitement, I forgot about the numbing pain. Only realized as I undressed that I was fine."

"Scarred, though. Healed Orien's knife wounds too." It *was* her body that showed the brunt of their adventures, but she wasn't angry. They'd survived, had a stone, and might live to find another. "Let me know when they swim away."

The sky was littered with stars. No light pollution diminished the full impact of their magnificence. It was a scene she wasn't familiar with.

Here, a shattered submoon arched across the sky. And not a single satellite pretended to be a shooting star.

"They're done," Eli said.

She swam to shore and walked out, accepting the offered bottle of water and protein bar. As cold as she was, she sat on the rock and leaned her back against the wall. Only time would dry her. As to warmth, that would come as soon as they settled down for the night.

As she ate, she tried not to notice his taut nipples, the curve of a hip, the soft-yet-muscled thighs. Nor did she want to dwell on their almost-kiss. Like she'd stated, it didn't count.

"I've been meaning to ask you..." He glanced at her, then at the stars. "Have you been experiencing something odd, like sensing my emotions?"

She shifted then found the same spot because it was a little warmer than the rock around it. "Yes."

A slow smile formed. "Phew. Was worried I was losing my mind."

"Must be a side effect of this." She flashed the blue tattoo crawling past her inner elbow. Day four's symbol would appear soon.

Capping the bottle and shoving the empty wrapper into the bag, she spread her thighs, shivering at exposing herself to a breeze. She tapped the ground between her legs. "I'm thinking you sit here, and warm my front while I warm your back. Let's hope our clothes dry soon."

He swiveled, thrusting his ass in her face, before he sat. "Watch your balls," he said, shuffling back.

Sighing, she cupped them until he leaned back. She slipped her arms around him, one across the collarbone, the other under his breasts, and pulled him closer until they were flush.

A sweet moan escaped him. "I didn't realize how cold I was."

She gritted her teeth, fighting the visceral reaction her body had to him. If everything he did aroused her, this would be a long night.

Strange cries, squawks, and chirps filled the air, peppered with fragrant flowers and wet sand. She rested her head against the rock, content to watch the submoon.

Their breathing evened out, and she was halfway to falling asleep when the caress of finger across her forearm snapped her eyes open. And of course, her cock had to harden.

"Stop turning me on, damn it."

"I'm not doing a thing. It's all you, buddy." Then he wiggled for added affect.

She tightened her hold, crushing him against her. "One more move and you're sleeping on your own."

When he brought his knees up then stilled, she slumped. It had been a trying day, not that she knew what time they'd arrived. Frederik had awoken them at two, and after all they'd been through, she was beat.

Now if her raging libido would calm the fuck down, she could get some sleep.

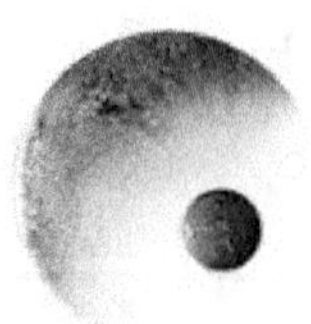

The moon, Lethara
At the base of a waterfall.
Onward, just hornier.
Day Four.

Jerking awake, Nova found her face buried in the curve of Eli's neck. It would be so easy to press a kiss there, to trail her lips to his jaw and angle it for a full-on kiss.

"I've gone mad," she mumbled, hugging him tighter.

"What is it?" he whispered, stirring.

"Nothing. Go back to sleep."

He wiggled, the bastard, twisting to gaze at her. "Did you hear something?"

Despite the growing ache in her groin, she didn't dare breathe. Their faces were inches apart, nose to nose. Even in the moonlight, she caught the warm amber in his eyes.

"My ass has fallen asleep," she whispered. It had, but as a distraction, it could work.

"Mine too," he rasped, his breath fanning her lips.

She made to get up, hoping to break whatever the hell this was. But instead of leaning away, he didn't move. Their lips met for a second.

It was long enough.

She groaned, cupped his cheek, and kissed him.

Like before, his lips were so soft, pliant, like rubbing hers across rose petals.

Tasting herself was nothing like she'd expected. It wasn't her mouth anymore. It belonged to him. When he swept a tongue over hers, all resistance crumbled. She delved in, desperate for something she couldn't put words to. The kiss—slow, luxurious, exploratory—ramped up the emotions swelling inside her. She refused to name them. This was nothing more than an adventure to him.

She was...nothing more.

She broke away. "Sorry," she said, slipping from behind him.

Standing with her back to him, she prayed the cool air would calm her...ardor. She glanced down, sighing at her impressive hard-on. It throbbed, making demands she struggled to silence.

In the distance, a dark red coated the horizon, like paint pooling at the bottom of a canvas. Dawn would be soon. She checked the coats and clothes, finding them damp but wearable. Grabbing her coat, she headed back to Eli...

When had she started to think of him as anything other than Thorne? The asshole had fucked and forgotten her, with zero regrets. The old hurt didn't rise to fuel her anger. She scowled. Great, she'd gone and forgiven him in the last three days.

She stomped to him and froze, catching his gaze on her. But what flittered across her mind was another woman, older, with his eyes, scolding him about his frown.

"A smile has potential to change the world. The right one at the right time is your power." She stroked his chin and ruffled his then-short hair. *"And you, my pumpkin, have the most beautiful smile in the world."*

"Nova?"

She blinked, snapping herself out of the vision. Odd things, he'd said. Studies had been done about memories being stored on a cellular level. That had to explain this madness. She'd been too long in his body and was now recalling his childhood. If they didn't swap soon, she'd have to suffer through his one-night-stands.

Including the night she'd given him her virginity.

"We can rest for another hour or two." She draped the coat over him, then squeezed behind him. The rock shared the warmth from her body.

As the world awoke, squeaks, shrieks, barks had her jumping. She tightened her arms around Eli, keeping him close. All their weapons rested beside the bag, the laser rifle leaning against the wall. That was near enough to reach. The sun peeked over the horizon. When its rays reached them, they added an extra layer of heat that made her groan.

A cup of hot tea would be heavenly, but without a way to light a fire and boil water, the chances of her getting anything remotely tea-like were slim.

Eli stretched, pushing up the coat. He clambered to his feet and scowled. "Got to pee."

"Saw some foliage to the west, but don't touch anything. Who knows what this moon's version of poison ivy looks like."

He marched across the shore, muttering about hating to drip dry.

Grinning, she dressed, peeling on the damp jeans and coat. Cold, wet socks had to do, made almost bearable in her equally wet boots.

"Where's your T-shirt?" he asked, striding to her, breasts jiggling.

She swallowed and cast her gaze down. "Cut it up for your wounds. Must have unraveled when you cooled off in the pool."

"Not that I mind...all of that." He gestured to her exposed chest.

She smiled. Being able to walk around shirtless was a benefit. "My turn." She abandoned him, choosing a different bush to hide behind. Her cock had softened, so she didn't have to use thoughts of strangling Orien just to pee.

She chuckled. "I'm getting better at this." She zipped up and headed back.

"Why do you say that?" he asked, tugging on a boot. At least he wasn't waltzing around naked anymore.

"No pee on my boots," she said, waving a foot. "Where next?"

"Follow the river, I suppose. Only way out of this place." He stood and held out a halved protein bar. "We can share."

She bit into it, rolling her tongue around its mealy texture. "Want to test the star stone before we try for another?"

"You think it will work?" He stopped and pulled the egg out of the bag.

With the protein bar clenched between her teeth, she placed her hands on the star stone and waited, praying for any reaction. A zap made her snatch her hands away. The blue tattoo extended another tendril and formed what she had to assume was the symbol for four.

"Well, I guess that answers it." He shoved the stone into the bag and offered it to her.

She sighed and looped it over a shoulder. "Right. We need directions."

Along the shore they strode, until he called her name, waiting for her to stop.

"Forgot the rifle." Back he hurried then froze. "Um, Nova-honey, there's something here. Bring the book." He flicked his fingers at her. "Quick."

She sprinted to him. Sure enough, along the wall was a line of letters, glowing in the morning sunlight. "How did we miss it?"

"The light, maybe," he said, taking the book from her.

"Why does it feel like a treasure hunt with super high stakes?"

He grinned. "Because it is."

"So, what does it say?"

He ran his finger over the page. "Y'know, I'm starting to know some of these symbols."

She shrugged. "You've been deciphering them. Practice makes perfect." She tapped wavy lines. "Let me guess, 'river?'"

"Life is in the motion, even when the path is not clear." He snapped the book shut and handed it to her. "We're to follow the river. I think this's a man walking on water. As silly as that idea is, that's my hunch."

"Wait," she said, lowering the bag to pull out the book with the cave locations. "We're here." She tapped the spot that looked like a convergence of rivers into a waterfall. "And if we follow the river, we land here." At an irregular circle that resembled a lake name 'Vael'Tir.'

"Shit, one of those islands, maybe?"

"Okay," she packed away the book, "we have a direction. If all goes well, we'll be swapped back by sunset."

"Then we'll worry about escaping this place without getting caught."

She smiled. "Baby steps."

Chapter Nineteen

The moon, Lethara

She kissed me!

Day Four.

It was a kiss Eli hadn't expected and hadn't instigated. A miracle in his book. As Nova marched ahead, he recalled her lips on his, the softness and sheer thrill in every flick of her tongue. She'd dominated when he always took the lead.

"Hurry up, Thorne," she yelled.

He frowned. "What happened to calling me Eli?"

"You're not dying," he thought he heard her say.

He broke into a jog, the rifle smacking his ass. "Think Frederik's all right?"

"I hope so."

"Yeah," he hummed, clambering over a fallen tree while she just stepped over it. "I'm hoping he got in touch with Graham. We could do with backup."

"I don't think you've realized that if we're stuck like this forever, you're going to jail."

"You'll bail me out." He grinned. "And vice versa."

"Deal." She tossed him a cheeky smile. "I don't know what I'm going to do with all my millions of credits."

He chuckled. "Billions."

She stumbled. "No shit. Well, as tempting as all that is, I want my meager bank account back, thanks."

"No craving for fame?"

She scoffed. "Nope."

A familiar whir whipped his gaze to the sky. A black metallic object gleamed as it trailed them.

"Shit," he muttered, catching the logo of a popular digital magazine.

"Orien?" she gasped.

"Paparazzi," he snapped. "Stay calm."

She snorted. "I *am* calm."

"Eli Thorne, E-Galactic." A feminine voice boomed from the drone's speakers. "We're so happy to have found you. Rumor has it that you're prepping for your next role. Any clues as to what we can expect?"

"I can shoot it from the sky," Nova whispered.

"Don't bother. They'll just send more drones."

"Okay, what do I say?" She shifted in front of him, shielding him from the camera.

"That you'll be reprising the role of Nebula Slim. There's no script, or I haven't seen it, yet."

She set the bag on the ground, then repeated him word for word. "I'd be happy to give you an exclusive once I return to..." She smirked. "Civilization."

"Thank you," the reporter said. "Who's the woman?"

Eli smothered a chuckle. *Time for improv.* "I'm Nova Blake." He gripped his hips. "I'm surprised you gained access to a restricted moon. Your name and designation, please."

"That won't be necessary. We have all the images we need." The drone shot up and circled back.

"Shit, not sure that was a good thing," she said. "Thinking you're out here for a role means no rescue."

"At least she left us alone."

An explosion whipped their attention at a plume of smoke. The drone crashed into the trees beyond the waterfalls.

"That had to be Orien's doing," Eli said.

"We're out in the open. Obviously." She waved a hand at where the drone had been.

"Yeah, let's find cover." He nudged his head to continue.

She did, picking up the bag and jogging onward. "Is this normal? People intruding?"

"You get used to it."

She scowled and veered left, skirting the side of the ravine a little farther from the riverbank. With no more drones to delay them, they covered a good distance.

At the edge of a forest, she faltered. "See any green goo?"

He stopped beside her. "Let's just assume it's there." He glanced at the river, white frothy waves proving the rapids might be a little tricky to navigate. "We've got no choice."

She clutched the bag's straps tighter across her chest. "I'd say to head back, maybe take the other side, but—" She nudged her chin at the opposite bank crowded with trees.

"Yeah, and with Orien too close, we're going to have to make a run for it." He gave her upper arm a squeeze. "I'm ready."

She smirked. "Just no more falling into caves."

"Well," he shrugged, "it did get us a stone."

She nodded, squared her shoulders, then broke into a sprint, weaving between trees, from boulder to root. He followed, tracing her steps as best he could. The wind and his breathing filled his ears. And a tingling.

"Do you hear that?" she asked, pausing on a thick patch of purple moss.

He halted next to her and scanned their surroundings. Tall grass, ferns, and gigantic mushrooms covered the forest bed. He tilted his head. "Sounds like bells."

"It's getting louder," she said, bolting onward but this time with even more urgency.

He peered deep into the shadows between the trees, the river muted and no longer visible. When a fern twitched, he chased after her. Patter and tinkles pushed him to go faster. He exploded into sunlight, cutting a path in a field of blue grass and white flowers that looked like praying hands.

He skidded to a stop where Nova had and doubled over, trying to catch his breath.

"Heard that, too?" she asked, hoisting the machete and the blaster.

"Yeah, like hundreds of little feet."

She walked back a few meters, studying the treeline. "Mm, would explain the bells."

He straightened, hands on hips and gazed across the field. The grass rippled as if God had run his fingers over it. Far in the distance was the shimmer of amber-colored water—the lake.

"I guess we're heading that way."

When she didn't answer, he glanced in her direction.

Ice stiffened every muscle.

Before her stood a man no higher than her knee. His bulbous head had tribal markings. Two googly eyes competed with large pointy ears for attention, but both lost to the wide mouth sprouting sharklike teeth. A fur of some animal covered his top half. A loincloth his privates, and below that were two knobby knees. His legs to his feet were bare, and the longest toe nails coiled over his toes—three per foot. One hand held a spear, chimes strapped to the shaft. In his other hand, he wielded a wicked-looking dagger.

The blades of grass split, revealing more of these...strange men.

"Run," she whispered.

And Eli did, sprinting at full speed toward the lake.

A horrific ululation drowned his ears, masking her footsteps. But he didn't dare to check if she followed. He didn't need to worry when she passed him, caught his hand, and hurried him on. The field gave way to dunes of black sand into a long shore where the amber-colored water lapped at its banks.

She spun, facing their pursuers.

"Think it was wise to run?" he asked, gasping for breath.

"He had *red* blood on his dagger." She raised her blaster, ready to fire.

On the crest of a dune, figures appeared, standing still, watching them. The air thickened with tension. This was it, the moment they'd die.

"We can try and hide," she said, gesturing to more forests on the opposite banks of the lake.

"Or we can swim," he finished.

"Yes." She tucked the machete under her armpit, ran her palm down her thigh, then regripped the weapon.

"You are foolish to swim here," a super-tall man said, peeking from behind a boulder. "The flesh-eating jedshe reside here. They prefer the calm to the force of the great waters."

"Stay back," Nova said, aiming the blaster at him and the two men who gathered behind him—looming like guards.

A fisherman on his own, not scary. Three men on a deserted bank, alarming. One bore a nasty scar from eyebrow to collarbone. She could kill two before the third would reach her or Eli.

Their gold-skin shimmered in the sunlight. It took a moment for Eli to look past that to the low-riding loincloths in woven fabric, falling to their sandaled feet. Their chests were bare except for blue markings similar to his tattoo. Long hair in bronze, copper, and gold fell down their backs, beaded and braided.

They had humanoid features for the most part minus the bridge of a nose. A gem was embedded in the speaker's temple.

And in his hand was a string of freshly caught eels.

Eli blinked at him, finally registering what he'd said. "You speak galactic?"

"I speak Lethari."

What? Something squeezed Eli's chest tight. *How's this possible?*

"Eli, why are you babbling?" Nova asked, coming to stand between him and the native warrior.

Eli angled his head to gaze at her. *She doesn't understand the man?*

Said man studied them, his gaze resting on their tattoos before he hollered at their hunters. "Under my protection."

Hands were thrown up in anger, spears waved, amid more ululation before one by one, the little men left.

"Do not mind the Skrillith. It is not often they find such a bounty."

"My thanks for the rescue." Eli leaned in to whisper to Nova, "I can understand him."

Her eyes widened. "Is he friend or foe?"

"I don't know yet." Eli pointed across the lake. "We need to reach that island."

The man gazed out. "For a Kovari Shol?" He hummed. "You must have the permission of my chieftain." He narrowed his eyes at them. "You are not like the others."

Eli raised his chin, meeting the man's dark gaze. "If we could return your star stones, we would."

"That is not what we call them. The Kovari Shol are older than we know. Come. I will take you to my village." He marched off, swinging his eels.

"He wants us to go with him. Says his chieftain can help us."

Nova gazed at the empty dunes then the island. "Do we go?"

"Wanna swim?" he asked, though the man's warning made his stomach churn.

"I am Amenkar," the man said, pausing to glance at them. "Do not fear me. I mean you no harm." He started along the beach.

Eli fell into step beside him, casting glances over his shoulder at Nova, who hesitated, eyed a loan Skrillith, and hurried to join him.

"My name's Nova," Eli said, "and this is Eli."

Amenkar bowed his head. "May Lethaar bestow their blessings upon you."

Eli reacted on instinct and dipped his chin to his chest. "And to you," he said, not sure what else to say.

A smile twitched the man's lips. "I like you, stranger. I sense no ill intent, no deep desire to change our world."

"It's beautiful and should remain untouched," Eli said, gazing at the winged whales swam in the sky, near the horizon.

"My village is not far." Amenkar wiggled his catch. "I come for the quet." He stopped again, whipped out a dagger, then sliced off a tail. The white jelly-like flesh wobbled on the end of his blade. He offered it to Nova.

She almost recoiled.

Amenkar brought the blade closer to her mouth. "He must eat to understand. It is a gift of the quet."

"Oh!" Eli grinned then frowned. "How? We were both healed—"

"It chooses who to bestow it upon." Amenkar's gaze switched between Eli and Nova. "I would say you did not seek them out for their powers."

"Nova, honey, eat the eel."

"Why?" She swallowed hard, her gaze on the gelatinous lump.

"Amenkar says that eating the eel helps us to understand Lethari."

"You ate one?" she squeaked, then with a grimace, slurped the fish into her mouth. Her eyes widened, a smile bloomed, and she licked her lips. "Like chicken, almost—"

She cried out and fell to a knee, dropping the blaster to clasp her head. But before he could react, she straightened, the pain scrunching her features smoothing out.

She blinked, color returning to her cheeks.

Eli helped her to her feet.

Amenkar handed her the blaster. Thank you," she said.

"A pleasure."

"I understand you," she whispered, awe in her parted lips. "Your world's magical."

Amenkar smiled. "It pleases me that you think so."

Geometric rocks stacked into great pillars of black stone pierced the sand like teeth. Eli clambered up a dune then gawked at more pillars lining the path. Each one carried a glowing symbol; his vision blurred, and words formed, speaking of legends and heroes.

"Are you reading this?" she whispered.

But he didn't answer her, fascinated by the people gathering to watch them. Small houses rose out of the sand, cobbles appeared beneath Eli's feet, and as he crested the dune, a city spread out. This was no village. Narrow roads formed a star and led to the center where he expected to find a castle, pyramid, or tall structure.

"This is Vael'Tir—the city of Lethaar." Amenkar swept out a hand.

From the white of their togas and loincloths to the splashes of scarfs and headdresses, Eli struggled to take in all the detail. Gold skin gleamed everywhere, and gold marked the houses with crests of animals he didn't know.

Chatter filled the air, from whispers to outright cries of alarm, demanding to know who they were. Amenkar marched on, waving aside anyone bothering him.

"The chief will decide" was all he said. On repeat.

"I'm starting to think this wasn't a good idea." Nova clasped Eli's hand. "We're moving away from the island."

"We need help, Nova-honey," he said. "And if playing nice with the local tribe gets us to the island safely, I'm willing to risk it."

She harumphed but said no more.

When they reached the center of the city, what lay before them would forever be embedded in his memory. There *was* a structure, except it went down, carved into the black rock. Forests surrounded the hole like silent guardians. Along the sides, stairs headed into its depths, lit by flickering blue flames that burned without fuel. Like the one in the cave. Narrow waterfalls in muted orange plummeted into the shadows, cooling the air rising to bathe him in a fine mist.

A sense of rightness settled on him.

He trailed Amenkar without hesitation. Nova stayed on his ass, almost too close. But he wouldn't complain when he needed her near. Anyone leaving the reverse pyramid dipped into tiny alcoves to let them pass. None bothered Amenkar. The deeper they went, the more the rock pressed on Eli. He couldn't shake the timelessness of the stone steps smoothed by many feet over thousands of years.

"It's incredible," Nova whispered.

They reached the bottom where a pool dominated the center. In it, a few eels swam.

Eli paused beside it. "Amenkar, why do you fish for eels when you have pools of them?"

"These are sacred." The man didn't pause. "Come."

Behind the pool and opening into the rock was an archway about fifteen feet tall. Poems of grandeur lined the curves. Two men stood guard, hefty lances in their grips, but they didn't twitch when Amenkar strolled past.

Blue flames illuminated the tunnel, then into a hall they went, bigger with taller pillars than the cave they'd found the star stone in. People lounged on cushions and soft rugs, platters of food and drinks nearby.

White-clothed servants rushed around, seeing to their needs. Ethereal music softened the hum of conversation.

Which stilled, all gazes on them. Along a broad path Amenkar continued, pausing in front of a dais. He climbed it and settled on a cushion.

His guards kneeled. "My chief," they said.

Eli gawked at the distinguished man. Amenkar was the chief? Why deceive them? Or had the man not trusted them? Eli had expected a throne at this rate, instead, similar to the others, there was a rug, many colorful cushions, and platters.

On instinct, Eli dropped to a knee, tugging Nova down with him.

Amenkar rose, his broad smile lost amid the gold of his skin. "I found these two, or should I say, they found me? They were hunted by the Skrillith, and they bare the Kovari Shol's touch." He circled Nova but didn't linger. He caught Eli by the shoulders and lifted him. "Your hair is beautiful. It is like ours." He flicked his hair with gold strips woven through the braids.

"Thank you for the compliment, my chief," Eli said.

"You say you are here for the Kovari Shol." He shifted his gaze to Nova. "My apologies. Such power should never have left this world." He grimaced. "To make amends, I must offer you a Lethari welcome."

"We don't want to inconvenience you, my chief," Nova said. "We simply wish to be free...of each other."

The man glanced between Eli and Nova. "A hot bath, food, and a soft bed cannot be declined. Not when you both smell like a yuxmet." He chuckled. "Spend a moon, and at the next sun, I shall have my men escort you to the temple. If it chooses to grant you its Kovari Shol, I have no power to deny it."

When Eli opened his mouth to back her up, Nova nudged him with an elbow and hissed, "He said a hot bath. Shut up."

Two women appeared and escorted them away. When Eli peered over his shoulder, he caught the chief whispering to the scarred man carrying a lance. An unknown tension tightened their posture.

That didn't bode well.

He prayed he'd read the room wrong.

Chapter Twenty

The moon, Lethara
The city of Vael'Tir.
Keep your hands to yourself.
Day Four.

Nova was led into an enclosed alcove, shielded by stone and flames. In the center of the small room was a hot springs, steam and bubbles rising off its orange surface. The heat was delicious after the night spent clinging to Eli for warmth. Beside it was a jar of what looked like honey, a sponge of sorts, and a stack of white cloths. She turned to smile at Eli but found herself alone.

Rushing to the entrance, she almost slammed into a glowering old man dressed in a white loincloth. His hair brushed his ass, braids and beads interlocking and releasing as he hobbled toward her.

"It is not often I serve one such as you," he spat. "But if our Chief Amenkar deems you worthy, I cannot object. Come, remove your offensive garments. Why do you wear so many? What are you hiding, boy?"

"Nothing, as long as I get these back." She set the bag against the wall, along with the blaster, dagger, machete, and rifle. Hesitating for a minute, she wasn't sure she could expose herself to a stranger. She'd walked around bare chested which pretty much invalidated her self-consciousness. Realizing the man waited, she stripped off the coat and handed it to him.

"This...is soft," he said, stroking the leather. "What manner of animal is this?"

"Cow, if it's real leather." She knelt to undo her boots and peeled them off, then the wet socks.

"How can it not be real? I hold it." The man waved the coat at her.

She swallowed a chuckle. "Please, call me Eli," she said, removing her jeans. Dropping onto her ass, she swung her legs and sank them into the water. A moan escaped, the heat melting the aches from her abused calves.

"You honor me with your name." He bowed. "I am Khepan if you should need to summon me."

When she reached for the jar, he cried out and waded into the water, coming to stand before her.

"I must prepare you for cleansing," he said. "This is my duty to honor the Great One, Lethaar."

She held up her hands as if in surrender. "Cleanse away," she said, hoping not to offend him.

Khepan urged her to stand on steps she hadn't noticed, then poured the honey onto the sponge. Every inch of her was scrubbed, even her ass. Twice. A layer of foam coated the pool by the time he was happy.

Her skin glowed pink from his attention—she was, no doubt, missing a few layers. The sponge had been coarse, but in a good way, giving her a head-to-toe scratch. He patted her dry with the cloths, not missing a drop, then tutted when he tried to braid her hair and found chunks missing.

"Beads are bestowed upon the wearer for their good deeds. I will give you mine."

"No," she spun, catching his hand. "You honor me, but I should earn my own."

He smiled, his two front teeth missing. "You will not be here long enough."

"True, then my lack of beads should not matter."

"You come for the Kovari Shol as most do." He stroked the blue tattoo. "Few have made it this far. Some bring evil with them, but Lethaar protects us."

"Tell me, Khepan, the last one we touched, it shattered. Will this happen again?" She frowned. "Destroying another...Kovari Shol would sadden me."

"It depends on the life within the shol. If it has seen millennia, it will die." He leaned in to whisper, "It chooses to be discovered. I sense you carry one now. Perhaps that is why my chief shows you favor." He flicked out a loincloth. "Refreshments await. I am certain my chief longs to converse with you."

She stared at the strips of fabric and grimaced.

"Your garments will be cleaned. For now, this is what our males wear."

She nodded and let him dress her. The loincloth was snug, like a pair of boy shorts. Two strips draped to the floor, covering her front and back.

"Do you like this man?" he asked, tucking and fastening as he circled her.

"You mean the one whose body I'm in?" She shifted from one foot to the other. "I didn't at first."

Khepan chuckled. "The shol does choose the most volatile of matches. I believe it is bored with the easy and fainthearted."

She stilled. They'd been arguing when they'd touched the star stone. But not with the second. *Mm, maybe that's the key?*

"This way, Eli," Khepan said, gesturing to the archway. "Your things are safe."

She gazed at the weapons, checked that the safety was on, then hurried after the old man. With Eli's long legs, it didn't take her long to catch up with his hobble.

Women stared at her, their cheeks darkening when she smiled.

"You are a curiosity. The last stranger was older with silver hair. He did not have a shol with him." Khepan scowled. "But he wanted them all."

Orien. "He's chasing us, and if he finds us here, I fear for your people."

"I shall warn Chief Amenkar." Khepan left her on a cushion-littered rug, darting away on his spindly legs to the dais.

She sat, choosing a spot with the best view, then spent a good deal of time trying to arrange the strips to best cover her. A serving girl offered a drink in a tall goblet. The liquid was purple with herbs floating on the surface. Nova thanked her and took a tentative sip. The honeyed nectar was tart with a hint of mint. She hummed, smacked her lips, and drank some more.

"Thank you, again, Bigeeli," Eli said, snapping Nova's gaze to him.

Her mouth dried, her insides churned, and her cock sprang to life. He'd never looked lovelier. His skin gleamed, the flames flickering over him like he'd been coated in gold flakes. His copper hair streamed around him, thick braids adding volume. He wore a loincloth, too, along with strips of matching cloth that diagonally covered his breasts from one shoulder to hip. Bracelets clinked on a wrist and an ankle, and when he sat beside her, he brought with him the sweetest fragrance that rivaled the tartness of the fruit juice.

"Fuck, Eli," she rasped, fighting the rising desire. "You made me beautiful."

"You've always been that to me," he said.

She met his gaze and tumbled into the turbulent depths of his eyes. An intensity promised more than she could handle, if she had the courage.

He sniffed the goblet a girl placed in his hand. "Damn, but it feels so good to be clean."

She chuckled around her galloping heartbeat. "Yeah, and I learned a few things about the stones they call shols." She took a gulp of juice to coat her tongue. "Orien's been here before. I suspect it didn't end well."

"Shit." Eli stiffened. "He'll probably follow us."

"My thoughts exactly. And their lances, as impressive as they are, can't compare to our modern firepower." She pointed to the dais with her goblet. "Khepan went to warn the chief."

She choked on a sip when Amenkar strode toward them, his strips flapping aside and exposing muscled thighs that implied an impressive workout regime. He was handsome with his bronze eyebrows arching over dark eyes. That chiseled jaw that seemed a little too dominant. When she'd been younger, she'd had a girlfriend or two but hadn't deviated from men for long. Now, she'd do both without batting her eyelashes.

She buried her nose in the goblet and thought about strangling Orien. Her hard-on tenting the strips wouldn't go down well. Her cheeks flushed in anticipation of that embarrassment.

"Khepan tells me you know Lord Orien?" Amenkar demanded. Four men gathered around him, including the one with the scar that ran from his eye to his collarbone.

Why hadn't the eels healed him? She dragged her gaze away.

"He believes it's my fault the shol shattered," she said.

"We escaped him, stole a ship, traveled here, and found a...shol." Eli rose.

"I had hoped you were not chosen," Amenkar said, running his gaze over Eli, lingering on the curve of his waist and bare legs. "You seek a pair." He held out his hand. "Give me the shol."

"I left it with my things," she said. "Khepan—"

"Will collect it." Amenkar raised a hand, and Khepan hurried past them. "You do not know that these are not mere...stones. They are ancient, carry a life of their own, and do not react to just any stone."

"So the one on the island might not work?" Eli asked.

Amenkar scowled. "How do you know of the temple?"

"We have maps drawn by Orien's people." Eli pointed to the bag Khepan placed at Amenkar's heels. When the chief nodded, Eli dove in and brought out the book, flipping to the pages to show the man.

Amenkar's eyebrows hit his hairline. "We do not even know these locations. Your Lord Orien has been determined."

"He is not our anything," Nova said, climbing to her feet. The scarred man calmed his men who'd shifted when she came to stand beside Eli. "If I could kill him, I would."

Amenkar studied their faces, listened to whatever Scar whispered to him, then hummed. "What you do not know is that the stones are more than fertility idols and are beyond our understanding. Those touched by it can open an ancient vault rumored to hold the secrets to godlike powers."

She gaped. "You can't be serious? Is the vault's location on the map?"

"Yes." Amenkar frowned. "You must know, when the shols were birthed, gods roamed this world. The vault was not built to hoard these powers or to guard them. Whatever is inside was meant to remain hidden."

Fear summoned a shiver. She glanced at Eli. "Orien isn't a good man. That sort of power in his hands would lead to destruction."

"No one should open that vault," he said, leaning into her.

She slipped an arm around his waist and pulled him close.

Amenkar's expression darkened. "Eat, rest. On the next sun, if Orien does not arrive before then, we will escort you to the temple. It is the shol's choice to welcome or kill you."

The black-cladded men ushered them behind the chief until they reached his dais. At a flick of his hand, she sank onto a cushion, servants offering her goblets or fruit from a platter. Her stomach churned at the dark cloud hovering over them so eating was O.U.T. Damn, she'd kill for a tea.

Eli crowded her to whisper, "Is it me or is Amenkar a handsome man? I mean, his physique's magnificent. I never thought I was a thigh girl, but have you seen his?"

She glanced at her thighs, trying to compare them to the Lethari's. With a huff, she tugged the strip of cloth over them. "Quit fangirling," she hissed. "There's no fucking anyone with my body."

"Ah, Nova-honey, tomorrow's the day we swap back. Can't I just have one teensy, weensy orgasm as a woman?"

She glared at him then shifted attention to the chief. "Can you defend this city from Orien?"

Amenkar grinned, blasting her with a bright smile that was devastating as it was nerve-wracking. "Of course. We improved our defenses after he killed the last chief."

"He did what?" Eli froze, the goblet halfway to his mouth.

She smacked his arm. "I told you he killed for that stone."

"I don't need I-told-you-so. We're past that," he muttered.

"Tell me." Amenkar ran his thumb along the side of the goblet. "Were you lovers before the shol changed you?"

She gaped, then cleared her throat. "How did you know?"

"You are not the first," he said.

She shifted on the cushion. "No, we're enemies."

"Were," Eli said, meeting her gaze. "Or do you still hate me?"

She stared at him, memorizing that hope in his eyes and his signature smirk teasing the corner of his mouth. "Not anymore."

Amenkar hummed. "It is as I expected. Bigeeli informed me of your markings bearing his name."

At the shock twisting Eli's face, ice burned like hot lava in Nova's stomach.

"My name? As in Eli Thorne?" His brow knitted. "Why would you have my name on your ass and in Lethari?" His eyes clouded with confusion.

"Bigeeli must have read it wrong," she hurried to say, looking everywhere but at him. "I got it a decade ago. I didn't know the writing was Lethari."

"Nova." Eli set his goblet aside and grasped her shoulders, forcing her to meet his gaze. "Why my name?"

"Youthful stupidity. You know this." She tried to shrug free, but he held firm. Heat bathed her face with embarrassment, and a vise squeezed her throat shut. Breathing had become unimportant under his potent focus. "My name's November, my maiden name was Rogers. My mother thought—"

"It funny to name you and your sisters after months of the year." He sat there, his mouth opening and shutting without another word. "I...remember," he finally whispered.

"We spent one night together." She dropped her chin, hoping to hide any telltale emotions revealing how he'd broken her heart. A giggle escaped her, no doubt from sheer hysteria. "I was your biggest fan. Got the tattoo a few weeks before *that* night."

He crushed her in a hug, running his hand up and down her back. "I'm so sorry, Nova-honey. I was high or drunk but that doesn't excuse my behavior." He leaned back. "Wait, is that why you hated me?"

"Besides the fact that you're egotistical, entitled, spoilt, too handsome for your own good, and a sex addict? Sure, let's just say it's because you took my virginity and had your manager kick me to the curb."

He slumped, horror and sadness drooping his expression. "Fuck, that's bad."

"I see why the shol chose you." Amenkar waved Bigeeli over. "I will admit to being disappointed. You are beautiful, Nova." He caught a strand of Eli's copper hair, letting it slide through his fingers. "Bigeeli will escort you to your chambers for the evening. If you do not mate, you will be killed."

Silence settled over Nova, shock stealing her voice.

"What?" she squeaked. "Say that again. I think I heard you wrong."

He bowed his head. "A mating will fuse your souls in what Letharis call a soul tie. Without its protection, the next shol will kill one of you and leave the other in this body."

Eli grinned, rubbing his palms together. "At last," he whispered, gripping her by the arm and dragging her off the rug to where Bigeeli waited.

"Fuck or die?" she muttered, trailing the old woman from the hall. "And we only have Amenkar's word on it? No, no, I refuse to believe sex will save us."

Eli was too happy, almost skipping along. "You've done me before—"

"Do not think to use that as a reason—"

He kissed her, making her stumble. "Has anyone told you that you protest too much?"

The room they were ushered into had no windows. And as soon as she crossed the threshold, a stone was rolled in front of the door.

"Shit," she gritted out, facing the room. The massive bed on the floor was covered with cushions and thick furs. A blue flame burned in a wall-mounted sconce. Beside the bed was a jug and two goblets. Next to that sat a platter piled high with fruit.

It had the look of a harem. Excitement skittered along her skin, even as nervousness tightened the knot in her stomach. "Eli, we can't—"

He kissed her again, rising on his toes to do so.

She pulled back and bumped into the wall. "Quit doing that."

He laughed and peeled off the cloth covering his breasts. They bounced free, nipples taut. Next went the loincloth until he stood naked before her.

"Your turn," he rasped, slipping a finger between her stomach and the loincloth. He tugged, bringing her closer. And damn if her cock didn't find that fucking hot. "I want Nova. I don't care what body you're in."

She would've rolled her eyes at that bit of nonsense if her heart didn't twang in response. Out of the men she'd met since Seth's death, Eli tempted her the most. The cool air on her hard-on had her glancing down. How had he managed to unravel the loincloth without her noticing?

Her cock was good and ready, urges driving her to push forward, to sprawl Eli on the bed, to layer her body over his.

"This is madness," she said as a last attempt to stop the inevitable.

"Tell me about it," he said, wrapping his arms around her and drawing her in for a kiss.

Chapter Twenty-One

Eli couldn't believe this was finally going to happen. Nova's reticence wasn't due to a lack of attraction, not when she sported an impressive erection. But her fighting this...them said much about her state of heart, highlighting that he liked her more than she liked him.

She jerked back. "We're just taking his word—"

"Yes." At some point, they had to see where this attraction would lead. Why not now? But she wouldn't want to hear that from him. "Another night with me isn't too much to ask for, is it?"

She scowled, stroking his arms looped around her neck. "That was long ago. We're different people now."

He didn't want to talk. Not when they were so close heat poured off her. "Nova," he whispered, running his lips up her neck.

Her breath hitched. When she shut her eyes on a blissful hum, he slid a hand lower, over a nipple and back, desperate to keep her distracted. Desire thrummed, more intense than he'd experienced. As a man, it hit him hard, roaring commands, dominating his thoughts. For a woman, it was more subtle, addictive, curling around his core, tightening and aching until he yearned to be filled. Such an odd sensation as if he was empty and only Nova could give him a sense of completion.

He shook the thoughts aside, and with a lunge, flipped her onto her back. Before she could protest, he stroked a hand lower, aiming for the sweet spot just below her balls. When a woman touched him there, he'd harden to snapping point.

He hoped to inspire the same reaction in Nova. In passing, he brushed the cock he knew too well.

Her groan sent a tremor through him. "Eli," she rasped. "Do that again."

Against her skin, he smothered a smile, shimmying lower to exhale a hot breath over the head of her cock. His now hers, it didn't matter. Not anymore. Her hips lifted off the furs, a drop of dew forming.

He chuckled and licked her from balls to tip, catching a taste he recognized. She cried out, arching her back, her fingers digging into the bedding. A garbled sound escaped her, bringing him such joy.

It would be too soon, too intense for him to go for the kill and suck her into his mouth, so he crawled over her, feathering kisses where he could reach: from a hip up her waist to a nipple hard with need.

Because he could, he caught her lips with his, sweeping back and forth with the lightest of touches. Each swipe promised a proper kiss he had no intention of delivering. Instead, he nipped at her bottom lip, dipped the tip of his tongue into her warm depths, and repeated until she writhed, her fingers now scraping his shoulders and back.

When he stopped, holding still for their breaths to merge, he met her gaze. Her dark green irises softened with an expression he could only hope was affection. His heart swelled, overflowing with what she invoked, his sassy cat. Inch by inch, he descended, not once breaking eye contact until he pressed his lips to hers.

She tugged him down, her tongue coming in to play. She was hungry for him, just the way he liked it. He met her assault with his own, diving in to relearn and memorize every crevice of her mouth. When he shifted back, feathering a hand lower to cup her balls, she whimpered.

The sound was so fucking delicious. He gave her a gentle squeeze, then a swirling caress over her perineum.

"Oh, Eli, I can't..." She grabbed his wrist, stopping him. "If you keep that up, I won't last. I want...*need* more. Now."

"You're so greedy," he teased, shaking her hand free to run his palm up and down her cock.

She glared at him. "It's been a while." She flopped back, her body shuddering.

"Want to come now or in me?"

She studied him, her eyes smoky with desire. "In you."

His heart soared. *Victory!* "Right answer."

When he tried to climb on top of her, she threw out a hand, catching him between his breasts.

"No, you need to be readied. I don't..." she swallowed hard, "want you walking funny tomorrow."

He laughed. "*I* want that with every fiber of my being."

She smirked. "A little foreplay?"

Curious, he sprawled beside her, tracing patterns over her abs. "Sure."

She lunged, sending him onto his back. Every part of him was coated with her hot, velvety skin. He moaned in agreement; this was an improvement. She nipped at the inside of his knee, along an inner thigh, then pressed a kiss to his belly, so close to where he ached for her that his hips lifted on their own.

She hummed, feathering kisses to a breast. Latching onto a nipple didn't prepare him for the heat, the suction, the sharp bite of teeth scraping over sensitive skin. The same had been done to him thousands of time, but her body's intensity was unparallel. She cupped the other breast, tugging and flicking the nipple until he couldn't tell where the pleasure was coming from. It bathed, rose and fell, ebbed and flowed.

Breathing was lost on him. Everything tightened in anticipation, and that ache he'd been suffering with for four days ramped up until words tumbled off his tongue.

"Please... Nova, show me what I crave."

She did, rubbing her thumb over the seam between his legs.

"Oh," he cried out, spreading his thighs without her asking. Craving? No, this was an obsession, an addiction he had to assuage. If she walked away now, he'd crawl after her, unafraid to beg.

How... How did women resist this compulsion?

He gazed at her, her focus on her hand doing nothing more than an up and down motion. When she dipped a finger between his folds, she smiled. "Mm, and here I thought you wouldn't be wet for me."

He panted, his cheeks on fire but unable to match the burning where she touched. The sensations were celestial, some cosmic blessing he couldn't describe.

He cried out at the stroke over his nub. His mouth opened and shut, no words forming. He dug his fingers into the bed, keening when she swirled that tight bundle of nerves. He'd done this to many before, had watched them unravel as if he was a sex god, but he'd had no idea what she was feeling, how ungodlike his so-called powers were.

Any man could do this to her.

Darkness lashed across his chest. No man would touch her again.

Thoughts whipped away, like feathers on a gale. He climbed a mountain, the angle sharp, the pleasure divine. Then with a flick of her thumb and a bite of a nipple, he tumbled into liquid ecstasy the kind he'd never known.

And it didn't end, tearing through him, arching him and drawing feminine growls.

"Ready for more?" she asked, catching his thighs and spreading them wider.

She nestled at the juncture, pausing to rub his seam with the head of her cock. Catching him under his knees, she hoisted his legs to rest on her chest. The position wasn't uncomfortable.

With a slow intrusion, she inched her way inside him, grinding her hips until she was so fully seated that a soul spark fired, wrapping around his heart and yanking hard.

Then, he knew, he loved her.

Fuck.

Orgasmic tremors ran along his insides, and as she withdrew and slammed in, a fresh wave leaped to life. He reeled. *This*...was different from the earth-shattering cliff-diving joy she'd thrummed out of him. *It*...was addictive, calling from deep inside him. The craving shifted, begging her to do it again, to summon that visceral reaction.

He propelled toward that mountain, but this time, when he exploded off it, all sound was silenced. He stilled, his body tense, unable to speak, to describe what raced along his veins, his skin prickling, his heartbeat roaring in his ears, his mouth drying, and his nipples puckering.

"That's it," she crooned, gyrating her hips and driving him higher.

"Nova," was all he could utter.

"Come for me, Eli," she whispered in his ear.

He did, again, the pleasure hitting him too soon, so unexpectedly. Waves crested, one after the other, before he'd had a chance to descend.

With a groan, she arched, her hips pinned to the back of his thighs. Another growl slipped past her clenched jaw, pleasure twisting her features into something primal. When a shuddering breath escaped her, she met his gaze then flopped onto him, catching herself in a push-up just before flipping them over. On her back, she adjusted him to warm her side.

"So, what did you think?" he asked, running his hand up and down her stomach before resting it on her chest.

"Good." She smirked. "But I *know* yours was better."

"Fuck," he whispered. "I never realized a woman's body is a massive erogenous zone."

"An exaggeration, but sure," she said, sinking deeper into the furs while keeping him close.

Being the snugglee was different to having the control of a snuggler. He liked it, cuddling into her. "Did you feel it?" he asked, keeping his voice low.

"The soul tie?" she asked, angling to meet his gaze before brushing her lips across his, gentle and unexpected. "I think so."

She nudged him aside and sat up, swinging her legs off the furs. But not fast enough for him to miss the shine in her eyes. Her shoulders shook as a sob escaped her.

"Sorry, Eli, it's not you," she said, waving without looking at him. "It's...just that I haven't been with anyone since Seth died." She leaned back to gaze at the ceiling, slapping her thighs in the process. "And it was *never* this good. Sex was just a weekly chore. His mind and heart mattered, y'know. I loved him for that alone."

Eli hugged her from behind, resting his chin on her shoulder. "Are you sad we did it? Wish we hadn't?"

She shook her head. With a swipe of her palm across her cheek, she met his gaze. "This was bound to happen as determined as you were." She chuckled, but it didn't hide the sadness in her eyes.

"True. I don't regret it, Nova."

She flicked a dismissive wrist. "You, the hedonist, would enjoy multiple orgasms."

He offered a soft laugh. "Want to stay rich, famous, sexy..."

"You asked me that before." She cupped his cheek, running a thumb over his bottom lip. "My answer hasn't changed."

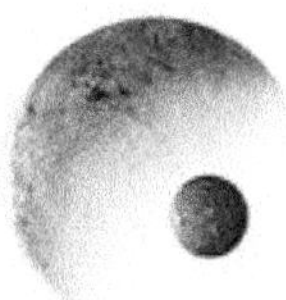

Eli's bladder woke him, or so he thought. In the silence of the room, the scraping of the door warned him moments before Bigeeli poked her head in. "More of your people have arrived. Chief Amenkar has summoned you. First, I will take you to be purified."

Eli scrambled to his feet and wiggled into his loincloth and chest strips while Nova did the same. Now wasn't the time to reveal how he felt about her. Perhaps after this adventure...if she wanted to stay in contact. If she did, then he'd know whether he had a chance...to win her heart.

"Think it's Orien?" she asked, combing his hair with her fingers.

"If it is, we need weapons. I'm not getting recaptured without a fight. Last time, when I denied knowing you, I didn't think I could help you from within a jail cell. I meant to get you released by sweettalking the asshole. Little did I know, he was onto me from the start." Eli gave her a rueful smile. "A hard way to learn I'm losing my touch."

Her stroking slowed, and she tugged, pulling his head back to meet her gaze. Then she caught his lips for a sweet kiss. "Thank you for not giving up on me."

His eyes stung, tears demanding release. He gathered her close and fought for calm. Now wasn't the time to cry. "Bigeeli, where are our things?"

"Close to my chief," she said. "Come."

She led them into a narrow cave. A gentle waterfall tinkled down the sides and at the base were stone-carved stools. Beneath them was a channel with running water.

"Please, use. My chief awaits."

Eli didn't need to be asked twice. He peeled his loincloth down and sat.

Nova chose the farthest stool, relieved herself, then rinsed her hands in the waterfall. She wiggled the loincloth back on and waited for him at the entrance.

When he made to pass her, she touched his elbow.

"Eli, I couldn't have done this without you." She tucked a braid behind his ear, making his lobe tingle.

He stared after her before hurrying to catch up. This woman... He should've realized why he'd wanted to spend time with her. Sure, she'd been obvious on how she felt about him, but such women he'd met before and walked away from. With her... He hadn't been able to, making up excuses that he found her entertaining, or that he was curious as to why she hated him.

He stroked his backside cheek where the tattoo sat.

Perhaps they'd had a soul tie from that one night? It was nice to think so because falling for her this hard shouldn't have been this easy.

Chapter Twenty-Two

The moon, Lethara

Amenkar's 'throne' room in Vael'Tir.

From good to oh-shit to argh-what-the-hell-is-that?

Day Five.

Nova kept her head up, hurrying to the throne room with determination in her stride. If only she could be done with all things Orien. In truth, she wanted to while away the day in Eli's arms, but more sex would be wasting time they could ill afford.

"Tell me, is this a countdown?" She showed the woman the tattoo climbing her bicep.

Bigeeli cackled. "Figured that out, did you?" She stroked a gnarled finger along a tendril. "So many suns you have." She shifted back to hold up eight fingers. "If the markings reach your heart before you form a soul tie, you die."

Nova frowned—the knocks kept coming.

Find a stone or be stuck as Eli.

Got a stone, but one wasn't good enough. So locate another, like they're as common as mud.

Have sex and form a soul tie, or the next stone she touched might kill her. Done, only to learn that the first stone was trying to kill her anyway.

"It is poison from a shol shard," Bigeeli added.

"But I wasn't cut when the stone shattered." Or maybe she had been and, in the ensuing chaos, hadn't noticed it?

Bigeeli laughed, the sound so young and joyful. "The slivers melt on the skin when it finds its victim." She hummed and veered toward the dais. "The boredom of gods... It is sad that your lord took a shol off this world. The gods do not need a bigger realm to play in."

"He's not my anything," Nova snapped. "Sure, he's human, but that's it."

A crowd had gathered, forcing Bigeeli to weave a path through. "My chief," she said, dropping to a knee.

"It is done?" Amenkar asked, rising off a cushion.

"It is," she said, staggering to her feet and stepping aside, exposing Nova and Eli behind her. Standing tall beside the chief was a familiar face.

Nova gasped, joy exploding through her. "Frederik? How... Where's... I mean, hello."

He smiled, looking good in jeans and a gray, dirt-stained T-shirt. "I'm happy you are well, Mr. Thorne." He cast a glance at Eli. "Lord Orien will soon arrive."

"Shit," she said. "We can't let him find—"

"He has been here before," Frederik said. "Your escape made him even more...determined."

"I know," she said, catching Eli's hand and drawing him closer. "We must leave now. Try and lead Orien away from here."

"Wait." Eli scowled at Frederik. "Does he know you helped us? How are you here without him?"

"I had a friend alter the security footage. As an actor, we have many vids of Mr. Thorne we could use. As to escaping Lord Orien's party, I claimed to be unwell. He thinks I am at the landing site." Frederik bowed to Amenkar but said to Eli, "Tell him to lie to Orien, that he never saw you. Orien might believe him."

Eli did as asked.

Amenkar stiffened. "Deception is not rewarded in the great skies." He flicked his fingers, summoning the scarred man. "Zal, to the temple. Go now. Bigeeli, their things."

She scampered away.

"Come with us, Frederik." Eli hitched a thumb over his shoulder. "If he sees you here, he'll know."

"He's many things, but he's not an idiot. He must have guessed someone helped you."

Frederik's complacency gritted Nova's teeth. Zal approached, Khepan trailing him with their bag and weapons. Bigeeli carried their clothes draped over an arm.

"Zal will take you as far as he can," Amenkar said.

The scarred man bowed his head in greeting. "We must hurry. The bridge closes at midnight."

When he ululated, Nova jerked back at the loud cry.

The crowd parted. He strode toward four black-clad men waiting by the pool. Behind them, descending the stone stairs was Orien, a young man scampering after him. She blinked, praying she was imagining things.

"Fucking you delayed us," she hissed at Eli.

"And I don't regret a moment of it," he said. "Besides, I'd rather face him here than in a cave, alone."

He had a point, but she wasn't in the mood to acknowledge it. "Just us against him is better than endangering these people."

"He might not—"

She squeezed his hand hard. "He *killed* their last chief. We *have* to do something."

"At last, Eli, Nova, I've found you." Orien grinned, skipping down the final steps with his arms open wide.

"We weren't lost," Eli snapped.

"I know, I've been behind you every step of the way. You located another star stone. Faster than my entire team." Orien pinched his lips. "Perhaps instead of studying you, I should hire you."

"Not a chance," Nova said, folding her arms across her chest and sidling in front of Eli to shield him.

Orien marched past the pool, ignored Zal and his men, and headed toward Amenkar. He bowed his head, not even bothering to kneel. Surely they taught archeologists to have better manners than this?

"My chief," he said, his words translated by the young man. Orien paused to stare at Frederik, his left eye twitching. "Thank you for helping me re-capture these...thieves."

"What the hell did we steal?" Nova demanded, bristling.

"My future," Orien said with a sweet smile. "I want the stone you have."

"What stone?" Eli asked.

She grimaced. He was right. Amenkar still had it. They would've traveled to the temple without it.

Orien drew his blaster and aimed it at Eli. "You've destroyed one stone and stolen another. Now, give it to me or someone dies."

The translator announced to all Orien's threat. Nova glared at the idiot while the crowd shuffled back.

Zal raised his spear with a heart-clenching war cry. He took two steps and slumped to the floor. A dark wound in his chest smoked around the edges.

Nova gaped, switching her attention between Zal and Orien with his blaster pointed at the fallen man.

The crowd scattered amid cries and ululations of despair.

In the chaos, Zal's guards surrounded their chief, forming a wall of muscle between him and Orien.

"What the fuck, Orien," Nova yelled, kneeling beside Zal.

The man lived but with a gaping hole in his chest. Dark blue blood poured from the wound. She held his gaze, trying to convey she'd do what she could.

Eli twirled the machete like it was a rapier and smacked the blaster out of Orien's hand. The older man leaped back, dodging Eli's slash.

Applying direct pressure to the wound, she spared them a glance, then caught Frederik's gaze. "Help me get Zal to the pool."

Khepan joined them. Between the three of them, they managed to carry a groaning Zal to the eels.

"Why didn't you run?" she asked Khepan, her breathing ragged when they hefted Zal into the water. The silver weeds shifted, making way for his bulk. The eels swarmed him, slipping around his body to gather at the wound. She rested her elbows on the rocks and washed the blood from her palms and fingers.

"I was there when he killed my chief." Khepan grimaced. "I prayed to the gods for his death. I mean to witness it."

"Fair enough," she said, drying her hands on the front strip of her loincloth. For so long, she'd wished she could see the life leech from Seth's murderer, even though she didn't know who'd done it. Hence why she blamed Warden. "And how did you convince them we're the ones you came to see?" she asked Frederik.

"They know your names. I just repeated them until they took me to their king." He hitched his thumb at Zal floating in the pool. "What's with that?"

"The eels heal," she said, her voice soft.

She was mesmerized, unable to drag her gaze away.

Eli and Orien were in an epic sword fight, dodging swipes and lunges. Orien used a lance, no doubt Zal's, and had more reach. Eli moved like a snake, ducking and striking. Blood stained Orien's shirt and cargo pants, appearing to be the weaker of the two.

Never would she have thought Eli could move like that or had any skill with weapons. He met Orien's thrust with the blade skidding along the lance's shaft until their faces were inches apart. The scene was incredible, his copper hair trailing him like a falling star.

"It's like your movie *Bang Bang, Binary Baby*. Ms. Blake moves like you did." Frederik beamed.

"Yeah, but I don't know where this is heading. Worst case scenario, she dies. Best case, Orien finally gets his comeuppance."

Frederik palmed his blaster—looking like a toy gun in his bulky hand. "I can't fire. They're jumping around too much." He met her gaze. "I would prefer not to kill anyone, Mr. Thorne. Even if it's Lord Orien."

She got it. Ending someone's life wouldn't sit well on anyone's conscience. Well, maybe not true for Orien. She didn't want to pull the trigger either.

A yelp snapped her focus to the swordfight.

Orien had jumped to the side, his eyes wide, his expression dazed.

Eli was covered in blue sparks, skittering over his body like static electricity brought to life. They traveled along the machete's blade, painting Orien's face aglow with the tip of the weapon a breath away from his neck. Eli's hair floated around his head, forming a halo. Orien threw aside the lance; it clattered across the floor, distracting her for a second. In that time, he dived for the discarded blaster.

Frederik gasped.

Boom.

Orien flew back, landing on a pile of cushions. Blood bloomed across his chest.

"Shit," she said, sprinting to him. She cast a glance at Eli amid a blaze of blue. "The pool's not big enough for two men."

Frederik stood beside her. "You want to save him?"

"You shot him," she snapped. "I get it, you hate his guts, but if he dies, how will we explain it to the authorities?"

An image of the half-eaten man fallen into the cave came to mind. What would Orien have told the man's family? Would he have even bothered?

"I will take him," Amenkar said, skirting around his guards.

"You have more eels...quet?" She rested on her heels, letting his men carry Orien away.

"Khepan, ensure they reach the temple."

The old man bowed and headed toward Zal, who'd sat up dead center of the pool, his brow furrowed in confusion.

He climbed out of the water, met her gaze, and knelt. "My thanks. I will fulfil this task, my chief."

Amenkar flicked a dismissive wrist, as done with this day as she was. "Use the yuxmets. Midnight is soon."

"Come with, Frederik," she said.

He stared at the translator then smiled. "I must stay."

He was too big to force, so she said, "All right, then ask for raw quet. One bite will open your mind to their language."

His eyes widened. "We didn't know this."

She shrugged. "Ms. Blake stumbled on it." She offered Eli her hand. A little jolt was more than bearable if she could keep him near, needing the comfort.

He hesitated, his focus on the sparks skittering over his body even though they'd faded.

"After everything we've seen, this bothers you?" She arched a brow.

He huffed and laced their fingers. "How'd you feel if you were short-circuiting?"

She held his gaze. "Calm like you," she said.

Bigeeli steered them into a covered alcove, shoving their garments at them. They were damp but wearable. Clean was clean in Nova's book. Unraveling the loincloth took moments, and when she peeled on the cargo pants, a sigh escaped. It was good to be covered. Socks and boots hadn't dried fully, but she didn't care. This part of the adventure had to end, and dilly-dallying because of laundry would be stupid.

If only she'd had a cup of tea.

Clothed, armed, and ready, she marched to where Zal waited. Without a word, he led them up and out of the sunken palace. The night was darker than expected with the waning submoon.

When she neared the top, she froze. "The stone," she gasped.

"It is in my possession," Zal said.

Relief slumped her shoulders, and she hefted the bag to settle it better. Eli grabbed the rifle. And behind him, the crowds reformed in trickles. Her stomach gurgled, reminding her she'd turned down the offer of food multiple times.

"Protein bar?" Eli suggested.

She flashed him a tight smile, dug into the bag, and pulled one out. "Wanna share?" she asked.

"All good," he said.

She chewed through the bar while they reversed their steps until they reached the pillars lining a path to the lake. But Zal and his men veered left and stopped at a sand-covered building.

The stench was...indescribable, so bad that her nostrils burned. She covered her nose and blinked the tears from her eyes.

A rumble preceded the schlurping of a long-haired animal lumbering out of its shed. The closest she could compare it to was a giant rhino. Its brown-gray hair was matted and covered its face, a wet nose peeking out. A girl hurried toward them, leather reins in hand.

Nova froze, sheer horror churning the undigested protein bar. She shuddered. "I *am not* riding that."

Chapter Twenty-Three

The moon, Lethara

Leaving Vael'Tir.

Onto the back of a beast and into the darkness of hope.

Day Five.

Eli slid onto a great beast. The girl had led a yuxmet to stacked bales, allowing him to mount with ease. It brayed, sticking out a purple tongue with drool dripping off. He'd ridden worse—all sorts of earthly animals cosmetically altered to resemble 'alien' creatures. The most interesting had been an animatronics that had moved with surprising agility.

As an actor, his job was to bring a character to life. All the props helped to fully realize the role he had to play. And for that, he was grateful. Layers of a mask was how he saw it.

"Sword fighting and bareback riding? What else can you do?" Nova gritted her teeth and accepted the reins.

What followed was a comedy of errors since she didn't know to swing her leg, to hook her hand in the mane or reins, to hoist herself up and over. In the end, the poor girl and Zal had their hands on her ass to shove her on.

Eli cried he was laughing so much, but he knew better than to make a sound. She'd skin him alive.

He was sniveling by the time the pack of yuxmets cantered toward the lake in the direction of the island. Nova muttered curses and threats they all ignored, especially the yuxmet she was riding.

Zal paused at the waves lapping the bank, the last of the cobbles fading into sand beneath the yuxmets' three-toed feet. He slumped, his hand on his hip, gazing over the rippling water kissed by moonlight. A cool breeze toyed with Eli's braids. The stench wafting off the yuxmets was becoming more bearable. Or it had killed his sense of smell.

Nova kept glancing over her shoulder, no doubt expecting Orien to charge after them. They were so close to being their normal selves again. Perhaps, by this time tomorrow, all would be as it was.

He frowned. With Nova 'hating' him, and he in love with her? No, his life...*he* had changed.

The seconds became minutes. The yuxmets shuffled, grumbling about standing motionless. In their place, he'd do the same.

"We wait," Zal said into the silence. A pat of his ride's rump drew a wail from the beleaguered yuxmet that echoed into the night.

"Is it just me or is this madness?" Nova leaned in to whisper, then almost toppled off the side. Once she righted herself, she sat like a plank of wood, her arms stiff, her lips pursed.

"We don't have a choice," Eli said. "We need another stone. And if, as Amenkar said, they have to like each other, the temple's stone might not be the right one."

Her shoulders relaxed for a moment, then she teetered, yelped, and stiffened again. "Fine. Argh. We have four days left. We can't afford to waste time."

He met her gaze. "See. No choice."

She frowned, wiggled the bag over her lap, then palmed the blaster strapped to her thigh. "Why are we waiting then? Where's a boat?"

"Not needed," Zal said, pointing at the submoon.

"Right," she mouthed at Eli.

He grinned. The yuxmet shifted beneath him, bumping into hers.

"Quiet," Zal snapped.

The pack stilled, even Eli's heart skipped a beat. The water shimmered, swished, then before them, a narrow, cobbled path appeared.

"Go," Zal called, and as one, the yuxmets lurched forward.

They cantered like thundering elephants along what looked like slippery stones. The wind whipped Eli's hair back, and laughter bubbled out.

"Zeet, zeet," Zal called, spurring his yuxmet on with a wild bray.

They clambered onto the island's shore, wet sucking noises following the Yuxmets' footprints. Zal drew his ride to a halt and leaped off. "We will wait here. You have three hours before the tide returns."

Eli whipped his gaze along the farthest shore, trying to see the ocean. A lake had minimal tidal forces, but a lagoon...

"My thanks, Zal," Nova said, dismounting her yuxmet like a lump of soft butter off a knife.

"At the center of the island is a gate."

Nova adjusted the bag, then raised her hands, offering to help Eli down. He caught her shoulders, and when she gripped his waist, he was airborne. For that second, she was his anchor, his world. Then his feet touched down, and she stepped back, unknowing that her touch had scorched him.

Something about her expression triggered a vision. Nova in a white gown flashed across his mind. She was admiring herself in a mirror, joy in the bloom on her cheeks. The ceremony came into focus, the guests few, but the man waiting at the altar seemed familiar.

Eli caught her hand, stopping her from moving away.

"What is it?" she asked, peering into his eyes.

"Seth... Did he have a mole on the top of his cheek?"

She blinked then a slow smile formed. "He wanted to have it remove. Why do you ask?"

"Y'know, memories," he said.

When she opened her mouth, no doubt to ask him a question or two, he ushered her toward Zal, who held out the star stone.

"Thanks for the escort, Zal," she said, taking the time to check the weapons were loaded while Eli shoved the stone into the bag on her back.

Zal gave her a tight bow. "May Lethaar guide you."

They followed the trail, clear in the moonlight. The air was crisp, summoning a shiver or it could be from the gaping entrance ahead. He pulled his coat tighter. A craving for tea struck, and he swallowed, blaming the chill. Something hot in his belly wouldn't go amiss.

Movement drew his attention. Nova had half-emptied a bottle of water. At that rate, she'd need to pee soon. He grinned. Easier for her than for him. He'd just learned how to squat and not drench his feet, but accidents still happened. If they didn't find a stone, he'd have plenty of time to get better at it.

The pathway dipped, carrying them into shadows lined with black pillars and thousands of glowing names. He stroked one, wishing Zal had come with to explain their significance.

The wind ceased. The chirping and whirring of insects calmed, almost as if the surroundings took a breath. He peered over his shoulder, casting one last glance at the scattered submoon.

Lord, please let this be the last adventure.

He faced forward and scurried after Nova who'd created too much distance between them. The darkness engulfed him, forcing him to blink to adjust his vision. When her form appeared, he realized she'd stopped.

"What is it?" he asked, pausing behind her.

Before her gaped a chasm with nothing more than a rotten rope-bridge. One anchor had broken free from the rocky wall.

"Can we jump it?" He knew the answer to that without having her confirm it. Maybe in his old body he might have made it. "I'll go across first," he offered.

Tightrope walking, balancing on window ledges, on the backs of horses, hovers, or antique motorcycles were all part of his skill sets as an actor.

"Whether you go first or I do makes no difference. I'm *not* crossing that."

He studied her face in the blue flickering light of the torches. Her eyes were wide, her lips pinched.

"We have to try." He grabbed her by the hips and tugged her back. "Take the bag. Toss it over when I reach the other side."

"Eli." She caught his hand. "Please... Be careful."

He flashed her a smirk. "I'm lighter than you, so this should be easy. Want me to go ahead and see what else is waiting for us?"

"No," she said, lifting her chin. "Let's tackle this one hurdle at a time."

"I could throw you across," he teased.

"Don't you dare," she snapped. "Neanderthal." Her lips twitched with a suppressed smile.

"Okay, here goes." He wrapped his fingers around the thick rope that formed the railing. It had a decent heftiness to it. Then with a careful step, he placed one foot on the braided rope that formed the spine of the bridge at the base of a 'V.'

It creaked under his weight. He sucked in a breath, took another wobbly step, then exhaled when the rope held. His other hand he stretched out in a stupid attempt to help balance better.

Nova stayed silent, probably holding her breath. He grinned, finding her too adorable for words. Inch by inch, he crossed. Midway, he peered past his feet to the chasm below, half expecting giant alligators to be snapping in eagerness. Instead, he caught glimpses of frothy waves hitting boulders.

The nearer he got to the other side, the more he wished he had another railing to cling to. The bridge had taken to swaying. Perhaps he was moving too fast? But he didn't want to slow, not when he was almost there.

He touched down on the stone ledge and let the tension ease from his shoulders. "Right, Nova-honey, your turn."

She blinked at him while running her palms up and down her thighs. "I don't know, Eli."

"You only have to do this twice in your life then never again."

"Twice?" she squeaked.

"Yeah, once to the stone then back to Zal." He beckoned at her. "Come. You're in my body and stronger than you realize. If the rope breaks, just hold on and I'll pull you up."

She harumphed. "So not helpful." And yet, she grasped onto the railing.

"Don't look down. Keep your focus on me and your feet."

She placed her foot with care. The rope creaked but didn't groan. When she took another step, he praised her, offering her words of encouragement, though if later questioned, he wouldn't be able to state what he'd said.

What mattered now were the right sounds. Still, at midway, she halted and did as he had, staring at the bottom and at what awaited any poor soul who fell.

"I can't do this," she whined, her body stiff. She'd twisted to grip the railing with both hands.

"Nova," he said, "Take one more for me. Please. Just one more."

She met his gaze and wormed forward. Not quite what he'd meant, but she'd made progress.

"Another," he said.

Little by little, she drew closer. If he reached out, he could brush her outstretched fingers. When she realized she was almost across, excitement threw caution to the winds and she made too large a movement forward, sending the bridge rocking. She screamed and lunged, landing on the ledge in an undignified sprawl.

"Not a word to anyone, Thorne," she mumbled, staggering to her feet.

"You did so well," he crooned, giving her a tight hug. "Now hand me the—" He gaped at the bag sitting on the other end. "Shit."

"I'm so sorry," she moaned. "And we *need* it. The stone's inside."

"I'll get it," he said, holding his hand to the railing in an attempt to slow its violent movement. Back he went, choosing to focus rather than to rush and be reckless. But with the bag on his arm, his balance was off. Returning to her took more control and patience.

He shot glances at Nova. Her face was pale. Concern showed in her wringing hands and shallow breathing. He took comfort from it, that she cared. When he was a few feet away, he tossed the bag to her, letting out a sigh when she caught it midair. The last few yards were easier, and he made it to the ledge without the bridge offering too much complaint.

She hugged him then, something he'd always cherish. It wasn't coerced or forced, but her choice. He buried his face in her chest, but too soon, she pulled away.

"One problem at a time, right?" Her smile didn't reach her eyes, but before he could ask her about it, she marched down the narrow tunnel toward the blue light.

The next chamber was blindingly well-lit. Pictograms lined the walls, and he somehow sensed they were older than the names at the entrance. They told stories with stones at the center of them all. The scenes had a whole submoon and not the shattered one.

"Look at the floor," she said, her feet almost touching squares carved with more pictograms. He recognized none of them. "I suspect these are trapped. If you don't know the word or legend, you can't cross." She knelt and tapped the closest one with the carved shape of a yuxmet. The tile crumbled and fell into a black void similar to the bottom of the chasm. "Yes, to our doom." She squeezed his thigh, using it as leverage to climb to her feet.

"Maybe the wall paintings will give us a clue." He read the nearest one, trying to unravel its mystery.

"Or we can use the path." She rested her hands on her hips and grinned at him. "See where they're worn from frequent crossings?"

Sure enough, a zig-zag of shiny stones showed the way.

Buzzing with excitement, he kissed her temple. "Has anyone told you that you're a genius?"

She laughed. "Not lately." Her giggling trailed her as she leaped from tile to tile, the rifle smacking her butt.

He went slower, weighed down with the bag. Each step he took, he held his breath, then released it when the stone stayed underfoot. "Why can't things be easier?" he asked when he joined her on the other side. "Why the traps, the danger? I get it, these are tombs, but I haven't seen treasure to warrant this much security."

"Let's hope the rest of this is—" She screamed, tumbling back and into Eli.

Before them stood a frail woman, her skin burnt gold, her blue tattoos glowing brighter than Amenkar's.

"My apologies, young ones. I did not mean to startle you. I am Senmut, a Tazoc." She touched her temple then Eli's and Nova's. "I guard the Kovari Shol, as is my birthright."

"But the one we found had no such guardian," Nova said.

"Not all our temples are accessible like they used to be so many centuries ago." She gave them a wan smile. "We live in a changing world." With a flick of her fingers, she asked them to follow her. "I sense you carry a shol." She paused, studying them. "And another has touched you." She hummed as she waddled onward. "That one was old and taken by a monster from the stars."

"Orien's an asshole," Nova muttered.

The old woman cackled. "Indeed." She ducked and dropped to her haunches to waddle along, a bright light at the end of the enclosed passage.

"Tell me, Senmut, what do the names lining the entrance mean?" Eli called past Nova, who'd dropped to all-fours to crawl behind the older woman.

"Those are my sister shol guardians who have served the Kovari Shols for millennia. I await my replacement. I was hoping when I heard you coming that my time was near." She huffed when she straightened in the next chamber. "I have been here since I was a girl."

"How do you survive?" he asked as he cleared the low-lying rock. Before him stood a massive chamber, imposing pillars in black stone holding up the carved ceiling. In the center was a pool packed with silver plants, quiet swimming in the crystalline depths. A waterfall cascaded from a high ledge, frothing the pool's surface. A variety of fauna and flora dominated one wall, and pictograms filled every available space.

Nowhere was a stone or a pedestal.

"Parcels are delivered through a crevice."

"And you never leave here?" Nova asked, her eyes wide.

"No, this is my purpose." She waved them onward while sinking onto a nearby stone bench. "The shol is behind the waterfall."

"You're not worried that it might shatter?" Eli asked, pulling the stone out of the bag.

"Mine is too young to die. Besides, you have already been touched. Why would it want to touch you a second time?"

"To free us, maybe?" Nova arched a brow then glanced at Eli. "Ready?"

He palmed the stone and marched to the waterfall. Sure enough, behind it sat a pedestal. "Okay, do we touch both at the same time?"

Nova shrugged. She splayed her fingers on the two stones. Since Eli was holding theirs, he had only to touch the one on the pedestal. A vibration began. He squeezed his eyes shut, half expecting another explosion.

Instead, the humming became a squeal, and fire burned from his bicep to his shoulder and into his chest.

He snatched his hand away, breaking contact.

"What the hell?" Nova demanded, whipping her gaze between the stones. She rubbed her chest as if it ached. Like Eli's.

"Let me see your shol." Senmut wiggled her fingers.

Eli handed it over, hopeful that she might guide them. She growled and muttered, turning the stone over. She even shoved it close to the other stone, triggering that hum.

She angled her head as if she listened intently, then she cackled. "That dear boy. This is Vael'Tir's shol—the one Amenkar guards."

"I knew not to trust him," Nova snapped.

"He swapped them," Eli said, like stating the obvious would reveal the man's motives. It didn't. "Why would he do this?"

Senmut closed her eyes for a few moments. When she gazed at Eli, her expression softened with sadness. "It seems his intentions toward you were not benevolent. Perhaps hoping you would die when the stones repelled each other? He loved the old chief dearly, and when the monster killed him, he was devastated."

Nova snorted. "And he claimed that lying denied him access to heaven. The ass." She gasped, her face paling. "We left Frederik alone with—"

"He's a big man; he can take care of himself," Eli said, but he hoped he spoke the truth.

Senmut shuffled back. "The mate to Amenkar's shol is across the lake at an abandoned temple. It watches over the great waters."

"Why can't we go back and get *our* stone?" Nova asked. "Shouldn't take us long."

"Would he give it to us?" Eli asked her. "Like you said, we can't trust him. And if Senmut says this one's mate is a little farther away, I'm willing to chance it."

She threw her hands into the air, then faced Senmut as if something had dawned on her. "Do we need a soul tie to save us or was he lying about that, too?"

The guardian narrowed her eyes, peering into Eli's. "Some believe it protects you, but in truth, none are needed." A toothless grin formed. "You carry many." She glanced at Nova then cupped her cheek. "And yours is lost. Seth was such a kind man."

A bolt of pain hit Eli hard, reminiscent of the day he'd learned of his parents' deaths. The same intense sorrow flickered across Nova's face. Her cheeks trembled as she struggled to control her emotions, even as her eyes glistened with unshed tears.

Visions of a man's body being brought out on a hover-stretch accompanied the sheer agony of grief. Behind his blackened body was a mining rig with the familiar 'Warden' signage. That explained her determination to destroy every scuttle or scout she came across.

"Come, you must hurry," Senmut said. "Your time is shorter."

Nova squeaked then wiggled, pulling the T-shirt down. Sure enough, the tattoo had spread, now crawling across her chest. The symbol for six had formed.

"But it's not day six yet." She gritted her teeth. "When I next see that man, I'm going to...punch him."

Eli coughed to cover a chuckle. "I'll hold him down."

"You must leave here, return to your guide, then hurry on foot to the west of this island. There is a tunnel that travels under the lake and into the temple. It should be navigable, except for a few...vukuub. They are fearful of noise, so holler like a yuxmet and you should be able to slip past them." She met their gazes. "Do not be bitten by any of them. The quet cannot heal you from such venom."

Eli bolted for their bag and shoved the stone in.

Senmut caught Nova's hand and placed an egg-sized stone onto her palm. "You cannot enter without bearing a gift. But you must vow to leave this shol in the temple."

"I promise," Nova said and pocketed the stone. On impulse, she hugged the older woman. "Thank you for your guidance."

Within minutes, they'd crawled through the passage, zig-zagged over the booby-trapped floor, then shimmied along the bridge. Nova hadn't hesitated, no doubt fueled by anger.

When she reached Zal, she wagged her finger in his face. "Why the hell did you give us the wrong stone?"

Chapter Twenty-Four

The moon, Lethara

A Lethaar Temple, near to Vael'Tir.

A mad dash to freedom and despair.

Day Six.

The poor man hadn't known. Nova realized that when Zal just blinked at her.

"I apologize." He held up his hands, palms outward. "How is it the wrong shol? My chief gave it to me…" His eyes widened. "I see."

"Now we have to head to another temple." She slumped, the weight of this made heavier by the time restraint. Although, given weeks, she doubted she'd dawdle. "I can't say how long we'll be or how we'll find a way back to you. I suggest you head home, Zal."

"The temple that watches the great waters?" he asked, gathering the yuxmets' reins. "I will circle the lake and meet you there. Wait for me for my journey will be longer than yours."

She gazed at the yuxmets, desperate to ask if they had boats. But since she hadn't seen one docked or dragged onto shore, the answer had to be no. "My thanks, Zal."

Eli hovered west of her. She hurried to join him, and together, they jogged to where the tunnel was supposed to begin. If she judged by the architecture of the temple and the city, she expected it to be pillar-lined.

"We can do this," Eli said.

"I know we can," she said, rolling her shoulders. "Just tired, hungry, and could kill for a cup of tea."

"I didn't say anything," he said, peering at her.

She shrugged. He had, but she wasn't going to argue with him. She wanted this done and behind her. Never again would she bemoan her fate as a pilot. She'd taken that cushy job for granted.

"There," he said, pointing at a hole in the ground.

She groaned. "Really? We don't have rope." Anger was swift to strike, flooding her body with adrenaline. She was ready to punch something.

"It has a ladder, sort of," he said, peering inside. "Notches in the rock."

Great! I'm going to break my neck.

"I'll go first," he said, dropping the bag beside her before turning his back to her so he could descend.

Part of her wanted to run in the opposite direction, to chase after Zal. She far preferred a Yuxmet than what lay below.

"They have blue flames that burn eternally and stones that play with people's lives, but no magic that could whoosh us to a destination?" She stomped her foot. "I could *strangle* someone."

"Save that fire, honey," he said as he located a rung at a time.

She glared at him surrounded by darkness, only his face illuminated.

He smirked. "She's so adorable when she's angry."

She jerked back, torn between basking in his admiration and smacking him. "What the hell, Thorne? Why are you talking to me in third-person?"

His eyes widened then narrowed. "Back to Thorne are we?" And down he went, disappearing from view.

Panic gripped her. The night air, the chilly breeze, the vast and unknown sky surrounded her with a sudden sense of loneliness.

"Thorne!" She sprawled on the ground to stare into the hole. When he didn't answer, she said, "Eli?"

"Better," he said, his face appearing.

Relief coursed through, draping over her shoulders like a warm blanket.

"Are you coming?" he asked. "And bring the bag."

And just like that, the panic was back. She clambered to her feet and looped the bag's strap across her chest, getting it settled at the base of her spine. Then with a deep breath, she sat on the edge, dangling her feet into the abyss.

There, for a few minutes, she debated whether she should believe an old woman. Unfortunately, Zal was off, planning to meet her. He'd reacted as if what Senmut had said was fact. Nova wasn't up to chasing after him. But worse than that was the guilt lashing her conscience for agreeing to his plan.

They'd needed a way to return. He'd offered. But what if something happened to them, would he know? Would he wait? Could he perform some sort of rescue?

"Nova, honey," Eli said, "We can't waste time, remember?"

And down she went, notch after notch and slower than a sloth. Thankfully, if she fell, he might cushion her fall or die beside her.

What a great comfort that thought is.

Hands grabbed her waist and yanked her off the wall. She squealed then stumbled when her feet hit the ground.

"Not funny," she snapped.

"Whoa, someone's hangry," he said. "I could do with a protein bar. Do we have any left?"

He rooted through the bag, yanking it down as he dug deeper. With it still in place, she had to bend backward. But since her stomach gurgled, she wasn't going to stop him from finding anything to eat.

He leaped away, waving a bar. "Think it's our last. Next time Amenkar offers a meal, we take him up on it."

She hummed in agreement, having already bitten into the half he'd given her. The mealy texture didn't matter, nor the fake sweetness. She'd eat ten of these if she had them.

She froze. "Wait, how can I see you?"

"Mirrors reflecting moonlight," he said while he chewed.

She shifted into the pool of light and looked up. Sure enough, tiny discs were embedded into the rock walls and beamed light from one to the other. "That's clever."

He cracked open a bottle of water and gave it to her. "We head this way." He hitched a thumb at a blue flame in the distance. "If you see anything move, scream."

She scoffed. "You do realize it's pitch black, right? I doubt these mirrors project the light into the deeper recesses of wherever the fuck we are."

"That's what Senmut said we needed to do."

"And not to get bitten. Gotya," Nova said, rolling her eyes since he couldn't see her.

"Nova," he said, his tone serious. "The moonlight, remember?"

"Oh, yes." She ducked her head, her cheeks warm.

"Yeah, wish we had a torch...that works." He headed on, placing his feet with care.

While sipping water, she followed, her ears pricked for any sounds.

The air was stagnant, the smell that of wet rock. And yet, they couldn't see enough to know what was on either side of them.

Then blue light exploded into life, blinding her. Crying out, she threw up her arm, sloshing water down her chest. She handed him the half-empty bottle and dabbed at her face with the coat's sleeve.

"One of those," he said, stepping off a raised and marked stone. The light faded, leaving spots in her eyes. And on again when he repeated the action.

"So much better," she said, accepting that they were in a tunnel. Carved black rock was on all four sides: bottom, left, right, and top. Words lined them, noticeable for their lack of glowing.

"More shol guardian names?" he asked, studying the closest one. He drained the water, capped the bottle, then slipped it into the bag.

"Could be," she said. "Or the names of those who died here."

He chuckled. "Pretty bleak thought."

With the tunnel lit, he strolled ahead with too much confidence. After everything they'd been through, her level of distrust had ramped to para-noia.

"Make noise?" She coughed to clear her throat, then started to sing. As soon as the deep baritone left her mouth, she stopped. Damn. No wonder he was such a superstar. When she sang, crows joined in.

> *"Oh, I once met a lass on the moons of Magree,*
> *She said, "Mind the low grav or you'll float off o' me,"*
> *We tangled in orbit 'til our thrusters ran dry,*

Then she launched me away with a wink in her eye!"

Eli watched her, a grin splitting his cheeks. "Please, continue," he said when she hesitated.

She drew in a deep breath and added a little gusto for the chorus.

"So grab all the booty, boys, plunder the skies,
From her Milky Way curves to her bright starry eyes,
We'll pillage their ports and we'll board every ship,
And we'll dock nice and snug for a lovely long trip!"

They hurried along the passage now accompanied by her singing. She threw in a few skips as she got into the swing of it.

"We danced on Uranus 'til morning was near,
Her asteroid belt slipped and her moons did appear,
And when her black hole pulled me close with a spin,
I was sucked into bliss — never seen her again!"

For the chorus, Eli joined in, making her wince. Still, he was laughing and enjoying himself.

It was the only space shanty she knew. By the time they were climbing a slope and hopefully out of the tunnel, her voice was hoarse and he'd improved his shanty repertoire.

Her hope crumbled for they weren't leaving the tunnel. A cavern opened up, an altar at the center of a pyramid of steps. Many long tendrils dangled above it, throwing out a circle of red light.

"I should've expected this," she said with a sigh. Climbing to the top would give her the best view. They had to find a way out.

"Looks like a stone used to sit here." He stroked the indent in the altar. "See any clues?"

She didn't answer, unable to blink. Something had moved in the shadows. A shimmer, nothing more, but her instincts warned they weren't alone while her mind claimed she was imagining it.

"What is it?" he whispered, crowding her to peer in the direction she'd fixed her gaze.

"I saw a ghost." She flicked a dismissive hand. "It's probably not a real one, but whatever it is, it's transparent and coated with a rainbow hue like an oil slick."

"Invisible isn't good," he said.

Her shoulders dropped an inch at him not doubting her. That went a long way to bolster her. "We need to find the stone if this is the temple. Or—"

"The next tunnel?" He spun on the spot, sweeping his gaze across the vast cave. They couldn't see the sides—the tendrils didn't illuminate far enough. "I don't want to venture into the darkness to find the exit."

"Same," she said, taking a step down.

If she circled the altar, she might stumble on worn stones showing the past foot traffic. It was the only hope they had. By her broken sense of direction, she'd say the tunnel was north or west of them.

"Wanna use my butt tattoo?" he asked, a smile teasing his upper lip.

"Tempting if it was strong enough to project. Can you summon your sparks?" She gestured to all of him. "You could be my personal glow stick."

He chuckled. "I don't know how I did that."

"So, we're back to the beginning." Her eyes widened. "What if the correct path illuminates like the other one?"

"Yeah! Go around and tap marked stones?" He ran down the steps to the base of the pyramid, stomping across the paving regardless of whether they bore letters or not.

Movement in the corner of her eye had her blurting out another verse,

"On a wormhole-bound freighter I met Venus May,
She said, "Mind how you steer or we'll both drift away,"
But the stars were aligned and my course set just right,
We made landfall together all through the night!"

Whipping her gaze at the 'thing' showed nothing was there.

"See it again?" Eli called from west of the pyramid.

"Thought I did." She hurried to him, mostly because Senmut had said west. They might be screwing themselves over by not checking all sides, but she was desperate. It was a gamble.

"Nothing yet," he said, stamping the stones. "We could cut off a tendril. Maybe it will light the way?"

She grimaced, not wanting to harm anything. For all she knew, what looked like a plant was a living creature.

He ventured out until the ring of darkness started. There he paced. "Could be a leap of faith."

"Again?" she moaned.

He glanced at her, drew in a deep breath, and moved into the shadows.

"Eli!"

Blue lights lit the path, and he stood there, beaming at her.

This man was going to kill her. She stomped across to him, ready to smack him.

"Fuck, she fires my blood," he rasped.

"Quit it," she said, "You were lucky we did it once. I knew better than to trust their chief, but no, you were all gung-ho about getting naked."

He chuckled. "You don't regret it, Nova." He held her gaze, waiting.

She huffed. "No, I don't." Before he could ask her any more revealing questions, she marched past him, aiming for the archway in the rock wall.

It was then a shape formed on the path between them and freedom.

Her voice lodged in her throat.

Chapter Twenty-Five

"So grab all the booty, boys, plunder the skies,
From her Milky Way curves to her bright starry eyes,
We'll pillage their ports and we'll board every ship,
And we'll dock nice and snug for a lovely long trip!"

Eli squawked in Nova's caterwauling. He even adored that part of her. No one was perfect, and her dismal singing voice made him love her more.

The shimmering crab-spider splintered into fragments like a kaleidoscope. For a moment, five white eyes lingered before they too faded.

"Run," she hissed, bolting ahead.

The flat cobbles lost the light once they'd gone over them. He didn't care as long as they showed the way.

Sweeping movement stirred a breeze across his neck, but he didn't think about it, not willing to peek over his shoulder. He echoed Nova's frustration. As much as he'd enjoyed this time as Nova Blake, he wanted to move on, to confess his love, maybe begin a new life with her. God willing.

"Is it me or can you smell fresh air?" she asked, increasing her pace.

She glanced at him, then behind them, jerking to a halt. "Run!"

Squeezing past him, she headed back to the cavern, hollering and waving her arms. Then she was chasing him, urging him to sprint with his shorter legs. The rifle smacked his ass, driving him onward.

The entire time, she screamed like someone was trying to kill her.

When he exploded out of the tunnel, it took him by surprise. He swiveled, blaster in hand to face whatever was chasing them. She skidded across the ground, rolling onto her back as she fought for air. He waited, his ears filled with her ragged breathing while he focused on sound or movement coming from the darkness.

White eyes watched him but didn't approach.

For the longest time, he held its gaze until it slowly retreated.

Only then did he lower his weapon and collapse beside her. "We made it," he said.

She sat up and studied their surroundings. The swish of distant waves and the salty tang of the ocean registered. And there, on a slight rise, stood a gazebo-like temple—a black construction without a roof. Stalwart pillars circled an empty altar.

"Shit," she said, staggering to her feet and jogging the final distance.

He followed, disbelieving that Senmut would send them to a stoneless temple. There had to be a catch. Nova stroked every inch of the altar, probably searching for a trigger switch or a clue. He swept his gaze out across the peninsula and beyond to the moonlight-kissed ocean the color of old blood. The flying whales on the horizon seemed closer and yet remained surreal.

He rested his temple on a pillar, squeezed his eyes shut, and drew in calming breaths. When he pulled back, his gaze snagged on glowing blue letters.

His heart skipped a beat. A quick scan confirmed he wasn't imagining it. Each of the eight pillars had a few words.

That is creation.

one another

To understand

That is union.

to be known.

one another.

is to become

To be seen,

"Oh," he gasped. "It's a puzzle."

She gaped at him. Her cheeks flushed red. Unshed tears glistened, and she pursed her lips. "I...can't even deal with this."

"Just write it all down and shuffle them until they make sense." He held out his hand for the bag which she happily tossed to him. "We can do this."

A poor journal sacrificed a few pages which he tore into eight strips. On them, she scrawled the words, handing each one to him as soon as she was done.

The waves, squeaks and cries of nature, and his steady heartbeat filled him with a sense of peace.

"'To understand' is pillar one; put the bag there and grab a few items."

She did as asked, then with machete and books in hand, she waited.

He hummed and switched the strips, undecided between 'is to become' and 'one another.' "I'm going to guess here. Mark number two as 'is to become.' And 'one another' as three."

"Mm, to understand is to become one another..." She palmed another book to place at the next pillar.

"Yeah, there are two 'one another.'" He waved a strip of paper at her. "And they don't make sense with what's left."

She tapped her chin with a book's spine and studied the words. "What about, 'To understand one another is to become one another?'"

He grinned. "That could work. Okay, that leaves 'That is creation. That is union. To be known, and to be seen.'"

"The first two have a finality to them. They'd be at the end, right?" She gave him a shrug. "Besides, even if we figure out what it means, how does it help us?"

"I don't know, maybe touch them in order? With our joined hands, with the stone, or with the egg?" He jumped to his feet. "I'm guessing here."

Her smile was sweet. "And doing a fantastic job, too." She touched, stroked, then kissed the first pillar's words. Nothing happened. "Okay, so not that. Or we have them in the wrong order."

He lifted the bag to dig out more items and blinked at the number carved into the base of the pillar. It was caked with black soil and barely noticeable. "Look!" He knelt and brushed aside the dirt. "I was right. This one's first."

They moved through the temple and dusted off the symbols.

"What's it say then?" she asked, wiping her hands on her ass.

He shifted to the center of the temple to take them all in. "To understand one another is to become one another. To be seen, to be known—that is union. That is creation."

She squealed, bouncing on the spot. "Since it talks about union, let's try touching them together."

He laced his fingers with hers and pressed them to the first words. They lit with a muted hum. Giggling, they ran between the pillars in order then faced the altar.

Excitement pulsed between them, and if they'd had the time, he'd kiss her, especially when she glowed with such joy.

Grating rumbled beneath his feet. He fought the urge to step back, worried the bottom would fall away and swallow them whole.

The altar split in half and spiraled outward. In the center a stone rose on nothing but air. When it was high enough, the grating returned and the altar reformed.

"I'm not ready to test the stones." She squeezed his hand still clasped in hers. "What if this one speeds up the timer again?"

"Then we leave this moon, get married, and learn to live like this." *Which I'd love to do with you, Nova-honey.*

Her panic faded, and she drew him into a hug. "I suppose that wouldn't be *that* bad," she said. She pressed a kiss to his temple then pulled away, dropping the bag between them. "Let's do this."

He stole another kiss. It was meant to be swift, a mere brushing of lips, but she crushed him to her and deepened it. His heartbeat deafened him. Breathing became inconsequential, and only the taste of her mattered. When he broke away, desire zinged along his veins.

He studied her as he rummaged through the bag, then dropped it at her feet, their stone in hand. "Ready?"

She splayed her fingers on it and reached out to the other. He did the same.

A low humming started on both stones and grew louder, making his palms tingle.

Between them, a light began, growing brighter until it was blinding.

"Is it going to shatter?" she whispered, peeking at him through her narrowed eyes.

Before he could answer, the colors swirled in the stones' depths.

Both shot up then spun around each other, whirling so fast they blurred. He snatched her against him, needing her warmth to calm him. This could end so badly.

Or it could go well.

His chest swelled. An explosion of heat poured outward from there to his shoulder, down his bicep, stopping at his fingertips. He held up his hand and blinked at the disappearing tattoo.

"It's...working," she said, showing him her palm. Tears traveled over her cheeks and dripped off her chin.

"You've been amazing, Nova," he said, stealing a fleeting kiss.

The light and hum grew bolder. He squeezed his eyes shut and cuddled into her embrace. 'I love you' burned the tip of his tongue, urging him to confess, but he hesitated. Time slowed. The air charged with electricity, tickling the hair on his head and arms.

Boom.

A force threw them backward. He bounced off a pillar. But all he registered was that she was no longer in his arms.

When he opened his eyes, the altar was as they'd found it with no stones in sight. He scrambled to his feet, pain ricocheting in his skull. Gripping the lump forming, he gaped at the altar.

Only then did he realize he was taller than moments ago.

He was Eli Thorne again.

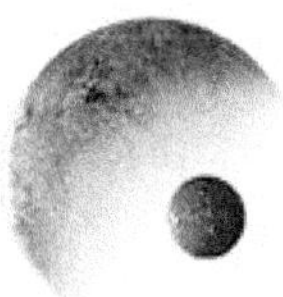

"Eli?" Nova moaned, struggling to stand. Her shoulder throbbed, and her hip burned. A steady pain in her core was an all too familiar sensation—her periods were due.

She froze, sat up, and stared at her knees, peeked inside her shirt at her cleavage, then cupped her face. The presence of her eyebrows, nose, lips, and chin sparked a cry of joy.

She was Nova Blake again.

And yet, what was inside her was deep loss, lingering like a devouring shadow.

She whipped her gaze to the altar in time to catch Eli climbing to his feet. Her heart swelled, heat exploded outward, and she swallowed a gasp by biting her lip.

I love him.

How the hell had that happened? When? Did that even matter? Loving a movie star was a one-way-road to misery. He'd be away all the time. Like Seth had been, and she'd coped with that just fine. The crux was Eli's fans. Many women would throw themselves at him. Could she trust him to resist temptation?

That was all moot when there was no sign that he loved her, too.

Oh, no. She wrapped her arms around her stomach and bowed. *This's bad, Nova. You're such an idiot.*

"You okay?" Eli cupped her cheek, snapping her from her sorrow.

"I could do with a cup of tea," she said, forcing a smile. "It worked, Eli. Can you believe that?"

"Yeah, now we need to leave this moon."

She waved a dismissive hand. "First, a real meal. A bath, maybe. That's a luxury right there, and if things go our way, we can hitch a ride."

"If I had a comm device, I could announce my willingness to leave, and a random news outlet would send a shuttle in the hopes of an exclusive interview."

She grimaced. Before this...adventure, she would've scoffed, thinking he was bragging, but now she knew. He endured the attention, used the fame for his own ends, and somehow had mastered it.

"I'm glad this happened with you," she said. "I don't know anyone who can swordfight their way out of a situation."

He grinned. "Got taught that in *Shadow Huntress of Andromeda*."

She squealed, clapping and bouncing on the spot. "I saw that one! You were Cassidy Collin's side kick."

He shook his head. "Trust you to have seen my worst performance."

She snorted. "All you did was walk around shirtless."

"Exactly. I learned little from that role." He laced their fingers and tugged her toward the altar. "Come, we need to leave the egg."

"Oh, yes," she said, digging in his right pocket where she'd slipped it. But when she went to place it on the altar, it clung to her palm. "It's stuck." She couldn't yank it free.

"That's not possib— Sorry, forgot our souls were swapped by magic. Here, maybe if we do it together?" He cupped the egg and guided her to the altar.

When he pulled away, she rotated her hand, hoping gravity would be on her side.

Nope, the egg stayed in place.

"Mm," he frowned, "and if you put it in your pocket?"

She did, and when she removed her hand, the egg stayed behind. "Why's nothing simple on this freaking moon?" she ranted. "I'm not cutting up my pants for this. Leave it. We'll ask Zal when he gets here."

Eli hummed, his gaze on the eastern bank of the peninsula. "Think we have time for an ocean dip?"

Excitement skittered into life. Never had she been in the ocean. She'd heard of Eternis, a paradise only the rich could afford to visit, but since the *Valiance* didn't tour that galaxy, she hadn't had a chance to go planetside.

"I'll have to strip," she said, striding down the embankment and onto the soft black sand.

"I can bear a little nudity if you can," he called, the muted thud of a boot hitting the ground.

She giggled, wiggling out of boots, pants, shirt, and underwear to stand on the damp sand. He strode toward her. A long time ago, he'd been young, his physique not the mountain of muscle he now was. Broad shoulders were the same, sure, but those abs. And even though she'd been him a few minutes ago, nothing compared to looking at the eye candy he was.

"If you keep devouring me with those gorgeous eyes, Nova-honey, you'll have to take what I give you," he drawled, circling an arm around her waist.

She didn't bother to suppress her reaction to his touch. "I'm up for it, if you are."

And over his shoulder she went.

She squealed and kicked her feet, grinning at finding his dimpled ass filling her sight. He swatted her backside while trudging into the frothy waves. Skinny-dipping at night on an alien moon was all kinds of stupid, but she ached to know him as Nova. Kind of like a refresher of memories. Soon they'd walk away from each other. And even though their adventure wouldn't be forgotten, she wanted to cram these last seconds with as much of him as possible.

The water was warm, thicker than normal, and clinging to every inch of her when he sank into the next wave. She could do nothing but gasp when he plastered her to his front, a hard-on pressing into her hip.

Their lips met in the middle, kisses frantic, hot, needy, hands stroking each other in a frenzy. Zal could arrive and catch them in the act, but she didn't care, her body thrumming with desire. Her core twanged, making demands she didn't want to ignore.

He grabbed her by the ass and hoisted her until she peered into his upturned face. This annoying, arrogant, egotistical, sexy-as-hell man had somehow gotten her to love him. She caressed his jaw, trailing a path over the stubble to his baby-soft bottom lip.

"Nova," he rasped, sliding her down until his cock pressed against her opening.

She moaned, wrapping her arms around his neck and arching.

His breath caught a second before he pushed in. She tightened her arms, relishing the tingling stretch as he impaled her.

"So good," he growled, angling his head to kiss her.

His tongue dueled hers while he pistoned in and out. The lights in her eyes became incandescent with every spark of joy he garnered. She squeezed her eyes shut and held on, burying her face in the curve of his neck with every one of his hip thrusts.

Ecstasy was so near, too exquisite for her to handle. She planted kisses across his skin, his jawline, his chin as the orgasm neared. It hit her hard. She leaned back using his shoulders as an anchor, breaking contact to scream his name.

He held onto her, a groan slipping from his lust-hardened features as he joined her in the sweet fires of pleasure. His breathing was ragged as he gathered her closer.

Her insides trembled, mini firebolts shooting along her channel. The ache deepened; she craved more. Tears blurred her vision, but she tucked her chin, not wanting them to spill free. This was...

"Beautiful," he whispered, feathering kisses along the shell of her ear.

She smiled. "You read my mind."

"No, not this time." A small frown furrowed his brow. "Why couldn't I hear your thoughts?"

She shrugged. "Probably why the egg's stuck to me even though Senmut gave it to you?"

He laughed. "True. I'll hurt myself trying to understand it all."

The rainbow lights flickering across his face ended their cuddle. She twisted to find the cause and slid off him in the process. In the deep burgundy of the water, quets glowed. En mass, the eels circled them, casting out their colors while weaving between their legs.

"Maybe we shouldn't linger?" he suggested and offered her his hand.

She took it, and together, they waded to shore. A breeze cooled her wet skin. She didn't rush to dress, preferring to stand there naked on a deserted beach on an alien moon. Moments like this should be treasured. She glanced at Eli and found him gazing at the star-strewn sky, a ring-planet dominating most of it.

'I love you' was on the tip of her tongue, but she'd be a fool to utter it. Despite all they'd been through, the best scenario was friendship. The thought of it cracked her heart. She glanced out to the horizon to hide her wince.

She was coward. Picking at Warden Mining Corp from the safety of the *Valiance*. Treating Eli badly because of what she'd done so many years ago.

But she wouldn't apologize for any of it. She could only vow to do better.

"Family first," she said as she dressed, patting the egg still in the pocket. It had to be her imagination that it warmed to her touch.

"Yeah. I'd invite you along, but I figured you'd want some time away from me."

A vice crushed her chest. She *had* been mean to him.

She forced a smile and peeled on her T-shirt. "To clear my head, yes. We could meet up if you like." She tried to hide her hope, but it slipped into her voice.

"A month from today?"

She wanted to ask why so long, but who knew how far he had to travel. It could take a week just to reach them. Instead, she grinned. "Sounds like a plan."

"I'll treat you to tea."

That drew a laugh. "Sweet talker."

Chapter Twenty-Six

The moon, Lethara

From the beach to Vael'Tir.

Time to head home? But first, there'd better be tea.

Nova had dozed, resting her temple against Eli's arm as they waited for Zal. The braying of the yuxmets stirred her, but Eli threw his arm around her and gathered her into the curve of his body. Leaving the warmth and comfort took a Herculean effort. She held his gaze as she straightened, then before she could second guess the instinct, leaned in for a kiss.

He met her halfway, humming when she drew back.

Zal halted the beasts amid a cloud of black dust. The burgundy sky had begun to tint orange as the sun rose.

"Is all well?" he asked, dismounting with far too much agility for a man of his age.

"It is." She beamed at him then clambered to her feet. "Just two more things to accomplish and you need never see us again."

He frowned, his focus switching between her and Eli as they approached him. "I will always welcome you into my home, qidhari."

She squeezed his bicep. "I meant no offense, Zal. We have loved ones who worry about us. It's time we returned to them." She dug her hand into the pocket and pulled out the egg. Without hesitation, she flipped it over to show him how it stuck to her palm. "What's happening here?"

He blinked at the egg defying gravity and grinned. "I am not surprised it chose you. Such is the way of things on Lethara. We do not question the shols." He looped the reins around his hand when the yuxmets shifted, seeking vegetation among the cobbles.

"Zal," she said, trying to ensure she had his attention. "Choosing me means what to a shol?"

"After all we've been through, I think it means it stays with you." Eli adjusted the bag across his shoulder then moved to the side to stroke a yuxmet's matted brow.

She gaped at him, then turned it on Zal. "Is he right?"

"Yes, it is so."

Eli chuckled. "You might as well name it."

Panic rose, squeezing her chest tighter until breathing became a struggle. "I can't...keep it. What does it eat? How long does it live?"

"Some shols like darkness; others thrive on light. You will need to discover this for yourself." Zal tutted and swiveled on a heel, gesturing to her to hop onto her ride.

Hop. She was mid-scoff when she was airborne, hoisted by Eli with a firm grip on her waist. Settling on the bareback took the wind out of her sails, and she harumphed as if her dignity had been insulted. All she could do was shove the egg into a pocket and snatch at the reins.

The yuxmets lumbered back without too much complaint.

"Aren't they tired?" she asked, holding her hands high to avoid touching its hair. The rolling gait gyrated her hips until a pain began to build at the base of her spine.

"Yuxmets can travel for days on a mouthful of water." Zal patted his ride on the neck. "They do enjoy a good meal, though."

They fell into a comfortable silence, the world around them coming to life in a kaleidoscope of colors. Flowers thrust out their petals, some plants with long leaves swayed in a non-existent breeze. And in this natural chaos, her stomach gurgled.

"Bacon, eggs, waffles, Tarnis syrup, and a pot of tea," she said, rubbing her stomach. The stone buzzed when she bumped it, so she stroked it until it calmed.

"Sounds amazing. Lost opportunity on my part," Eli said. "As you, I should've eaten as much cheese as I could stomach."

She laughed. "Sure, from the fine selections we were offered."

Zal handed them each a strip of pink leather. He gestured with pinched fingers to his mouth.

Too starving to care what it was, she bit off a piece, fighting to tear it off, then moaned when it melted on her tongue amid a variety of sweet and salty flavors. "So good," she mumbled around her second bite.

"Thank you," Eli said, almost done with his. "What is it if I may ask?"

"Salted Yuxmet skin they shed every three weeks."

Her tongue dried, a piece lodged in her throat, and she cupped her mouth to hide a gag.

Zal guffawed. "They do not feel the loss, and we do clean and spice the strips."

She nodded, a finger to her lips while she chewed, debating whether she could spit it out or endure the pain of swallowing.

Eli held out his palm, and she hastily handed over her last piece. Right then, she'd never loved him more.

"Long ago, when the Lethaars walked this world, their adventures were entertaining, but now that their influence reaches the stars, things have worsened for my people." Zal's serious tone snagged her attention.

She hurried to swallow without choking herself.

"They created the stones to toy with each other's favorites, turning enemies to lovers, matching souls for the joy of it. Eventually they would restore balance, which is why there was a set number of moons to limit the time the victims suffered. Anything longer would have been cruel. In other instances where chiefs fought amongst themselves, the shols taught the value of perspective—seeing the problem through the other's eyes. When the gods...abandoned us, they left their creations, as well." Zal raised his gaze to the sky, his smile rueful. "It was wrong of Amenkar to give you another shol. Thankfully, Senmut could guide you to its mate. Perhaps my chief's deceit was written in the stars." Zal grinned at them. "For here you are, once again whole?" He arched a brow.

"I have learned much," Eli said, his gaze meeting hers. "For me, it's been more than worth it."

She nodded, not trusting her voice. Her heart thumped as if it wanted to squeeze past her ribs and return to him. She almost rolled her eyes. *Waxing poetic? Really.*

They'd return to their normal lives: her as a pilot. Him as a famous actor. Worlds apart even when they'd swapped souls and formed a soul tie.

"Amenkar is fighting a changing world. Many visitors are finding our paradise. This is inevitable and cannot be thwarted."

"True, but you're without the power to stop them." Eli tapped his chest. "I am not. This...adventure will be shared. I'll beg my government to help protect your untouched world."

Zal's smile was slow to form. "I do not understand your words, but I do read your heart, my friend. And perhaps, your gov-in-mint will see the good in you, too."

What Eli could achieve was possible with his wealth and influence. If they could get off the moon. Priority number two, okay, three. Bath, meal, tea. Make that fourth on her to-do list. Senmut had offered some explanations, but Nova wanted everything confirmed. She had so many questions like why had Amenkar switched stones and lied about soul ties? Senmut had said it was because of revenge for the former, and an erroneous belief for the latter. Could Nova be happy with that?

And what had happened to Orien and Frederik? She'd find out soon enough if Zal led them back to Vael'Tir.

Also, what the hell was she supposed to do with her own stone? Raise it? Did it even grow? Having touched bigger stones, she had to assume they did.

She and Seth had wanted children, but when every month had passed without falling pregnant, they had to accept it wasn't possible for them. Now she was a mother to a shol.

She smothered a chuckle. The teenage years would be a bitch. And if this thing grew, would she have to resort to carrying it on her back? No, no, she'd have to find what it ate, then maybe choose a suitable spot for it. Maybe on a shelf with other souvenirs?

Why couldn't it have chosen Eli?

She glanced at him, then stilled. In the far distance was Vael'Tir. The weak sunlight warmed the crown of her head and her shoulders. But as pretty as the sight of the city was, what made her breath catch were the many hovering shuttles.

"What the hell?" she whispered.

"Mm, the circus has arrived," Eli grumbled and tightened his hold on the reins. "Time to wear the mask, Nova-honey."

Resignation flittered across his handsome features, proving she'd only ever seen his fake façade and never bothered to look deeper. She did now. Zal had said seeing different perspectives, and she had to agree, the soul-swapping had been effective, if stressful.

The yuxmets carried them behind a copse of asparagus trees, hiding them from view. They approached the city's entrance from the south, drawing no one's attention. She tried not to stare, unable to truly see past a wall of black-clad warriors, their lances beside them, piercing the sky like porcupine quills. Beyond them stood Frederik, a giant wall unto himself.

Zal steered them toward the shed, letting her dismount using the bales. Eli had leaped off, patting his ride's flanks while thanking it.

'You measure a man by his kindness to critters, November,' Mama used to say. Seth hadn't harmed animals, but he hadn't sought them out either, choosing to treat them like one would a hovercycle. Understandable when owning pets was for the extravagantly rich.

"Thank you for fetching us, Zal." She grabbed his hands for a squeeze.

"I will forever serve my qidhari," he said, squaring his shoulders.

Not sure what to say to something that sounded formal, she nodded and let Eli lead her off. "Any idea what qidhari means?"

"Must be ancient if their current language no longer carries the word."

She blinked at him, finding his intelligence impressive.

"Frederik," he called from behind the warriors.

The man turned and grinned. "It's about time you arrived. Seems like the universe has learned of your...vacation."

Eli grimaced. "It was unavoidable. Any chance I can get Artivar's governor on a call?"

"I have spoken to him, promising to reveal all on Orien's dealings. Your name will carry weight, of course." Frederik strode toward them.

In a blur, drones blocked out the sunlight even as they bathed her and Eli in blinding light.

"Come, Amenkar has given me the use of the nearest house. There, we can talk." Frederik marched along the cobbles amid flashes and cries for comments.

Eli clasped her hand and drew her against him. "Don't pay them any attention. Just walk."

She did, one foot in front of the other, while wishing she could use her blaster on everything not Lethari.

Frederik veered through the first door on the left and gestured to a rug and cushions. A white loincloth-clad woman offered fruit from a platter. Nova chose a few pieces in pink, purple, red, and white, not sure what they were but hoping she'd enjoy them.

"Why did you help us?" Eli asked, sipping from a goblet as he sat on his haunches.

She joined him, popping the first sliver of fruit into her mouth and moaning when sweet juice exploded across her senses.

"At first, I saw you as nothing more than another naïve financial backer. But when you spent the evening trying to convince Lord Orien to use Ms. Blake instead of having her prosecuted, it made me realize there was more to you than your reputation. And once you offered me a position, I knew something was wrong. Your interactions at breakfast proved my instincts were right." He settled his great bulk on the rug, taking up a large portion of the confined space. "Then on board the *Laurus,* you both had me second guessing my conclusions. You treated each other like a couple on the verge of marriage." He smiled. "I'm a romantic at heart. As Eli Thorne, the famous actor, I thought you wouldn't do good by Ms. Blake, but you suit each other very well. You love her, and that's good enough in my book."

Nova coughed on spit. There was no other way to describe what lodged in her throat. Tears sprang to life, and she dipped her chin to hide her expression. Eli loved her? What had convinced Frederik of this miracle? And she sure as shit didn't want Eli to see the hope on her face.

Whatever had made Frederik believe this, she wasn't going to kick a good horse in the mouth.

"Thanks, Frederik," she managed to rasp. "Without you, we wouldn't have made it here. Who knows what Orien would've done to us had he not found the anomalies he was looking for."

Eli watched her, his gaze intense with a potency she couldn't describe. She shoved a mushy white thing in her mouth to stop herself from blurting out what he made her feel.

"So, where is Orien?" she asked, desperate for a change of subject.

Frederik's expression hardened. "I haven't seen him since you left. Amenkar refuses to talk about it, but I suspect he's...dead."

In that second, her mind blanked.

Eli dragged his gaze from her. "I can believe it if he killed their previous chief like they claim."

"He was alive when Amenkar's guards took him away." She sucked a droplet of juice off her finger.

"I should feel guilty about shooting him, but I have blood on my hands because of him." Frederik scowled. "I doubt Artivar's governor will be happy with not knowing Lord Orien's fate."

"I'm tempted to lie." She huffed, popped the last pink-like peach into her mouth, and wiped her hand on her pants. "After what he did to me...*us*, he can rot in hell."

"Nova-honey," Eli said, his expression sad.

"He would've bribed his way out of any punishment. You know that," she snapped.

Eli bowed his head. "I do. Still..."

She wasn't going to feel guilty about not mourning the ass. "I didn't get him killed. Accidents happen. And after what that poor man suffered, losing half his body?"

"She's right. Barry's wife just gave birth to twins. They'll never know their father." Frederik slapped his thighs and stood. "On other news, they delayed the premiere until you'd been located."

Eli laughed. "That must've angered the organizers."

"Your agent put up a million credits for a reward. I have one of Orien's shuttles on standby—you should slip through without issue." Frederik paused outside, waiting for them to join him.

The chances of a bath and a pot of tea were fast escaping her.

"What about you? Are you coming with us?" she asked, running catch-up when both men had long legs.

"Thanks to you suggesting I eat a little quiet, I am now the official Lethari ambassador." Frederik beamed. "My place is here until I can ensure Lethara is a no-go zone."

"The job offer still stands," Eli said.

"I will reach out to you when I'm done here." Frederik led them into the city, along the path Amenkar had taken them.

"Um, Frederik," she rocked on her toes, "if you can, find out what qidhari means, please. Zal calls me that."

"Will do, Ms. Blake."

This time, they didn't descend to the throne room but continued along the edges to where a shuttle waited—*Viator V*.

"I trust you can fly this without destroying it?" Frederik asked, his tone clipped.

"Pirates fired upon us. Not our fault," Nova said, fighting the urge to pout. "Besides, we didn't blow it up."

Eli offered Nova the crook of his elbow. "Shall we?"

She hesitated, taking a second to stare into his gorgeous eyes.

"I do believe we have a premiere to attend," he said.

She grinned, happy to spend more time with him. "I did promise."

"Until the clock strikes midnight, you're mine."

She fought a blush and slid her arm through his. "Wine and dine me, Mr. Thorne."

He dipped his head, keeping his heated gaze only for her. "Fly us home, Nova-honey."

She boarded before him and sank into the pilot's seat.

"Travel safely," Frederik called and walked off.

Eli sealed the door then moved around the compartment while she powered up the engines. Only when he paused beside her, did she catch the delicate aroma of Lady Grey tea.

"Computer, fly us to Artivar Station," she called and reached for the cup as the shuttle rose upward.

"Manual pilot deactivated," the computer intoned.

"Think we'll return?" Eli asked, leaning a hip against the console with a disappearing vision of Lethara behind him.

"My egg might need to," she said.

He folded his arms across his chest. "Chosen a name for it?"

She shook her head, content to sip her tea, and relishing the warmth in her belly. This was...happiness.

"What about Barry?"

The memory of half a man plummeting past the vines flashed across her mind. "I like it," she said.

"Computer, time on Artivar?"

"Ten A.M."

Eli hummed. "Connect me to Graham Whitney."

Nova stiffened, wishing she could leave before his agent answered. But doing so would raise suspicion. Perhaps she could hide behind the cup?

"One moment, please."

"Eli? Is that you?" A man's face filled the forescreens.

She winced. Yes, the same man who'd whisked her out of Eli's bed while insulting her looks. Was she allowed to hate him on sight? Then again, the poor man, having to deal with all of Eli's one-night-stands.

"Of course it's me. This is Nova. We're on our way to Artivar. It's a five-hour trip."

"At last!" The older man's expression warmed, revealing his fatherly love for Eli.

Her heart broke then. She couldn't hate someone who loved him as much as she did. If not more so.

"I'll let everyone know." Graham's grin threatened to split his cheeks. "Expect a full-blown welcome."

"Wonderful. Nova's my date. Please take care of everything."

Graham studied her then, his expression curious then worried. "I'll...need your sizes."

"Sure," she mumbled, rolling her shoulders and burying her nose in her empty cup.

"She's the *Valiance'* pilot," Eli said, his gaze on her.

"Oh," Graham said, then added, "Oh! I'll let Marco know. He's been so worried."

"Thank you," she said, flashing a smile she was far from feeling. Returning to civilization was unexpectedly soul destroying.

"See you in five," he called and hung up.

"We have hours of time to kill. Any ideas?" He took her cup from her, hefted her to her feet, then looped his arms around her waist, pulling her snug against him. "Chess? Tic tac toe? Thumb wrestling?"

"How about a shower?" she suggested, gliding her hand to his fingers and tugging him toward the bathroom.

"Mm, I like the way you think," he said, giving her his signature smirk.

But this time, he was all sincerity.

Chapter Twenty-Seven

Eli didn't want Nova out of his sight, not for a second. But when they docked, Graham whisked her away despite his protests. He stared after them, wishing he could follow. But he knew the drill: head to his apartment, shower, put on his tux, and hurry to the premiere. Tons of interviews awaited him, more so than normal after the events of the past six days.

So quickly he'd gone from alone, his arrogant self, to...what? He couldn't claim to be dating Nova when they'd yet to discuss it. They'd agreed to visit family. Maybe in the month they were apart he could work up the courage to ask her to be his?

For now, he did as expected, trudging along the private corridor then up to his penthouse suite. He crossed the sterile apartment to the wall of windows overlooking the docking bays. The ships coming and going intrigued him and summoned a sense of timelessness. This view was why he'd bought this place.

He scanned the ships, searching for the *Valiance*. A futile attempt on his part when massive ice haulers were the size of thumbnails. Offering the windows his back, he scanned the lifeless décor in steel and white. After the vibrancy of Lethara and Nova's bold red hair, he missed color.

The state-of-the-art shower couldn't compare to the one he'd shared with Nova a few hours ago. He didn't linger, choosing instead to sit on the bed in his towel and stare at nothing.

A stomach gurgle reminded him he needed to eat something other than yuxmet jerky, protein bars, and a glass of alien juice.

"Alexa, order a pizza." Would Graham make sure Nova ate, too? Eli was tempted to task him to do that. A chuckle had him shaking his head. She could take care of herself.

"The usual?" Alexa asked, her mechanical voice sultry. He could've chosen a unisex monotone, but his past self had thought otherwise.

"Yes." He rose, crossed to his closet, and chose a tux at random.

As he dressed by rote, he replayed memories from the moment he met Nova to their last few hours. The urge to pat himself down as if he'd lost something made his fingers twitch. He was midway through snapping the magnetic clasps on his boots when the elevator chimed, announcing his pizza had arrived.

He gave his damp hair a glance. Hopefully it would dry while he ate. His five o'clock shadow had darkened, on its way to beard status. He did need a shave, but he hadn't bothered. Something was off, like his appearance was no longer his core focus. To be expected when his future was uncertain, but still, he prided himself on his ability to change course without too much fanfare. A director wanted snow instead of a desert? No problem. Shaved head? Sure. Blue skin? Why not. Jump off a cliff? Anytime.

But he'd never been in love.

"Evening, George," he said when the elderly concierge exited the elevator, pizza in hand.

"Mr. Thorne. Welcome home. The papo sure made our lives a misery." He waddled to the kitchen and placed the pizza box on the counter.

The aroma had Eli's mouth salivating.

"Glad to be home," he said, though his voice lacked warmth. "Want a slice?"

"Kind of you to offer, Mr. Thorne, but the missus made my favorite." George smiled, cracking his laugh lines that resembled old road maps. "Mr. Whitney has a hover waiting to usher you to the premiere. When you are ready, of course." He left without another word.

Eli ate half the pizza in silence. Alone. Solitude hadn't bothered him, but to be fair, he'd never met a woman quite like Nova. He left the rest of his dinner, brushed his teeth, ran his fingers through his still-damp hair, and headed down. Swarms of reporters greeted him the second he stepped onto the landing pad. Drones flashed as they took photos and footage. Questions were thrown at him without letting him answer, but he waved with a wide grin in place.

The silence in the self-driving hover was welcome, a stark contrast to how he'd hated it in his apartment. He savored it while he whizzed along the rails. Graham would greet him on the red carpet. And beside him would be Nova.

Excitement sparked in his chest, and he formed a genuine smile. She'd probably been put through the wringer: hair, make-up, gown adjustments. In truth, he'd never thought about his dates suffering to be on his arm. Not even after starring in *Alien in Lipstick* when he'd learned firsthand what women endured. But the past six days as Nova had opened his eyes.

That growing ache in his core was no longer there. Her monthly cycle loomed. And yet, she'd barreled through the adventure without mentioning it. That implied all women went about their daily lives in some level of pain.

The hover stopped, and the door slid open. "Destination on your left."

He peered out and blinked, blinded by more lights.

"Eli, over here," someone called.

"This way, Eli."

Where's Graham?

He ignored them all and climbed out, sauntering along the red carpet. His swagger was back. He grinned, remembering when Nova had sashayed in his body. At set markers, he paused, posed, smiled, waved, then carried on, his target the interviewer to the side of Eastwood Hall's entrance.

"Oh, Eli, it's so good to see you're well." The platinum blonde beamed, sweeping out her hand to the many cameras trained on him.

"Happy to be here," he said.

"All are dying to know what you've been up to. I'll admit, your disappearance caused quite a furor."

He laughed. "A vacation, no more." He peered into the center drone. "I do believe I owe E-Galactic an exclusive, and two station-secs a five-star dinner. Please, reach out to my agent."

A splash of burgundy caught his attention. *Nova.*

He whipped up his head and froze.

Gliding toward him was... Nova? She looked...*magnificent.* Her gown hugged every delicious inch of her, shoulders bare, a high sweetheart neckline, but the fabric had the appearance of leather. It shimmered like dragon scales from her toes to her cleavage.

His breath caught.

A rushing consumed his hearing.

His heart thundered in his chest.

She smiled at Graham trailing her, then with two fingers, caught the hood and flipped it back, exposing her rich burgundy hair piled on top of her head.

She was a vision in crimson. Against the red carpet, she should have blended in. She didn't, not with those amber eyes, the lushness of her deep red lips with her pale-almond complexion, and that outfit, right to the red-metallic, spine-shaped brackets running over the curve of her ass to nape of her neck, forming a choker. Matching gauntlets adorned her forearms.

"Missed me?" she teased, looping her arm through his.

"Always," he managed to rasp. "Beautiful, Nova-honey. You've surpassed my expectations."

She flicked a dismissive hand behind her. "Blame him."

Graham's smile was tight. "Argued about everything. How did you survive six days with her?"

Eli gazed at her upturned face. "It's been longer but far too short."

She beamed.

"I'll confirm a few things and meet you in the cinema." Graham hurried off.

"I should feel guilty about being difficult, but that man's so used to getting his way." She swept a hand down her body. "Wanted me in purple. Said it was the new black." She rolled her eyes.

"You've eaten?" he asked, ushering her to the next interview marker.

"Noodles. You?"

He nodded and faced a brunette. "Hi, Mindy. This's Nova."

Despite the crowds, noise, shouted demands, and flashing lights, Nova didn't move. She remained poised and smiling, sometimes cuddling his upper arm or whispering an observation.

"And...is this more than friendship?" one interviewer asked, gesturing to Nova.

Her cheeks flushed a peach color. "Too soon to tell."

He knew what he wanted. More time wouldn't change that. Lacing his fingers through hers, he twirled her then drew her against him for a quick kiss. Well, that was the plan. He got as far as a twirl with Nova an arm-length away.

"Eli, be a dear and come pose with me." Cassidy squeezed between them, leaving Nova adrift.

She blinked then circled Cassidy, coming to stand at his right. He looped an arm around her, keeping her close. In a show for everyone to see, he kissed her temple.

"In a bit, Cass." He gestured with his chin at the last interviewer.

Her pout didn't ruin her classic beauty. With her deep brown hair pulled to the side, she could've charmed a hungry Skrillith. "But—"

"You signed the same contract, Cass. Marketing comes first." He ushered Nova to the next marker.

"That's Cassidy," she hissed, peering past him at the woman. "You didn't mention she's in this movie."

"Plays a spoiled girl." Like always, but he wouldn't go into that. "We're the golden couple, don't you know?" His tone had a note of resentment to it.

Actors supported each other, and if he said anything, he'd be breaking that unspoken code. Besides, whiners impacted their own reputation more than their intended targets.

And of course, she was seated to the right of him in the cinema. His step faltered, but he pasted on a smile and fulfilled his part of the contract. *Smile and wave, boys.* But he leaned toward Nova, ensuring their clasped hands were visible to all.

"I know that look," Graham said, gesturing to a server to hand them bottles of purified water. "There's no sneaking out before the party."

"Wasn't going to," Eli said, "for about fifteen minutes. Can't make any promises after that. And could you get us a pot of Lady Grey, please."

Nova smiled at him like he'd given her a million credits.

Graham huffed and placed the order with the server. "We'll talk about this later," he said when the lights dimmed.

In the shadows, Eli could pretend he was alone with Nova. He pressed his shoulder to hers and brought her fingers to his lips. "Where's Barry?"

"Cleavage," she said, then laughed. "Scared the shit out of poor Graham." She gasped. "But...I think I found what he doesn't eat."

"Oh?" He smiled, ignoring the director giving a speech.

"Bright light." She squeezed and released his forearm. "I'll show you...later." Her expression turned serious, but she faced forward.

The movie started. He paid it no attention, not when Nova reacted to scenes with such gusto. *Lord, I love her.* He watched her more than the screen.

Tonight.

He'd tell her.

No way could he wait a month.

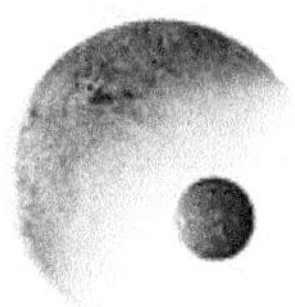

So much for stating she was unremarkable. Graham had remembered Nova and was using her given name from minute six of their 'acquaintance.' She'd endured the hairstylist, trying on dress after dress, fighting with the make-up artist who thought she needed war paint, but Graham had soothed her frazzled nerves with the best noodles she'd ever had. Not to mention pots of tea when she asked.

Eli's reaction had made it all worth it.

Tingles had swept through her, that he found her mesmerizing. Barry had started to hum from within her cleavage. And to be honest, she *did* look amazing.

Here she was, pretending to be his *friend*. She'd gotten to 'meet' Cassidy Collins, but that woman had leveled such a nasty glare on Nova, that getting to know the famous actress didn't appeal anymore.

Thankfully, despite her many attempts to drag Eli away from Nova, he'd resisted. She wasn't going to lie. Him choosing her over *the* Cassidy Collins sent a thrill through her. The movie started, but he couldn't care less, more concerned with the tea the server brought. Once she had a cup, he settled in the seat and said no more.

He played a sweet cowboy sheriff so out of his depth. His quirky comments and often fourth-wall breaking made her laugh. He'd hated this role—she'd gotten that impression when he last mentioned it. Something about being signed for the sequel but the role not worthy of a nomination.

Not everything had to be serious. Laughter still warmed her chest when Cassidy tried to distract him with an anecdote. He was polite, borderline friendly, but didn't encourage conversation more than necessary.

Midway through the movie, Nova stood. "Gotta pee," she whispered and waddled off, the mermaid style of the skirt limited a hasty getaway, which was fine when she was squeezing her knees together in an effort to pinch her bladder.

Easier said than done, and the classical music softly playing in the bathroom didn't calm her panic. The issue was, Graham had all but stitched her into this impossible-albeit-gorgeous creation. If she didn't find a zipper soon, she'd be wearing a wetsuit.

Too many cups of tea had led to this, of course.

An elderly woman in a crisp uniform stood beside the vanity. "May I offer assistance?"

Nova could've kissed her. She was on the verge of begging Eli to follow her into the ladies. Hidden zips from heel to hip helped her *peel* it up. The fabric was like a second skin.

The relief was instant. After she washed her hands, studying her make-up in the mirror, she fiddled with the zips to seal herself in again.

"Thank you so much," she said to the woman. "I wouldn't have made it without you."

"Oh, it was a pleasure," the woman said. She gestured to Nova's cleavage. "Your gem's showing."

"That's Barry," Nova said, shoving him into place, but he vibrated and tried to climb out. "Quit it," she hissed at the stone. "It's there or nowhere, get it?"

He must have because he calmed and stayed put. If this was what having children was like, she wasn't ready. She hurried along the passage, wincing when her new shoes pinched. Nothing beat worn-in boots. Enshrouded in darkness, a familiar figure stood near the door into the cinema.

She'd spot Eli anywhere. Planning on retelling her ordeal to pee, a smile formed in anticipation of his laughter. But he jerked to the side, his arms going around a woman who'd slipped through the door and thrown herself against him.

Nova's eyes widened, her steps faltered, but she didn't stop. She expected him to shove the woman away, maybe call security.

But when the faceless woman kissed him, he just stood there.

Ice slithered down Nova's spine even as a cold chill swept over her. This... *This* was what she'd feared. Anger uncoiled, warring with her shock. She marched on, choosing to lean her shoulder against the wall like a 'casual' observer.

Fair enough, his eyes held panic. For such a philanderer, it could be because she'd caught him red-handed. Part of her tried to soothe her ruffled feathers with ill-timed facts. They hadn't discussed where their relationship was going. She had no claim to him until then.

"I'd give her an award," she said, forcing her tone to be cheerful. "Excellent performance."

At last, he shoved the woman aside, wiping his mouth with the back of his wrist. That was a nice touch.

"Eli," Cassidy whined.

Nova's shoulders dropped with relief. She'd gotten the impression he didn't care for the woman. "Oh, it's you." She looped her arm through Eli's. "Sorry I took so long, honey pot," she crooned. "All those cups of tea, y'know."

He chuckled and drew her closer to him. "I realized that stunning dress might be a little tough to get out of."

She giggled then almost rolled her eyes at her nonsense. "You can peel it off later." With one determined glance at a frozen Cassidy, Nova led *her man* back to their seats. The bitch didn't know who she was dealing with—a woman who blew up mining scuttles for fun.

"Why did you hesitate?" she hissed, sinking into her chair.

"Her kiss made me realize I only want your lips on mine."

She gaped. "Just wow." Her heartbeat fluttered, her breathing ragged. "You're good."

"I'm serious." He looked it. His potent gaze was fixed on her like she was supposed to know what to say to that.

"You're going to have to deal with her." She hitched her thumb at the door where they'd left Cassidy.

His chuckle was cold. "I've tried."

A server brought a fresh pot of tea with a plate of sandwiches. As distractions went, it was perfect. She smiled at the young man, who held the tray for her to help herself. A flurry of movement drew her attention for a second, just before boiling tea landed on her lap.

The pain was sharp, a spreading fire that sent her thoughts reeling. She bit her tongue, tasting the metallic tang of blood.

"Cass," Eli thundered, jumping to his feet and scooping Nova into his arms. "This's the last straw—"

"What happened?" Graham asked, running up.

Nova was in agony and having a parent-child chat with the instigator was beyond her level of patience. "In pain," she screamed.

Eli bolted, rushing her through the doors with Graham and a whining Cassidy chasing him. "Let it be known that I will not be acting opposite Cassidy Collins again. I don't care who it upsets. It's her or me."

A gawking Graham stumbled to a stop.

Cassidy collapsed to the floor with a dramatic sob then wailing like someone had stabbed her.

"Can you walk?" Eli glanced at Nova while carrying her through the front doors of Eastwood Hall. Drones and reporters swarmed them as they made their way along the red carpet. Security formed a protective circle, preventing fans and paparazzi from crushing them, but it wasn't enough. They slowed to a walk.

Graham appeared out of nowhere, gesturing to a waiting med-hover, a white cross emblazoned on its red side. "I have emergency services. Come with me, Nova."

Eli hesitated, grimaced, then lowered her feet to the carpet. "I'm so sorry about this."

"Not your fault," she gritted out, letting Graham drape an arm around her. He steered her toward the medic, who held the med-hover door open.

The sadness dulling Eli's green eyes and pulling his sexy mouth down was the last thing she saw as the med-hover flew off.

Chapter Twenty-Eight

"We saw it go down," Petr said, waltzing into the ward, his uniform mis-buttoned. "You're all over the news, babe." He punched his fist into a palm. "*That* woman… I will never watch another of her movies."

Nova grinned, almost throwing out her arms for a hug. *Damn drugs, making me loopy.* She pulled the hospital gown close, just in case.

Captain was on his heels. Sharon trailed him, her chin down like she'd prefer to be anywhere but here.

"It's so good to see you," Marco said, resting his hand on her toes tenting the bed's blankets. "I was so worried when Lord Orien whisked you and Eli away. Graham was panicking, especially with the comm silence."

She scanned the room, her eyes widening. Here was her family, something she hadn't considered before. "I won't lie… There were some scary parts I won't bore you with." Her thoughts buzzed as if she couldn't focus, and a warm lassitude had her sinking deeper under the covers.

"What did the doctor say?"

"All good," she mumbled, gazing at her gown draped over the back of a chair. *Oh, yes, the hot tea.* She pushed herself onto her elbow and peered around Marco. *Where's Eli?* "The leather protected me from third-degree scalds."

"What's that?" Petr tapped her fist.

She opened her fingers to reveal Barry.

"It's beautiful. Did Eli give it to you?" Petr stroked the stone's smooth surface.

Sharon whipped her head up, a scowl marring her delicate features.

"No, Barry's mine."

"You named it?" Sharon snapped, bitterness in her tone.

"He's a Kovari Shol—a sentient rock from Lethara. So yes, I named *him*." Unable to enjoy in peace the pain meds the nurse had given her, Nova sat up and shifted back, resting against a pillow.

"We're running out of docking time, sweetheart, so when you're released, we can start the next voyage," Marco said, then smiled. "On a happy note, you and Eli have generated such business that our trips are booked for months."

"That's wonderful," she said and meant it. At least something good had come from their adventure. She sighed. That was a lie. It hadn't *all* been bad. "I'll be ready to leave soon. Doctor just wanted me to stay for a few hours. He mentioned lasting effects?" She frowned, unable to recall his words exactly. "Something about monitoring it, just in case."

"I'm just glad you're all right," Marco said, giving her toes another pat. "I called your grandmother as soon as Graham let me know you're fine."

"Thanks," she said, accepting the bottle of water Petr handed her. "My sisters aren't home often, and Gramma never watches the news."

"Well, we'll let you get some rest." Marco raised an eyebrow at Sharon, and the three left.

The silence was perfect. She cuddled Barry and the bottle to her chest, slithering under the blankets until the pillow cushioned her head perfectly.

Back and forth, medical staff rushed past her door; no one entered. Time ticked on, and she had no idea how much longer she needed to stay.

"Where's Graham?" she muttered.

A man loomed in the doorway.

Her breath caught when Eli strolled into the room. He was in his tux minus the bow tie. He'd undone the top button, exposing his collarbone. *Damn, he looks good.* She licked her lips, her mouth dry despite the sip of water she'd had.

"He's taking care of things," Eli said, his attention on her. He swept a gaze over her, and the concern furrowing his brow smoothed out. "How do you feel, Nova-honey?"

"Fuzzy," she said, pinching the bridge of her nose.

"Doc says the pain will lessen by tomorrow, then gradually every day." He clenched his jaw, anger darkening his eyes. "I should've realized she was capable of—"

"You can't anticipate everything," she said.

"And don't we know it," he said, curling his hand around her fist. "Barry okay?"

"Yeah, the scald was across my thighs. He was more than safe." She slipped her hand free to press a kiss to the stone. "Right, buddy?"

"Nova—"

"We need to talk." She sat up, resting Barry in the blanket valley between her thighs.

"Yes, I—"

"If I don't know where we stand, I can't react to whatever-the-hell just happened." She arched a brow at him. "Should I be angry you kissed another woman?"

He opened his mouth to speak, but she held up her hand.

"Cassidy doesn't know either, so to her, you're as philandering free as usual."

He snapped his lips shut and glowered.

She waited.

So did he.

"Tonight, I pretended to be your *friend*." The word made her stomach churn.

"You are," he said, then clenched his jaw. "*And* the love of my life."

She'd been friend zoned. The blow to her solar plexus was visceral. "Well, that sets me straight..." Her mind reeled. "What did you say?" She shook her head. Damn drugs messing with her hearing.

"I *said*, you crazy redhead, that I love you." His expression softened, and that potency was there, blazing his affection for her.

She froze, her heart thundering in her ears like she needed extra sound dampening. "That's not residual sex hormones making you say that?"

He chuckled. "Nova... Just tell me you feel the same so we can move on, honey pot."

"I do...love you." She pouted. "You could've made it a little more romantic."

"On bended knee? In an alien paradise? On the back of a drooling yuxmet?"

She laughed. "Yes, you've had plenty of prime opportunities—"

He kissed her, snatching her breath. "I...adore...every...inch...of you," he said between kisses. "Let me love you. Inside and out."

She grinned. "Only you could say that and mean it." She cupped his face and held him still for a long gaze. "I feel the same."

"Forever?" he asked, nuzzling her palm. "My qidhari," he whispered.

She jerked back. "You know what it means?"

The slow smile he blessed her with held promises, happiness, and pure love. "Yeah. God's savior, and you did...save me."

"No regerts?" she teased.

His reply was without hesitation. "None. Ever."

EPILOGUE

On the Entertainment Cruiser (EC) Valiance.
The staff quarters belonging to Mr. and Mrs. Thorne.
Home Sweet Home.
Year of 2203, November

"Barry, will you stop that?" Nova snapped, bolting across the cabin to flip the music to Mozart. She'd hopped into the shower, not expecting her playlist to change.

Her egg, now the size of her hand from fingertip to wrist, had revolted, spinning faster until it blurred and sent out pulses of light.

What he ate was music. That had been fun to discover on her wedding day mid-dance. Finding out what kind he preferred had taken much longer.

He calmed, slowed his spinning, and settled on the plinth. There he bobbed, sending out a soothing hum. Learning this explained why he'd tried to climb out of her cleavage in the bathroom at Eastwood Hall. Classical music had been playing in the background.

A squeal whipped her gaze to the door when it slid open to Eli standing there with January in his arms. Her daughter cooed, her bright green eyes and mop of brown hair so like her father's.

"Oh, what's this?" Eli said, his gaze warming with his ever-present desire for Nova.

She stood in the middle of their living room, dripping on the floor with a hand towel pressed to her front. "Barry lost his shit again. Note: he hates country."

"So do I," Eli said.

"It was the soundtrack to *The Quick and the Quasarian*."

"Oh." Eli chuckled. "Everyone's a critic these days." He sauntered to her and swooped in for a kiss. "Want me to slip into something a little more comfortable?"

She laughed. "I'm already pregnant, Mr. Thorne. No need to implant anymore of your sperm, thank you very much."

He pretended to be aghast. "You say that like it's a bad thing." He settled January onto her play mat then gathered Nova against him for a long, leisurely kiss that curled her toes.

"Okay, maybe once more, just to make sure the pregnancy took." She was seven months along, her belly pushing him back even when he tightened his arms around her.

"Have I told you I love you, Mrs. Thorne?"

She hummed when he ran kisses down her neck.

He pulled back and stole her towel. His appreciative gaze never failed to amaze her. This was her man, the father of her children. Between movies, he traveled on board the *Valiance*. Never did he look at another woman, something she'd been so scared he'd do.

"Time for a quickie?" he asked, glancing at the digital clock. "Marco won't mind if you're late to dock, right?" He caught her hand and twirled her once more into his embrace. "For like an hour."

"You have ten minutes to show me what you've got, Thorne, or I'm walking out that door."

He chuckled. "I'd pay to see Marco's expression when you pilot the ship naked." His voice deepened. "In fact, make it happen."

Her core coiled with need, and she smiled at him. "Love you."

She was airborne, whisked into his arms and carried to their bed. "I'll never get tired of hearing you say that. To think I almost lost you..." His kiss carried all he felt for her, so intense it summoned tears.

She melted against him and let him love her...as he'd asked to so long ago.

ABOUT THE AUTHOR

Sevannah Storm is a fiction writer who immerses herself in fantastical worlds both magical and science fiction. She has a flair for the creative having studied art and interior architecture and spends her time drawing, oil painting, and writing. An avid reader from an early age, Sevannah finds her inspiration from various sources: games, novels, music, and the land of make-believe. The unique versus the practical has brought on numerous debates.

In her spare time, she does Pilates and rereads novels that snatch her breath away. Having embraced the social media world, you can find her on most platforms.

Her home is a land south of Wakanda, where animals roam free. Born in Zimbabwe, she grew up in South Africa. The crisp blue skies with cotton-candy sunsets expand her heart and soul, encapsulating a sense of freedom.

Words she lives by: "Know your pothole and dodge it. Don't work in a pencil factory if you're a vampire."

Sevannah loves to hear from her readers. You can find and connect with her at the links below.

Website/Newsletter:

https://www.sevannahstorm.com/

Facebook:

https://www.facebook.com/sevannah.storm

Instagram:

https://www.instagram.com/sevannah.storm/

Twitter:

https://twitter.com/sevannah_storm

Thank you for taking the time to read *Stealing the Star Stone*. If you enjoyed the story, please tell your friends and leave a review. Reviews support authors and ensure they continue to bring readers books to love and enjoy.